NAVIGATING
EARLY

ALSO BY CLARE VANDERPOOL

Moon Over Manifest

NAVIGATING EARLY

CLARE VANDERPOOL

DELACORTE PRESS

Text copyright © 2013 by Clare Vanderpool
Jacket art copyright © 2013 by Alexander Jansson

Visit us on the Web! randomhouse.com/kids
Educators and librarians, for a variety of teaching tools, visit us at
RHTeachersLibrarians.com

Library of Congress Cataloging-in-Publication Data
Vanderpool, Clare.
  Navigating Early / Clare Vanderpool. — 1st ed.   p. cm.
  Summary: "Odyssey-like adventure of two boys' incredible quest on the Appalachian Trail where they deal with pirates, buried secrets, and extraordinary encounters"—Provided by publisher.
  ISBN 978-0-385-74209-2 (hc) — ISBN 978-0-307-97412-9 (ebook) — ISBN 978-0-375-99040-3 (glb)
  [1. Adventure and adventurers—Fiction. 2. Boarding schools—Fiction. 3. Schools—Fiction. 4. Eccentrics and eccentricities—Fiction. 5. Appalachian Trail—Fiction. 6. Maine—Fiction.]   I. Title.
  PZ7.V28393Nav 2013   [Fic]—dc23   2012014973

The text of this book is set in 12-point Goudy.
Book design by Vikki Sheatsley

Printed in the United States of America
10 9 8 7 6 5 4 3 2 1
First Edition

To my husband,
Mark,
and
my children,
Luke, Paul, Grace, and Lucy,
the brightest stars in my sky

NAVIGATING
EARLY

The great black bear, awesome as Ursa Major, wagged her head from side to side, and her bellow shook the nearby passage of the Appalachian Trail. I say *her*, but the truth is, we had no way to tell. There were no female markings. No cubs in sight. But I knew. I knew her like I knew my own mother. It was in her bearing—her absolute authority over us two boys locked in her gaze. And it was in her unwavering will to keep us alive.

PROLOGUE

If I'd known what there was to know about Early Auden, that strangest of boys, I might have been scared off, or at least kept my distance like all the others. But I was new to the Morton Hill Academy for Boys, and to Cape Fealty, Maine. Fact was, I was new to anyplace outside of northeastern Kansas.

I've heard it said that Kansas has a long-standing history of keeping its sons and daughters close to home, but in recent years there have been some notable exceptions. General Eisenhower, for one. Everyone was so proud of the way he led the Allied forces during the war with Germany. He came back to Abilene for a big parade, but once all the hoopla died down, he left. I don't think he plans on taking up residence again anytime soon.

My father is in the armed services too. Captain John Baker, Jr. He's in the navy. You know what they say. There's two kinds of fellas: navy men and those who wish they were. My father heard that from his father, Rear Admiral John Baker, Sr. I'm the third John Baker in a row. Believe me, I'd rather be a whole of something than just a third. But you get what you get and you are what you are. That saying comes from my mom's side of the family. The civilians. They're the fun side. They call me Jack. My mom calls me Jackie. At least she used to.

But things changed. That's how I ended up at the edge of the country. To say I was a fish out of water would be a good expression but the wrong way to put it. Because there I was, a landlocked Kansas boy standing on shifting sands at the ocean's edge. And all I could do was burrow my feet down deep so I wouldn't get swept away.

I wasn't a complete stranger to sand. There was a good-sized sandpit near our house. And I'd read a story put out by the National Geographic Society that told of whole dinosaurs being found in the Kansas plains. They think Kansas might have once been covered in water, and after the water was gone, it was the sand and soil that kept the dinosaur bones from being scattered and lost.

Early Auden knew all about sand. But growing up in Maine, he had a whole ocean lapping up on his shore, washing it away. The first time I saw Early he was filling bag after bag with sand and stacking them like bricks. Just what he was trying to keep from washing away, I didn't know. It was a crazy thing he was doing, but something in me understood it. I just watched him—sandbagging the ocean.

I knew Early Auden could not hold back the ocean. But that strangest of boys saved me from being swept away.

1

The first time you see the ocean is supposed to be either exhilarating or terrifying. I wish I could say it was one of those for me. I just threw up, right there on the rocky shore.

We'd flown to Maine a few hours earlier on a military cargo plane. The big beast lurched and rattled the whole way while my father read over some manuals on naval preparedness and coastal fortification. I felt queasy before boarding the plane, was nauseous by the time we were over Missouri, and clutched the barf bag over most of Ohio, Pennsylvania, and New York. The captain—my father, that is, not the pilot—didn't say anything, but I knew he had to be thinking his son would never make it in the navy with such motion sickness. Besides, my green face wouldn't go well against a smart navy uniform. I watched him out of the corner of my eye, still not used to being around him.

I was nine when he left, and he'd been gone for four

years in the European Theater. When I was younger, I thought that was a place where they showed movies. But from what he said, and more from what he didn't say, there was nothing make-believe about it.

Last spring, the war in Europe started winding down, and my mom and I were looking forward to my dad's home-coming. We'd have our own welcome-home parade, with streamers and cowbells and homemade ice cream. I could imagine my father in his crisp blue uniform, with all his medals for bravery pinned above his breast pocket. He would plant a kiss on my mom's cheek and he'd ruffle my hair like he always used to.

But when my father came back to Kansas, it wasn't for a parade. It was for a funeral. My mom's. It was a misty day in July. Mom would have liked that. She always said that for her frizzy hair, a steady drizzle was the next best thing to a permanent wave.

So, long story short, there was no ice cream. My mom wasn't there for him to kiss. I wasn't nine anymore, so he didn't ruffle my hair. And from the start, we seemed less like father and son and more like two strangers living in the same house.

I guess that shouldn't have been a surprise, though. When he'd left I was a kid reading superhero comic books on the living room floor, waiting for my mom to call me to wash up for supper. When he came back, I was a thirteen-year-old boy with no mom and a dad I barely knew. And I didn't believe in superheroes anymore.

Anyway, that was how I ended up in a cargo plane head-ing to Cape Fealty, Maine, and Morton Hill Academy. It was the nearest boys' boarding school to the Portsmouth Naval Shipyard, where my father was stationed.

After a bumpy landing, a military jeep drove us to the school. As we approached Morton Hill Academy, I read the words etched into the arched stone entryway. It was the Marine Corps' motto: *Semper Fidelis*—"Always Faithful."

We passed through and arrived at the dormitory. Arrangements had been made with Mr. Conrady, the headmaster, to get me enrolled at this late date in August, and for that I should have been grateful. But right then, the only thing I was grateful for was that I would soon be out of that jeep and standing on solid ground.

Headmaster Conrady greeted my father by his first name and shook my hand so firmly I winced. He led us on a sweeping tour of the campus. Morton Hill Academy was a prep school for boys established in 1870, but from the names of buildings and fields he mentioned, I thought it must have been a military school. He pointed out the two classroom buildings, Lexington Hall and Concord Hall. Lexington was the upper school, for ninth through twelfth grades, and Concord was for sixth, seventh, and eighth. He showed us the dormitories: Fort O'Brien for the high school boys, so named for the fort built near the site of the first naval battle of the Revolutionary War. Camp Keyes, for the younger boys, was where I would be stationed—I mean staying. Pershing Field and Flanders Field House, the former named for a general and the latter for a battlefield in World War I, were the athletic field and gymnasium, perched at the top of a hill overlooking the ocean.

The newest buildings were the Normandy Greenhouse

and Dunkirk Commons, aka the mess hall. When Headmaster Conrady pointed out the white clapboard chapel, I wondered whether there might be at least one structure with a softer name, like Church of the Good Shepherd or Chapel of the Non-Weapon-Bearing Angels. No such luck. Armistice Chapel was a place of peace, but only if you signed the treaty and sat at attention.

The remaining building from the original 1870 campus—and the only structure that had escaped the onslaught of military names—was the boathouse, affectionately called the Nook.

When Headmaster Conrady prepared to leave us at the dormitory, he had a few words in private with my father. I gathered from the look on his face and the occasional glance at me that he was expressing his condolences for the loss of the captain's wife and offering words of assurance that the school would provide a healthy environment for his queasy son.

In a louder voice meant for me to hear, Headmaster Conrady said, "We'll take good care of him. He'll be a new man when you come back for the Fall Regatta."

I didn't know what the Fall Regatta was. It sounded like a dance, although at an all-boys school I didn't know who we'd be dancing with.

As Headmaster Conrady's eyes rested on me, I wasn't sure if he was waiting for me to salute. Instead, he motioned me forward, placed a broad hand on my shoulder, and lowered his bushy eyebrows.

"Son," he said, "the boys here at Morton Hill Academy are pretty much like kids anywhere. If you want to sit with a group in the lunchroom, they'll probably let you. If you want to go off and sit by yourself, they'll probably let you do that, too. So my advice to you," he said, pumping a fist in the air, "is jump in."

"Yes, sir," I said, my legs wobbling a bit. And with that, the headmaster finally dismissed me to my dorm.

He didn't say "At ease," but upon entering my room, I let out a breath that I had apparently been holding for some time. There were two beds. The room assignments had been made already, and since I'd registered for school late, I wouldn't have a roommate. Still, I only needed one bed, and I chose the one by the window. Then we—the captain and I, but mostly the captain—unpacked my things. Shirts went in a shirt drawer, underwear in an underwear drawer, and socks in a sock drawer—everything shipshape. I had already been given my own Morton Hill sweatpants and sweatshirt, and in the closet, my new khaki pants hung next to the navy blazer with the Morton Hill coat of arms stitched on it.

Then the captain pulled out a set of sheets from the closet and swiftly made my bed with military precision. Crisp hospital corners at forty-five-degree angles and sheets tucked in tight enough to bounce a quarter on. I'd slept in a bed made by my father before, and it was a little hard to breathe.

Even after the past couple of months, it still felt strange being alone with him. He'd been gone for so long, and now all of a sudden he was back—but only sort of. He seemed far away—like he was uncomfortable being off his ship and his sea legs hadn't adjusted to dry land.

I'd already pleaded my case for staying back home with Grandpa Henry and my mom's bachelor brother, Uncle Max, but the decision had been made to put me close to my dad. Nobody seemed to understand that I could be standing right next to him and he would still be a million miles away.

"Do you have all your gear?" he asked.

Gear? He made it sound like I was getting ready for boot camp. Maybe that was what he wanted. To put me someplace where I'd get whipped into shape and turned into a real navy man.

"I have everything I need," I said quietly.

I lifted my suitcase to put it on the shelf in the closet, but it wasn't completely empty. I pulled out the stack of my favorite monthly magazine put out by the National Geographic Society. I'd been a member since I was seven and had dozens of issues at home, but I'd grabbed only a few to bring along. I thumbed through to see which ones were in the stack. January 1940—"Whales, Porpoises, and Dolphins." October 1941—"Daily Life in Ancient Egypt." September 1942—"Strategic Alaska Looks Ahead."

Then I realized that the rest of the magazines were old comic books I thought I'd left back home. Superman. Batman. Captain America. These figures, who had once been part of my daily life, now seemed as foreign to me as ancient Egypt. And I didn't feel like getting reacquainted. Superheroes were for people who hadn't grown up yet. I shoved the whole stack of magazines in the bottom drawer of the desk against the wall.

The last item in the suitcase was a small box. I had put tissue paper in it, but the contents still rattled. I could see the red-and-white pieces of broken china without lifting the lid, so I quickly hid the box back in the suitcase and stuck the whole thing in the closet.

The captain suggested we get a bite to eat in the cafeteria. I said I wasn't hungry. So we said an awkward goodbye that involved a salute and a handshake as he told me to take care of myself. I winced. He'd told me to take care of my mom when he left four years earlier. Was he giving me a reminder that I'd failed? I wondered as I watched the jeep sputter off.

I stared at my newly made bed and was reminded of the time I built a car for the annual soap box derby. It had a roomy carriage with perfectly balanced wheels for a fast, smooth ride and was decked out in shiny red paint. I knew I'd win the big race. The only problem was, I left it outside the day before and the car got waterlogged and warped, and the shiny red paint peeled off.

My father was put out that I had left it in the rain and said, "Well, son, you made your bed, now you'll have to lie in it."

But my mom shook her head at him and said to me, "Yes, you made your bed, but for heaven's sakes, *don't* just lie in it!"

I stared at her, lost in my attempt to figure out what she was getting at. My mom had a way of using expressions that were as mysterious and confusing as an upside-down map.

She folded her arms. "Jackie, if you don't like the bed you're in, take it apart and make it right."

It took all night to make it right. To strip down that soap box car and rebuild it with new wood and fresh red paint. I don't even remember finishing it and almost fell asleep at the wheel the next day at the race. I came in second.

Standing there, looking at my crisply made bed, I took a deep breath. But just then I didn't have the wherewithal to take it apart and make it right for *me*. So I left the room.

The dormitory was deserted. Most of the boys wouldn't arrive until the next day. I didn't like the way my footsteps echoed in the hallway, and I needed some fresh air. That was it. Seeing the ocean, feeling the salty spray I'd read about in books, would help get the quease out. So I took off my socks, cuffed up my pant legs, and headed down the dirt path to the shore.

Suddenly, there it was. The ocean. With its never-ending swells and lapping waves. Its heaving movement that made everything around it look like it, too, was in sympathetic motion. I took one look at the swells and bent over—and that was when I threw up.

Once I was sure the waves wouldn't come and swallow me whole, I lifted my head but tried to keep my gaze off the moving water. I looked up the shore. It startled me to see someone, but there he was, surrounded by sand and trying to fit it in neat little bags. Stacking them to form a wall.

He didn't say anything, so I guessed he hadn't seen me. I turned and walked away. It might have been silly, walking away like that, but school hadn't even started yet, and who wanted to be known as the new kid from Kansas who couldn't hold his lunch just because he'd laid eyes on the ocean?

Besides, the sand made me think of my mom. She always described my hair as sandy brown, and noticing the different shades of brown and taupe and even red, I could see why. I felt the tears coming, and I gave in to a moment of remembering her.

My mother was like sand. The kind that warms you on a beach when you come shivering out of the cold water. The kind that clings to your body, leaving its impression on your skin to remind you where you've been and where you've come from. The kind you keep finding in your shoes and your pockets long after you've left the beach.

She was also like the sand that archaeologists dig through. Layers and layers of sand that have kept dinosaur bones together for millions of years. And as hot and dusty and plain as that sand might be, those archaeologists are grateful for it, because without it to keep the bones in place, everything would scatter. Everything would fall apart.

I glanced once over my shoulder, but the boy was gone.

2

The next day was filled with boys, boxes, and bulletin boards. Suitcases, books, and pillows. And everywhere there were moms giving bosomy hugs and tear-filled kisses.

I spent most of the day in the library, wandering from shelf to shelf, breathing in the familiar smell of books and wood polish and India ink. It felt good to be closed in among the stacks, which didn't pitch and sway. They were solid and stable. Maybe that's how cows feel when they come into the barn after a day in the open field.

The librarian introduced herself in a quiet, librarianly manner, saying her name was Miss B. She smiled and said it was short for Bookworm. I didn't say much, so she gave me a quick tour of the library, showing me the fiction section and resource books, and she got particularly excited at the poetry collection. When I didn't match her level of enthusiasm for Longfellow and Hopkins, she just smiled, encouraged me to have a look around, and returned to her card catalog. I wandered around the stacks until I found the *National Geographic* magazines. Standing in front of those bright yellow spines all lined up in numerical order, it felt, for a moment, like I had a place, a tiny spot where I belonged.

Then the door was flung open and two boys poked their heads in. Glancing around, they apparently didn't find who or what they were looking for and left.

There had been no opportunity for introductions, but even if there had, I wasn't sure what I would have said. *Hi, my name is Jack. I'm from Kansas and I wish I was still there.* Still, it would have been nice to have had at least a couple of names to put with those faces. There was a large trophy case on the far wall of the library. *Maybe some of those boys' pictures will be in there,* I thought.

The case was full of trophies and plaques from years of Morton Hill Academy victories. Basketball, football, track and field. Mixed in were pictures of young men in their team uniforms, smiling with the joy of winning and standing with arms over each other's shoulders in a show of camaraderie. I studied the faces—ripe, ruddy, youthful, as if they were faces from history. That was pretty much what they were, as the dates stretched all the way back to the late 1800s.

As I walked the length of the trophy case, the faces spanned the years, one blurring into the next. Then one stood out.

An older boy stood in a picture all his own. His hair was slicked back, and he had a strong, handsome face. Written at the bottom in white ink were the words *Morton Hill All-*

Team Captain, Rowing and Football, Class of 1943. The picture rested against a jersey with the player's name and number on the back: FISH–67. But it wasn't the jersey or the trophy that held my attention. It was his face. His smile. He smiled as if he held life in that championship cup and he could drink from it whenever he liked. He smiled as if that victorious moment would last forever.

Then I noticed my own reflection in the glass. My face was different. Not just because it was younger. Not just because I wasn't smiling. But because the past summer had taught me a lesson that, from the looks of it, the all-team captain had yet to learn: life can't be held in a cup, and nothing lasts forever. Suddenly, I felt sorry for Number 67 and all he didn't know.

Monday morning came like a cool Kansas rain shower on a hot, humid day. In other words, it was a relief. Because now at least I had a schedule. I knew that history came first, followed by Latin, English, and math. Science and phys ed were held in the afternoon.

I figured if I knew what was coming, maybe I'd get my bearings. That was what I needed. Bearing. At home you could walk outside and see for miles in every direction. You could always figure where you were, based on which church steeple or windmill or silo rose like a beacon out of the horizon. They were landmarks that served to keep a person rooted. Grounded. But then it struck me: to have landmarks, you had to have land. And the salt air filling my lungs reminded me that most of what surrounded me in this place was water. Constantly moving, changing water. I started feeling queasy again.

The history teacher was a short man with stubby fingers who seemed very excited about a bunch of Greeks who all must have been from the same family—Oedipus, Perseus, Theseus. His name was Professor Donaldson. He called roll, and every kid said "Here" except for one. Early Auden.

Latin. Mr. Hildebrandt. Same roll call. Same kid absent. Early Auden.

All the way until math. Then who showed up? Early Auden. And I recognized him. It was the kid from the beach. The boy with the sandbags. He was a little fella, about four foot something. His feet dangled just above the floor when he sat at his desk.

"Good morning, gentlemen." The math teacher greeted us as he set down his mug of steaming coffee. "My name is Professor Eric Blane," he said as he began writing on the chalkboard. "As many of you know, this is my first year at Morton Hill, and I'm looking forward to getting acquainted with each and every one of you."

He turned to face us, and we all stared at what he'd written on the board.

The Holy Grail

"We all know from the legend of King Arthur about Sir Galahad and his search for the Holy Grail—that sacred, mysterious, and oh-so-elusive chalice used at the Last Supper. For centuries it has been revered as a miraculous vessel and has been sought after by kings and princes, humanitarians and tyrants. There is supposedly a brotherhood of guardians to keep it *safe*. Or, might we say, keep its mysterious allure from being evaluated in the light of modern-day knowledge and skepticism."

Mr. Blane sat on the desk at the front of the room. "We're not here to discuss the authenticity of the Grail, but rather the nature and merits of a quest. Why does one embark upon a quest?" Mr. Blane looked down at his seating chart and glanced around the room. "Sam Feeney?"

A pudgy kid sitting next to me squinted an eye. "Arrgh. To find buried treasure, matey."

The other boys laughed.

"Spoken like a true pirate," said Mr. Blane. "But yes, to search for something. It can be treasure. However, it can also be a search for something less tangible. Ever hear of a quest for happiness? Or a quest for justice?"

"Buried treasure sounds a little more exciting," said Sam.

"Maybe. But what about a quest for the truth? Perhaps that was really Sir Galahad's goal. To demystify the miraculous. What if he was looking for the Grail—that miraculous vessel—to show that it was just a cup?"

The boys looked at the teacher with furrowed brows. "Jeez, Mr. Blane, you sure know how to take the fun out of a good story," said Robbie Dean Meyer, a red-haired kid I'd sat by in Latin. "And besides, isn't this math class?"

"Precisely. So what does this have to do with math?" said Mr. Blane. "What is the holy grail of mathematics? Something that is so mysterious as to be considered by many almost miraculous. Something woven throughout the world of mathematics. A number that is nothing less than never-ending. Eternal."

Several hands shot up at the last clue.

"Preston Townsend?"

"That would be pi, sir," answered an athletic-looking boy in the second row. His hair was precisely combed, and the way he sat back in his chair, poised with pencil in hand, he looked like he was about to call an important meeting to order. I figured his father must be a banker or a politician. Or maybe the governor of the great state of Maine.

"Yes, pi. The holy grail of mathematics. That mysterious number that has entranced mathematicians for millennia. It originated with the Babylonians, was used by the Greeks in measuring the Earth, was thought to be a miraculous number by some and the work of the devil by others. So what is the number pi? Robbie Dean?"

"That's a trick question, Mr. Blane. Everyone knows that pi starts with 3.14 and keeps on going. We all had to memorize the first one hundred digits last year. But pi is—"

The whole class joined him in saying, "A never-ending, never-repeating number."

"See, everyone knows that," concluded Robbie Dean.

"You mean everyone has accepted that as fact," countered Mr. Blane.

We shifted in our seats, unsure of what he meant.

"Alongside Sir Galahad, I believe, we can add another name to the list of great seekers. His name is Professor Douglas Stanton. He's a mathematician at Cambridge who is on a quest of his own. He has spent much of his career studying this number and has a theory that, contrary to popular belief, pi is *not* a never-ending number. That yes, it is an amazing number that has over seven hundred digits currently known, and thousands more that haven't been calculated yet. But he believes it will, in fact, end."

Mr. Blane brushed the chalk dust from his fingers. "Why do I mention this today? Because this year, we are going to embark on a quest of our own to expand our minds, to challenge what we think we know, and to push the boundaries of mathematics. If pi, the most venerable number, can be proven to end, what else are we blindly believing that might be put to the test? So"—Mr. Blane loosened his tie—"let's get down to the business at hand. Open your textbooks to page one, and let's begin."

I glanced behind me, but Early's desk was empty and the classroom door quietly shut.

3

Walking into the cafeteria that first day, I remembered the headmaster's words of advice about sitting with a group in the lunchroom.

As much as I would have preferred to be by myself right then, I made my way through the lunch line, picked up my tray of meat loaf, green beans, and Jell-O with banana slices, then ventured over to a table of boys I recognized from some of my classes.

One boy—it was the chubby Sam Feeney—moved over easy enough as he continued the conversation. "Anybody who thinks you can outrun a cutter with a gig is a pinhead. Let's ask the new kid. Baker, which is faster? A cutter or a gig?"

I had no idea what they were talking about, so I took the safe way out. I shrugged and said, "Six of one, half dozen of the other."

"Well, what about the oars?" asked Robbie Dean. "Do you prefer whiffs, wherries, or rum-tums?"

"Oh, you know. Whiffs or wherries, usually. But rum-tums'll do in a pinch."

They looked at me steadily, I'm sure wondering what to make of me, when Preston Townsend said, "So, what brings an inlander like you to Maine?" The way he asked the question, I decided his dad was probably a lawyer instead of the governor.

I felt my face get hot. "Just needed a change of scenery, I guess," was my weak reply.

"I hear it's so flat in Kansas that you can see all the way to the next state in every direction," Sam said. "Is that true?"

"I wouldn't know," I said. "What with the waving wheat and the brilliant sunsets, I guess we don't bother to look too far away." I was putting up a good front, but my diversionary lines were running out. One more question and my jitters would probably show through in either spilled milk or dripping sweat. Thinking fast, I decided to shift the focus to someone else's strangeness. "So, what's with the kid who never shows up to class?" I asked.

"Early Auden?" Preston answered. "Not much to tell. His dad was on the board of trustees, had a heart attack and died. So now the kid gets a free ride here, but he picks and chooses what classes he wants to show up for. Sometimes he takes a seat and then leaves as soon as the teacher says something he disagrees with. He's so weird that nobody does anything about it."

"Yeah," Sam piped in. "Last year he walked out of biology class and never came back just because Mr. Nelson said there are no venomous snakes in Maine. Early insisted there are still timber rattlesnakes up north and walked out."

"How come he's so sure there are timber rattlesnakes?" I asked.

"Who knows. He's all-fire sure about most things. Sometimes he has these weird fits when his eyes go all blank and he kind of twitches. They think having those fits messed up his brain somehow."

The bell rang, ending any further discussion about the odd boy. But I knew there had to be more to the story than that.

"See you at PE, Baker. And don't forget your rum-tums." Preston smirked as he got up from the table.

Coach Baynard stood at the deep end of the indoor pool, light reflecting off the water, which was in turn splashing ripples of light on the tile wall. The air was thick and moist, with the sharp scent of chlorine. He gave his whistle a firm blast that echoed around the room. Boys in black swim trunks lined up, displaying an assortment of bare legs: long, short, mostly skinny, a few chunky, hairy, white, knobby kneed, gangly, awkward.

Coach blew his whistle again, "All right, you yay-hoos, let's see what you can do with this." He hefted a ten-pound weight off the floor and threw it into the deep end. "Dive in, then push or carry the weight as far as you can without coming up for air. Once you surface, that's your distance. Robbie Dean. You're up."

Dean stood at the pool's edge, raising his spindly arms

with hands clasped above one shoulder, then the other, as if he were the reigning underwater-weight-moving champion of the world. "Let me show you how it's done, fellas."

After a few catcalls from the crowd he grinned and dove into the water.

The rest of us watched from the deck as he frog-kicked his way to the bottom, first pushing, then pulling on the weight. Robbie Dean got it halfway up the sloped floor before he came to the surface, sputtering and grinning. "Beat that, boys," Robbie Dean called.

The boys on deck pointed and hollered as the weight slipped back to its starting position at the bottom of the deep end. "You really showed us. Yeah, give us another lesson, why don'tcha?"

Sam Feeney was next. He got the brick up the incline before he had to come up for air. Preston Townsend did the best, pushing the brick halfway across the pool.

The coach called out another name. "Baker. You're up." I looked around, surprised, thinking there must be another Baker, then realized he was looking at me. "Come on, son. You know how to swim, don't you?"

Of course I could swim. My mom took me to the pond near our house from the time I was little. I could swim faster and hold my breath longer than any boy close to my age.

"I can swim," I answered, taking my place at the pool's edge. My big toe pressed into the eight-foot marker, etched in red. The lights playing on the tile wall left me feeling unsteady. But with everyone's eyes on me, I dove in.

I swam easily to the bottom, down by the drains. There

was the ten-pound brick, waiting for me to be the first one to push it all the way across the pool. But something else caught my attention. Something shiny, glimmering. A ring? I knew it had to be my imagination. My navigator ring was nowhere near this pool. Still, something shimmered near the drain. I'd been so excited when my dad gave me the ring, just before he left for the war. That was back when I thought it could make me a navigator like him, guiding a ship by the light of the stars. And that with that ring, I could always find my way. But after the scout survival camp last July, which I barely survived, I knew these things weren't true. Like I'd told my mom, it was just a stupid ring. But now it weighed heavily on me, pulling me under.

I reached for it in the bottom of the Morton Hill pool, the deep water pressing in around me. My ears hurt and my lungs were bursting. Then I couldn't see it anymore. Nothing glimmered. But it had been there. I pulled on the metal drain cap. It wouldn't budge. I felt sleepy, like my eyes couldn't stay open anymore. But I had seen it. It had been there.

Suddenly, I felt strong hands clamp around my arms and pull me toward the surface. Air. Light still splashed on the tile walls. And lots of faces stared at me.

Coach pulled me toward the side and some other hands dragged me out of the water.

"Is he breathing?" Robbie Dean whispered.

I sputtered and coughed, answering his question.

"Move out of the way," Coach barked. "Hey, Baker?

What were you doing? You were under for over a minute and didn't even touch the brick."

"I . . . I . . ." Tears were lurking just behind my eyes. "I feel kinda sick," I muttered.

"Right. You do look a little pale. Hit the locker room, kid. You'll get it next time."

It had been there, that shiny ring.

I grabbed a towel and stumbled my way to the locker room, only to hear a group of upperclassmen whooping and snapping towels at each other. I'm no genius, but even as cloudy-headed as I felt just then, I knew my skinny white legs would be all too easy a target in there.

So I opened the first door I came to and followed the stairs down a flight, to the open doorway of a dimly lit workroom. My head still spun as I leaned back into the coolness of the metal door marked *Custodian*. I closed my eyes, waiting for the feeling to pass, remembering.

Our Boy Scout survival outing was in the woods of northeastern Kansas. The scout leader set each of us out on a course that we'd have to navigate using only landmarks, the stars, and our wits. We'd been preparing for weeks. We'd gone over the North Star, the Big Dipper and Little Dipper—all the constellations. I could identify them all. But that day the sky was overcast. It was only supposed to be a mile out and a mile back. We'd have to rely on landmarks unless the clouds cleared. I knew I'd be done before it got dark and wouldn't need to use the stars anyway.

But as I walked on that humid July evening, each tree

looked like every other. One bush blended in with the next. Rocky paths meandered this way and that, leaving me so turned around, I could barely tell which way was up.

It was almost ten o'clock at night before I heard the scoutmaster and the other scouts calling for me. The whole way home I had to listen to the boys' teasing—how I couldn't find my way out of a bushel basket and how they were glad my dad had a better sense of direction than I did, or his ship would have never found the shores of Normandy on D-day.

But sitting there on the way home, miserable and stewing in the back of the jostling pickup truck, I had no idea how lost I was soon to be. If I had known about my mom— what would happen to her—what could I have done differently? I don't know that anything would have changed what happened.

Suddenly, I realized the water dripping from my swimsuit was making a small puddle around me. I opened my eyes and ventured past the doorway. The room was warm and hummed with a soft, crackling, airy sound. It seemed like a typical custodian's room, cluttered with all kinds of tools; hammers, pliers, wrenches. Anything you would expect to find in the custodian's quarters, only it was much neater. My dad would have felt right at home. A place for everything and everything in its place.

But as I let my eyes roam around, I noticed things you wouldn't expect. Like a cot, bookshelves, chalkboards filled with numbers, equations, and drawings. Not just any drawings, but kind of connect-the-dot pictures. A hunter, a scorpion, a crab. And a great bear. I recognized them. They were constellations. The bear was Ursa Major.

There was also a bulletin board with several newspaper clippings tacked up. The headlines read:

BLACK BEAR STALKS THE APPALACHIAN TRAIL

LARGEST BLACK BEAR TRACKS ON RECORD

**REWARD FOR KILL OR CAPTURE
OF GREAT APPALACHIAN BEAR**

There was still the sound—airy, like a long breath, only not that. I followed it until I came to an old phonograph with a record spinning on the turntable, but the needle was at the end, making only that rhythmic whispering sound. There was a collection of record albums, all neatly placed on a shelf. I was about to see which record had been playing when I heard a voice from a back corner of the room.

"They don't know where he's buried."

I spun around, gripping the towel about my shoulders. It was Early Auden.

4

"Where who's buried?" I asked.

"Mozart." He gestured toward the record. "He's somewhere in Vienna, but there's no gravestone with his name to mark where he's actually buried. Do you think he wanted it that way? To let his music live on, with him unencumbered by praise and accolades?"

I wasn't sure what *unencumbered* meant, and I thought an accolade might be a drink, so I just said what had to be obvious. "I don't know."

"I think he wanted it that way. He wanted to be buried in the white space. Do you hear it?" The boy talked funny. A little too loud. A little flat.

I listened, but all I heard was the sound of the record spinning at its end. "Nothing's playing. You'll have to move the needle."

"No. Mozart is only for Sundays. You were upset when you ran down here. So I put on the white space for you. To calm you down. That's what I do when I'm upset. I listen to the white space. Do you feel better?"

"Yes, thanks." I knew this kid was strange. I was just trying to gauge how strange. So far, I knew he stacked sandbags against the ocean, skipped every class but math, and apparently lived in the basement of his own school. The way he dressed was normal enough, if a bit overly careful, his plaid shirt neatly tucked into his khaki pants and his hair spit-combed down, with a tuft that had sprung free in the back.

Still, the question remained. Was he straitjacket strange or just go-off-by-yourself-at-recess-and-put-bugs-in-your-nose strange? I knew a kid who used to do that in second grade.

I was still making up my mind when he handed me a pair of neatly folded khaki pants and an oxford shirt, along with some deck shoes.

"There's underwear in the left shoe, and socks in the right shoe. Is that the way you do it?"

"That's fine," I said. "Thanks." I didn't make a habit of putting socks or underwear in either shoe, but it was a nice gesture, so I went ahead and crossed *straitjacket strange* off the list of possibilities. Pulling on the dry clothes, I was surprised that they were too big on me, because Early was kind of scrawny. Slipping on the shoes and socks, I looked around at the unusual array of hammers, chalkboards, and record albums. "What is this place?"

"It's my workshop. My father wouldn't let me have a workshop at home. He said I would be the death of him. But I wasn't. It was his heart. He had a heart attack."

"I see," I said. Even though I didn't. "But doesn't the custodian work here?"

"No. Mr. Wallace is the custodian, and he didn't like me hanging around down here, so he set up a new shop in the basement of the middle school. Plus, he likes to *tipple*. That means he likes to sneak a drink of alcohol once in a while. He also calls it *taking a wee half*. My favorite is when he says he's *going for a swalley*. But he prefers to go for a swalley without anybody around."

"Right," I said slowly, thinking Early knew a lot more than I'd given him credit for. "So are these your dad's records and chalkboards?"

"No. He doesn't own anything anymore, because he's dead." Early picked up a piece of chalk, and with what could only be called delicate hands, he began adding numbers to a series of numbers already on one of the chalkboards. There was a deep, croaking sound coming from near the record player.

"That's Bucky. He's a northern leopard frog. I've had him for two years."

"What about your mom?"

"She never had a frog."

"No, I mean, where is she?"

"She died when I was born early."

Aha. Now we're getting somewhere.

"So you live down here? In the custodian's room?"

"Yes. I lived in the dorm until last year, but it was loud. I like it here. It's warm and quiet."

"And if Mozart is for Sundays, who do you listen to the rest of the week?"

"Louis Armstrong on Mondays. Frank Sinatra on Wednesdays. And Glenn Miller on Fridays, unless it's raining. If it's raining, it's always Billie Holiday."

"What about Tuesday, Thursday, and Saturday?" I asked.

"Those days are quiet. Unless it's raining."

I shrugged. "Okay. What's all this?" I gestured to the numbers on the chalkboard.

He picked up where he'd left off, writing numbers on the board, one after another: *806613001927* . . .

"This is the part where Pi gets lost in a hurricane and saved by a whale, and he washes up on the shores of a tropical island right before the volcano blows."

I was leaning back toward the straitjacket. Then I asked Early Auden, that strangest of boys, the most important of questions.

"Who is Pi?"

Suddenly Early looked up from his numbers and locked me in his gaze, as if I were the one who should be wearing a straitjacket. No, I think it was more a look of him trying to decide if he could trust me.

His eyebrows drew together and he paused, chalk in hand. Finally, he took the eraser from its ledge and, standing on tiptoes, erased the hundreds of numbers that were written in neat lines all across the board.

"It's better if you start from the beginning." He took up a piece of chalk in his slender fingers and wrote three numbers and a decimal point on the board.

3.14

I recognized the number pi. Or the beginning of it, anyway. Kind of a coincidence that he had a whole chalkboard full of the number when we were just discussing it in class. But then, my mom always said, "There are no coincidences. Just miracles by the boatload."

"Yeah, Mr. Blane was just talking about that in math class, about it ending. But maybe that was after you left."

"I heard what he said." Early's voice got a little louder. "That's crazy talk."

"How do you know? People thought it was crazy talk to say that the Earth wasn't flat or that it moved around the sun and not the other way around." I couldn't resist. "People probably think it's crazy talk to say that there are no timber rattlesnakes in Maine."

"NO." Early clenched his hands at his side. "It's not like that, because the Earth *isn't* flat and it *does* move around the sun. And"—he huffed—"there *are* timber rattlesnakes in Maine!"

"And pi is just a number." At least, that was what I thought.

Early circled the number one. "This is Pi. And the rest of the numbers are his story. The story of Pi begins with a family. Three is his mother. She is beautiful and kind and she carried him in her heart always. Four is his father. He is strong and good. And here"—Early pointed to the number one, in the middle—"this is Pi. His mother named him Polaris, but she said he would have to earn his name."

The Stargazer

BEFORE THE STARS HAD NAMES, before men knew how to use them to plot their courses, before anyone had ventured beyond his own horizon, there was a boy who wondered what lay beyond. He gazed up at the stars with praise and wonder, but his wonder was not only born of awe. It was also born of a question: Why?

This question began as a spark in his breast and grew with the kindling only a boy's curiosity can provide. Why is the sky so big? he would ask his mother. Why am I so small? Why does the water creep up on the shore, only to retreat again? Why does the moon change its shape? Why do shells hold the sound of the sea? Why? Why? Why?

The mother didn't know the answers to his questions, but she did know that one day he would leave. And that day was not as distant as it had once been. She had named him Polaris, a big name for her little boy, and for now she still called him Pi. But the days passed. The moon changed its shape, and the ocean licked the shore and retreated over and over again.

Someday, when I am big, he thought, *I will put my boat in the water and follow it when it retreats. Then I will know why.*

And the boy grew big.

One day he went to his mother, and she knew. They both cried their tears, though they were not the same. His were youthful and exhilarating. Hers were old and earned. She had made a necklace of shells for him, so he could always hear the sea lapping on his home shore.

"How will I find my way?" he asked as he prepared to leave.

"Look to the stars," she said, ruffling his hair. "They will guide you."

The boy and his mother gazed at the stars as they had when he was small. "Remember those?" He pointed to a cluster that looked like a crab. And another that resembled a hunter. "Which should be my guide?"

His mother looked to the night sky. "What do you see?" she asked.

"That one." He pointed to a shining star. "That one—in the little bear. It's always there."

His mother said, "We will name that star, and it will guide you. And for me, I will know that it is within both our sights." She pointed to the little bear's bright light. "That star will be my Polaris. But"—his mother pointed to a larger group of stars—"the little bear has a mother. The Great Bear." Pi's mother gazed out into the rolling sea. "And a mother's love is fierce. The Great Bear will watch over you."

Finally, Pi cast off, waving as the distance grew between them. Then she called after him. He had forgotten the necklace of shells.

"Too late," he called from a ways offshore. "I'll get them when I return."

She watched as her son became the first to take the questions burning in his chest and set off by the light of the stars. Her Polaris would be the first navigator. But Pi had not yet earned his name.

5

Early continued writing numbers on the chalkboard as he told his story of Pi, but the talk of stars had taken me back to the one place I didn't want to be: The creek near our house, with the late-afternoon sun dancing on the water. After the survival outing.

"Come on, Jackie," Mom had said, trying to perk me up. "Let's skip some rocks. See if you can get four skips with one."

"I might get lost," I grumbled.

"Oh, you're just a bit out of sorts. You'll find your way next time."

"Fat chance," I said. "I can name every constellation in the sky, but put a few clouds in the way, and I get lost. A lot of good stargazing does."

Mom tilted her head back and looked up at the sky. "Sounds to me like you're getting ahead of yourself, Jackie.

That's like expecting a young lady to do your laundry before you gaze into her pretty eyes."

I looked at her, confused.

"You're jumping into the navigating part too soon. Maybe you should focus on the beauty of those stars up there apart from their function. Just take them in, admire them, stand in awe of them, before you expect them to lead the way. Besides, who's to say that one group of stars belongs together and only together? Those stars up there are drawn to each other in lots of different ways. They're connected in unexpected ways, just like people. Who'd have thought your father and I would make a pair? Me, a farm girl from Kansas, and him, a navy man from the East Coast." She smiled at the retelling, even though I'd heard the story from both of them over the years.

My mom had met my dad in a chance encounter. He'd spent some time in California and was heading back east to finish his last two years at the Naval Academy when his train got held up for some repairs in my mom's hometown. He got off the train to stretch his legs just as my mother was delivering a cake to the Granby house to celebrate their new baby.

My dad had said, "What's a fella got to do to get a cake like that?"

"I guess you'd have to have a baby," my mother answered, *grinning to beat the band,* my dad would say.

My dad *smiled a smile that went into tomorrow,* my mother would say. *And that was the end of that,* they both would say. He walked her down to the Granby farm, offering to carry the cake, missed his train, and they were married the next month.

My dad put aside a military career, which didn't sit too well with his father, John Baker the First, and lived the life of a farmer for the first nine years of my life. Then Hitler started bombing England and the Japanese bombed Pearl Harbor and all H-E-double-hockey-sticks broke loose. He joined the navy and shipped out before Christmas that year. He left me in charge, giving me the navigator ring and saying, *Take good care of your mother.* I didn't see him again until my mother died.

"We're part of the same constellation, your father and I," Mom said that day. "It's just not one you find in any textbook."

"That's a nice story, Mom, but it's not exactly going to help me find my way out of the woods," I told her.

"Sometimes it's best not to see your whole path laid out before you. Let life surprise you, Jackie. There are more stars out there than just the ones with names. And they're all beautiful." Listening to my mother was a lot like reading poetry. I had to stretch my mind to make sense of what she was trying to get across. And even when I did understand, sometimes I tried not to let on.

Gradually, I realized that the *click-clack* of chalk had stopped and been filled with the white noise of the record player. Sitting on the floor with my back against a file cabinet, I must have nodded off. Looking up, I saw the chalkboard full of numbers streaming out from the original 3.14. The numbers, Early had said, were a mother, a father, and their son, Pi.

Had I really heard this story or just dreamed it? Either way, it was a silly notion that these numbers told a story. And Early, that strangest of boys, was now sitting on his cot beside the record player, but instead of watching it spin, he was busy tying a rope in an elaborate knot, so engrossed in his work, it was as if that rope and its knots also had a mesmerizing story to tell.

"Um, sorry," I said, clearing my throat. "I must have dozed off."

"That's okay," said Early without looking up. "The next numbers aren't as good as the beginning. Pi just sails on the open seas awhile before anything happens again. I don't think you'd like that part."

"Okay," I said. "Well, thanks for the clothes. I'd better get back to the dorm."

Early was too engrossed in his rope and knot making to notice me leave.

I didn't see Early for a week, not that I went looking for him. My mother would not be happy about that. She had a knack for pairing me up with every misfit and newcomer. *Jack would love to have you come over to play,* she'd say without having heard any such thing from me. For my tenth birthday party, she said I could invite six boys to the bowling alley. But there ended up being seven, because Melvin Trumboldt had just moved to town and supposedly didn't know a soul. I fought her on that point, as Melvin got in trouble the first day of school for flushing all the toilets in the boys' bathroom one after another, and I knew he was well acquainted with the principal.

But she made me invite him anyway, and he turned out not to be so bad. Especially when he gave up the name Melvin and started going by Flush. I got sucked into his antics a couple of times, but Mom could never get too mad, as she was the one who'd forced us into being friends.

The point is, she wouldn't be too happy with me not inviting Early to join a table at lunch or play ball after school. But my mom wasn't here to watch over me. Besides, I was the new kid this time, and people weren't exactly banging on my door. Until about five o'clock one morning when someone was doing just that. Banging loud and insistent.

I was still coming out of a hard sleep when the pounding continued on the next door over, and the next one.

"Let's go, gentlemen. Crew call," an adult voice boomed.

I poked my head out the door. It was Mr. Blane, the math teacher. It was a school day, but no one had said anything about five-a.m. math class. He was dressed in gray sweatpants and a hooded sweatshirt with the Morton Hill crest on the front and the word *Crew* underneath. Was he getting us all out of bed to be the kitchen crew? Or the latrine crew?

Just then, Sam Feeney poked his bleary-eyed face out of his room. "Hey, what's all the racket about, Mr. Blane?"

"It's about rising to the challenge, Mr. Feeney. It's about discipline and strength. It's about working as a team."

"Really?" Sam muttered. "'Cause by my clock it's *about* five a.m., which is *about* an hour and a half before my alarm's set to go off." He stretched and, yawning, said, "Which means I'm *about* to go back to bed."

"Time waits for no man, Feeney. Suit up."

Emerging from my dorm room in my own Morton Hill–issued sweats, I finally clomped down the stairs. I made it out of the building and was the last one to catch up with the other eighth-grade boys on their walk down to the calm inlet called Wabenaki Bay. By the time we reached the water, the boats were all full, with groups of two and four boys to a boat. Those sleek vessels had names, painted on the sides, like *Torpedo* and *Jerry Runner* and *Spoiler*.

By the time I set foot on the swaying dock, the only boat left was a weather-beaten vessel named the *Sweetie Pie*.

"All aboard, Mr. Baker." Mr. Blane extended his hand with a flourish, as if the *Sweetie Pie* were the flagship of a magnificent fleet of rowing vessels and not the sorry, saggy swamp bucket it appeared to be.

"This is my boat?" I asked.

"Yes. I know she looks a bit rough around the edges, but she's yar," he said, before moving on down the dock.

"*Yar?*" I repeated. I stared at the boat, with its two seats. My face must have screamed confusion.

"Don't you know anything?" Robbie Dean asked. "Your boat's a double, which means it's for two people. But you're the last one here, so you'll have to row it as a single." He took up the rowing position in his boat, which was sleeker and obviously designed for just one person.

"But what does *yar* mean?" I asked.

"Quick to maneuver. Easy to handle."

"Quick to maneuver. Easy to handle," I repeated. "Got it."

"Now, remember, this isn't a race," said Mr. Blane. "We're just trying to get our legs pumping. So let's get you out and see what we have to work with."

One by one, the boats were pushed away from the dock. Most were two-man boats. Robbie Dean and Sam shoved away from the dock in the *Jerry Runner*, while Preston Townsend occupied the only other single, the *Spoiler*. I watched as they glided through the water, straight as arrows, their bodies moving forward and backward, legs pushing, arms pulling, in one fluid motion.

"Mr. Baker. Let's see how you fare. You know how to row, don't you?"

"Sure," I said. *It can't be that hard,* I thought. My arms and legs were strong from swimming and bike riding, even though I hadn't done much of either after everything with my mom. I eased myself aboard and tried to position myself in the seat, hoping to catch up with the other boats.

"Quit messing around, Baker," hollered Mr. Blane. "Turn around and get moving."

Turn around? I looked up, expecting Mr. Blane to yank me out of the water and put me in a beginners' rowing class with the sixth graders. But he was studying his clipboard and seemed to mistake my bumbling for messing around. I guess I *had* told him I knew how to row, but I didn't think he'd believe me.

Another boy rolled his eyes. "You don't face forward. See how they're rowing? You face backward."

Backward?

I turned around. This time, my feet found their place, and I started rowing—backward. In a direction I couldn't see. Still, it was a big bay. Nothing really to run into. I hunched forward as far as my body would reach and gave the oars a mighty heave. Mom always said I was as strong as an ox. And an ox had to be stronger than anything they had around here—like lobster and shrimp. *I'll be fine*, I told myself.

My heart began pounding, and for the first few strokes, I felt the thrill of gliding through the water. Until I realized I was veering off course. I tried pulling a little harder with the left oar and veered off course even more. *Must be the right oar.* I tugged and pulled. *Yar. Quick to maneuver. This boat isn't quick to do anything except go off in the wrong direction.*

Slowly, I veered back toward the center of the bay. *Uh-oh.* Too far the other way. And so it went. Too far this way, too far that way. I zigzagged back and forth across the bay. As I made a wide turn to head back, I saw that most of the boats had already arrived at the dock. Well, I could still make a strong finish. *There's no shame in coming in last as long as your head's up and your tail's not between your legs.* Three guesses who said that.

I had the dock in sight, as much as it could be as I strained to look over my left shoulder. The other boats were already out of the water. What was maybe a twenty-minute row for the other boys was taking me twice as long. The rowers stood on the deck, watching me make my approach. My shoulders and back ached, and my legs shook violently each time they crunched forward and pushed back. Even my hands were clenched, so tight on the oars that I didn't think I'd be able to pry them off. But I would finish, and it would be over.

I was already rehearsing my finishing line. *It took me a while to figure her out, but she sure is yar.*

Finally, I pulled the *Sweetie Pie* along the dock with a scraping noise that sounded like a cat on a midnight prowl. Preston, Sam, Robbie Dean, and the others all watched with pained grimaces on their faces, waiting for the boat and the noise to come to a stop. I stood up and felt the evil *Sweetie Pie* pitch left, then right, and before I could say Jack Tar, I was upended in Wabenaki Bay.

There were a few chuckles and shaking of heads as the boys lifted the remaining boats onto their shoulders and headed to the boathouse. I took my time getting out of the water, as I was not eager to catch up. Mr. Blane extended his hand and gave me a lift. "It's all right, Baker. I guess you're not as experienced at rowing as you let on. We'll work on it for next time."

Next time. That's just what Coach Baynard had said after the incident in the pool. That's what Mom had said about my next survival outing. How many *next time*s would there have to be?

"Here, help me get her out of the water," said Mr. Blane. I lifted the boat but wasn't sure how much I helped. "I'm sure one of the boys will help you carry her to the boathouse. I've got a faculty meeting in a few minutes." He patted me on the back. "You'll get the hang of it next time. See you in math class, Baker." Mr. Blane walked briskly up the dock.

"Yes, sir," I said, glad to be left alone. I stood dripping and shaking like one of our old barn cats, glaring at the source of my contempt. The *Sweetie Pie*. I gave her a swift kick and toppled her onto her craggy side.

Yup, she sure is yar, if by yar you mean wobbly, easily tipped, and likely to throw you in the drink.

6

I read somewhere, probably in a *National Geographic* magazine, that you can tell a lot about people by what they enshrine. I suppose every place has its temples. In my hometown, the church is at the center of everything: potlucks, baptisms, weddings, auctions, bingo. At my old school the baseball diamond was our shrine. The folks from town would fill the bleachers and pray for victory. As players, we were well versed in the scripture of baseball lore and knew all the patron saints: Babe Ruth, Lou Gehrig, Ty Cobb, and Joe DiMaggio.

The moment I set foot in the stone boathouse, I knew this was Morton Hill Academy's shrine. According to Headmaster Conrady, the Nook, as it was called, was the oldest building on campus. Inside were sturdy wooden beams, lobster traps, coiled ropes, and a colorful array of oars. The scents of lemon wax, polish, and apple cider vinegar were as powerful as any incense I'd smelled. But it was the boats themselves, gleaming and elevated like altars, that were the focal point.

I held my breath, waiting for the heavens to open and angels to begin singing as I walked almost in procession to a single boat called the *Maine*. It was in the center and seemed to hold the place of highest honor. I reached out my hand, thinking if I could just rub it like a genie's lamp, I could have my wish granted. My fingers touched the rich grain, and I considered my wish. That should have been easy, right? Everybody's got a special wish. I thought harder. Of course, I could have wished that Mom wasn't dead. I could have wished that my dad wasn't in the navy. I could have clicked my heels together three times and wished myself back to Kansas. But I knew none of those wishes would come true.

Letting out a sigh of defeat, I realized I didn't even know what to wish for. I looked down at the *Sweetie Pie* with scorn. Her tired frame and half-split oars seemed to reflect my own shabby state. I was too stubborn to ask the other boys for help, so I'd had to hoist and tug and even drag her back to the boathouse myself.

I pressed my hand to the rich wood of the *Maine* and let out a breath. It was a little wish, and I knew it didn't count for much in the great scheme of things. But it was all I could muster.

I wish I had a better boat.

Then I heard a noise and drew back my hand. There was a rustling sound in the corner. I peeked around another boat, and there was Early Auden. What *was* he? Some kind of second-rate genie? His back was to me, but he spoke as if he were looking at me.

"You row crooked." He reached into a canister of wax and pulled out a glob. "You're left-handed, and you pull harder on that side. That makes you go crooked."

"Is that so?" I asked, the spell of the boathouse broken. I went to look for the *Sweetie Pie*'s stall or rack or whatever fancy name they might call it, since they had a different word for everything. It would probably be in an out-of-the-way spot that wouldn't be a source of embarrassment to the other boats. Sure enough, there was an open rack next to the workbench where Early Auden was kneading some honey into the wax.

"Your body is stiff and your shoulders are too tight. You're working against the boat instead of with it."

"Uh-huh." I hoisted one end of the *Sweetie Pie* before Early helped me with the other end. He wasn't very strong, so it was still an ordeal to lift the boat onto its rack.

"And you slouch."

"Great." I slammed the boat in place. "Maybe next time you should just hop on and give me your instructions the whole way."

"Okay," Early answered. "But we'll wait a few days. Tomorrow you'll be too sore. You'll still walk funny, but here, this will help." He scooped dollops of the wax and vinegar and honey concoction into a jar.

"What?" I said. "No, I didn't mean—"

"Put your arms out. Like this." He spread my arms out to the sides in a T, then took a tape measure from a drawer and

47

began measuring. My arm span, height, and legs. "You're tall. And your sculls are too short."

He handed me a pair of shiny wooden oars with brightly painted paddles.

Right. Sculls equals oars. Got it. But at that point I didn't care.

"You need longer sculls so you can have a wider rowing span."

"Look," I said, "I appreciate it, but . . . I didn't mean I really wanted . . . What I'm trying to say is, I don't need your help."

Early smiled. "That's what *he* said."

"What who said?"

"Pi. Remember that part I told you, when he set out on his voyage? Remember that, Jackie?"

It hit me like a wave of ice-cold water, and I found myself holding my breath. My mom was the only one who called me Jackie.

"Remember, he wanted to set out. To be the first navigator. But it wasn't easy for him at first either."

My jaw tightened. "Yeah, I remember. But I don't want to hear another story about numbers right now. And my name is Jack."

"Jack Baker. I know you. You're from Kansas. Do they not have boats in Kansas?"

"Of course we have boats in Kansas. Only we use them to fish, not just row around in circles. Besides, the boat I got stuck with is lopsided, rickety, leaky, and ugly. And it has a stupid name. What kind of name is the *Sweetie Pie*? I'm surprised it doesn't have a pair of red lips smacked on the side."

I took a breath after my rant.

Then Early said, "If you don't like it, take it apart and make it right."

I kept my back to him. I didn't want his help. I didn't want his advice. What did he know, anyway? He was just an odd kid who nobody listened to.

Still, I remembered my mom's words about the soap box derby car that I'd left out in the rain. The same words Early had used. *If you don't like it, take it apart and make it right.*

Then I turned around, but Early was gone. Only the jar of waxy goop remained. My muscles were already starting to tighten up, but I didn't need Early's help, so I headed back to the dorm to get ready for class, leaving the jar in its place.

I woke up the next morning and could barely get out of bed. The muscles in my arms, shoulders, back, and legs ached as if I'd just walked the Appalachian Trail, then swum the English Channel, then gotten hit by a bus. It even hurt to open my eyes. But I did, and that's when I saw the jar of honey-colored ointment on my desk.

I sat up and tender-footed my way across the cold tile floor and reached for the jar. Opening it would be another matter. My hands had been clenched so tight on the mismatched oars of the *Sweetie Pie* throughout my zigzag course of the day before that now they felt the way my grandpa Henry's gnarled, arthritic hands looked like they must feel. But I made them clamp on the lid and twist.

The smell was shifty. It wafted up first as honey, then snuck up on me with a stiff vinegar-and-menthol punch. I quickly put the lid back on to keep the odor at bay. After a painful and fairly awkward trip to the bathroom, I went back to my room and thought about whether or not to use Early's ointment. Reasons for using it: Early said I'd still walk funny, but it would make me feel better. And the smell would keep vampires away. Reasons against: I'd stink to high heaven, and the smell would keep everyone else away.

But after the pool incident and then my latest embarrassment in trying to row the *Sweetie Pie*, I didn't figure I'd have too many guys wanting me to join their table at lunch anyway. So I stuck my fingers in the goop jar and applied it to my sore spots, which pretty much covered my whole body. Then I put on my khaki pants and blue oxford shirt and walked out of my dorm room to brave the sniffs and snorts of the students of Morton Hill Academy.

Semper Fi.

7

By the time I got to math class, the boys were giving me a wide berth. I slipped in the back row and took out my textbook.

After a lesson on congruent triangles, during which I struggled to keep my eyes open, Sam Feeney raised his hand. "Mr. Blane, I read an article about that professor you mentioned and his theory of pi ending. He's presenting his theory at the Fall Mathematical Institute, in Boston. How do you think he's going to show that pi ends?"

"Well, I've read quite a bit about it myself, and his theory is based on a trend that he has noticed in the most recently calculated digits of pi. Right now, we know pi to over seven hundred digits after the decimal point. But as you know, mathematicians are continuing to calculate more and more numbers.

"Professor Stanton has discovered that in the last one hundred digits of the most recent calculation of pi, the number one no longer appears. He believes that this trend will continue and that the numbers will continue to cease to appear until the entire number pi collapses in on itself and ends."

I looked around the room to see if everyone else was as befuddled as I was. They were.

"Imagine, if you will," Mr. Blane continued, "a pool table. There are fifteen numbered balls on the table. Each time one of the numbered balls is sunk in a pocket, that number ceases to play a part in the game. If balls continue to be knocked into pockets, eventually there will be no numbers left, and the game ends."

Robbie Dean's hand went up. "And Professor Stanton can prove that numbers will continue to disappear until the whole number pi ends?"

"That remains to be seen at the Fall Math Institute." Mr. Blane's eyes flashed with excitement. "It might make for a great field trip, if any of you are interested. There will be mathematicians there from all over the world. It could be the equivalent of Sir Galahad discovering the Holy Grail—or, rather, discovering that the Holy Grail doesn't exist."

"What if he's wrong?" I asked. "How would someone disprove Professor Stanton's theory?" I wasn't really all that interested in Professor Stanton's theory and didn't really care if he was right or not. But in my mother's words, I was being contrary, and it felt good to challenge what everyone else was so excited about.

"That would be called a proof by contradiction. Someone would have to find one of the numbers that is supposed to have disappeared. It would be like finding one of the missing pool balls. If it could be shown that a missing number was back in play, Professor Stanton's theory would be contradicted and rendered invalid."

There was a buzz around the room as boys considered the prospect. Then the bell rang.

"Class dismissed, gentlemen."

I didn't think Mr. Blane's revelation would spark such discussion, but that evening in the dormitory, a few boys congregated in Sam and Robbie Dean's room, relaxing on their Friday night. Granted, it didn't start out as a discussion of pi, but rather as a sort of pie-eating event. Robbie Dean's mother had sent an apple crumble pie for him to share among his friends, and there was a great deal of dispute over how big a slice each boy should get.

From the talk I overheard from my room next door, mainly through the vent that opened into both rooms, I gathered that Sam was insisting he should get a bigger piece because there was more of him to feed. Robbie Dean said his mother meant for him to share slivers, not full-fledged pieces. And Preston Townsend said that he had always been a favorite of Robbie Dean's mother, and he was sure that she meant for him to have a healthy portion.

I sat reading a *National Geographic* magazine on Machu Picchu, trying to convince myself that I preferred having a room all to myself and that I enjoyed the quiet. But the noises from next door, the eating, the chatter, the banter, presented me with a head-on proof by contradiction that I was fooling myself. I was lonely.

"It's too bad *this* pie isn't never-ending," said Preston. "I wonder what Professor What's-His-Name would have to say about that. The one who believes that pi ends. Stanford? Sanbridge?"

That's when I was called in.

"Hey, Baker," Sam called. "Put your *National Geographic* down and come here."

I shut my magazine and shoved it under my pillow, wondering how he knew what I was reading. It was true that most of my free time lately had been spent with my nose in a *National Geographic*, so it was a pretty safe guess. I poked my head in next door, trying to look casual and disinterested.

"Douglas Stanton," I said, giving away the fact that I'd been listening. Glancing around, I saw that the room was identical to mine—two beds, two closets, a sink, and a desk. But their bedspreads were red, there were pictures on the wall, and—I breathed in deeply—it smelled of apple crumble pie.

"Yeah, well, if he's like Sir Galahad, I'm a monkey's uncle," said Preston. "There aren't very many people I'd put in the same category with *him*. Who would you say?"

"Robin Hood," said Sam.

"The Three Musketeers," countered Robbie Dean. "Four, if you count d'Artagnan."

The three of them looked at me. "What about you, Baker?"

"I don't know. I guess I'd rather pick somebody real, not just a character from a book."

"Oh, well, that's easy," said Sam.

Then the three spoke in unison, saying one name.

"The Fish."

I knew I was going to sound dumb, but I said it anyway. "Who's the Fish?"

They looked at each other, confirming that I was both stupid *and* an outsider. Robbie Dean took on the role of the explainer. "The Fish—Number 67, class of 1943. He's only the greatest athlete ever to walk the halls of Morton Hill Academy."

Number 67. The boy in the trophy case.

"They retired his number, and that's his boat in the Nook," Sam added.

My eyes grew wide in disbelief. "The blue one? The *Maine*?"

"That's the one," said Robbie Dean. "We were all sixth graders that year. He was all-state in football, track, and rowing. But those pale in comparison to what he did in the Steeplechase."

I took a breath, knowing I was only going to make myself look worse. "Steeplechase?"

This time they rolled their eyes and groaned. Preston spoke up. "For crying out loud, Baker, what rock have you been living under? Oh, yeah, you're from Kansas." He said it as if Kansas were in some remote tribal region inhabited by illiterate natives like the ones in my *National Geographic* magazines.

"Shut the door," Preston ordered. I did and immediately regretted it. "Jeez, Baker. You smell like a medicine cabinet."

"Sorry, it's a kind of lotion for sore muscles," I said, leaving Early's name out of the mix.

The boys leaned forward with an air of secrecy as Robbie Dean set about relieving me of my ignorance. "The Steeplechase was a competition that used to be an annual event among the senior boys. It was named after the horse races that started in Ireland and England where the horses would run a course from one church steeple to another, jumping fences, ditches, creeks, and everything in between."

"We'd be hard-pressed to use horses here"—Sam picked up where Robbie Dean left off—"because we don't have any. But it's the same idea. You start at the chapel, then head to Dinosaur Log—"

Robbie Dean smacked him on the back of the head. "Don't tell him the course, you idjit."

"If it's an annual event, why is the course such a big secret?" I asked.

"Because they put the kibosh on the Steeplechase after Philip Attwater slipped off Dinosaur Log and nearly broke his neck," said Preston.

"Yeah, he had to go and ruin it for everybody," Sam grumbled. "That's why anytime someone messes up in a way that messes it up for everyone else, we say, 'Attaboy, Attwater.'"

Robbie Dean spoke up. "That's what we should have said to Sam when he ate too many desserts at lunch and threw up. Now we each only get one."

"That wasn't my fault," Sam insisted. "Coach had us running laps in PE after lunch and—"

"Yeah, yeah, and I'm sure he apologized right after you hurled three helpings of cherry cobbler on his shoes."

"So, does the Fish ever come back? Do you think he could still do the Steeplechase?"

The guys fell into an awkward silence. "No, he didn't come back," Robbie Dean answered, all the bravado gone from his voice. "After graduation, he enlisted. He took it on the chin in France. His whole squad was killed."

Nobody said anything more after that, but their silence and their awkward glances at each other made it clear that they preferred not to have their all-star image of the Fish ruined by an outsider coming in and forcing them to view their legend outside the trophy case.

And no one seemed to have much of an appetite for any more pie.

8

I must have fallen into a deep sleep, because I woke up hours later to the first light of dawn on a foggy Saturday morning. My body still ached from my first rowing experience, but I felt the need to get up and move.

Without really knowing where I would go or what I would do, I put on my sweats and headed out into the mist, first walking, then running. The air was damp, and I felt beads of moisture on my face and neck. The world around me was gray and quiet. I settled into the rhythm of my running. And let my thoughts run as well.

Steeplechase. It reminded me of the landmarks back home. The church steeple, windmill, silo, grain elevator. All could be seen from miles away. I knew where I was when I was there. But the very name of it captured my imagination. *Steeplechase.* It seemed a quest of sorts, like the quest for the Holy Grail—the runner searching from steeple to steeple, overcoming obstacles along the way.

And the Fish. To hear those boys talk about him, he must have been like Sir Galahad himself—courageous, adventurous, honorable. And he'd completed the Steeplechase faster than any boy ever had. No wonder he had become such a legend at Morton Hill.

I found myself running faster and faster, downhill, uphill, hurdling rocks and jumping fences, creating my own steeplechase as I went. My lungs were bursting and my heart was pounding. Was I trying to beat the legendary Fish? We probably weren't even running the same course. Was I chasing after him? What made him run so fast? The way I figured it, anybody runs that fast, they're either chasing after something or running away from it. Which was it for the Fish? Which was it for me?

Then I saw the log. I could understand why they called it Dinosaur Log. It looked like a long-necked brontosaurus stretched out over that waterfall and the rocks below. Sam had let slip that it was part of the Steeplechase. I stopped, my breath coming out in puffs of air as if from a dragon. A dragon being stared down by a brontosaurus.

I took the challenge and stepped onto the log. It was slippery with mist and moss, about twenty feet across. I figured it should only take about as many steps, but the sound of rushing water crashing against the rocks below, and the thought of Philip Attwater's nearly broken neck, made me pause. Still, the challenge lay before me and had to be met. I inched my way out, beyond where I could easily turn back. A few more steps, then I was halfway. That was when a double whammy happened. It started raining *and* I looked down.

The rain was falling at a slant, pelting me from the side, forcing me to shift my weight just to stand upright. I'd been in some stiff Kansas winds, but not while standing on a slippery log over a waterfall. My thick sweats hung heavy and clung to my skin. There were only three ways to go: forward, backward, or straight down. The rocks below, jagged and sharp, sent a shiver up my back.

I was halfway, I reasoned. Even if I turned back, that would be the equivalent of the full length of the whole log. But I wouldn't have crossed it. Wasn't that the whole point? To cross? To get to the other side? But for what? There was nothing different over there. Just the same rain, the same grass. And what other obstacles would I encounter?

I don't know if it was fear of falling or fear of getting across that turned me back, but I maneuvered myself around and inched my way off the log.

My arms and legs shook with cold and fatigue. I shoved my hands in the wet front pocket of my sweatshirt and listened to my shoes make squishing sounds as I walked back to school. Mom used to say, *Get out of the rain before it washes all the dry off.* By the time I got back to campus, every bit of dry had been washed clean away.

I knew the dorm would be full of rowdy boys just waking up to their Saturday. So I veered in the other direction, hoping to find an open door to the school, where I knew I had a change of clothes in my locker.

The hot shower water felt good on my cold skin and aching muscles. I let it warm me for several minutes before putting on a fresh pair of denims, a long-sleeved shirt, and dry socks. Unfortunately, I didn't have different shoes to put on, so I walked down the hall to the library in my stocking feet.

I stared at the picture of him in his Morton Hill Academy sweatshirt, his hair slicked back, smiling that smile. I remembered feeling sorry for Number 67, the Fish, the last time I'd been here. I'd felt pity for him because of all that he had yet to learn about life's cruelties. But something had changed. He was dead. There was no plaque memorializing him. No date to say when he was killed in action. But then, this trophy case wasn't meant for that. It was meant only to lock its inhabitants in a particular time and place. To make its onlookers share forever in their glory days.

The Fish. Did his exuberant face seem not so exuberant anymore? Where I had once felt pity, I now felt kinship.

If the Nook was the shrine of the school, the trophy case had become a sort of shrine for me, a place to pay homage to the Fish, my patron saint. I remembered touching his boat and sending up a wish, a prayer of sorts. But, I reminded myself, the only answer I'd gotten was that Early kid lecturing me about how horrible a rower I was.

So much for wishes or prayers, I thought.

I padded out of the library so quietly that even if somebody had been there, they'd never have known I was gone.

9

The rain was still coming down, and I'd either have to put on my wet tennis shoes to go back to the dorm or take off my socks and walk in my bare feet. I stood at the door, watching the rain make rivers on the window of the side door to the school, feeling the cold of the cement stairs creeping through my socks. Barefoot it was.

Then I heard a woman's voice—singing.

It was a rich, soulful voice full of tenderness and heartache. Something in me hurt like a wounded joint that aches when it rains. The voice was coming from the basement. As I walked down a couple of stairs, it dawned on me that it had been a while since I'd heard a woman's voice at all. Oh, there had been the ladies from church who'd brought over casseroles after my mom died, but they usually spoke only in sympathetic whispers. The woman at the funeral home was old, and she smoked, so her voice was deeper than my father's. And there was Miss B., the librarian, but she spoke in a hushed librarian voice.

No. I crept closer. This was the voice of a whole different kind of woman. She sang of wishing on the moon and begging of the stars. It was a song of dreams and longing.

As I got closer to the custodian's workshop, I could hear a crackly, whirring sound and realized with some disappointment that the singing was from a record. I remembered what Early Auden had said. He listened to Louis Armstrong on Mondays, Frank Sinatra on Wednesdays, Glenn Miller on Fridays, and Mozart on Sundays. Unless it was raining.

If it's raining, it's always Billie Holiday.

I had heard of Billie Holiday, the jazz and blues singer, but I'd never really listened to her sing. Her voice mixed with the music like molasses with warm butter.

I stood just outside the door, listening, glad I was out of the rain, when I recognized a familiar smell. Wood. Wood shavings, cut wood, split wood. I breathed in deeply. It smelled like my dad's workshop. And kind of like a soap box car.

Suddenly, I had a feeling I knew what Early was doing. I walked in, and there he was, leaning over the *Sweetie Pie*, laid out on a wooden frame. He had knocked out several sections of warped boards and was working at unscrewing the seat rigging.

I opened my mouth to tell him thanks but no thanks. I really wasn't serious about building a better boat.

"Her real name is Eleanora Fagan," Early said before I could speak.

"Whose real name?" I said, irritated at how he just jumped into a conversation, making me feel two steps behind.

"Billie Holiday's. I wondered if she changed it so people wouldn't confuse her with Eleanor Roosevelt. But I don't see how they could be confused, because one's white and one's Negro. Do you know which one is white and which is Negro?"

"Yes, Early, I know which is which." My irritation subsided a little. He was odd, but in a funny way.

"Plus, one is a singer and one was the president's wife."

"Yup, it'd be pretty hard to confuse the two of them."

The room smelled not only of wood, but also of other shop items, like kerosene, glue, and varnish. It was warm and homey. I picked up an oar and ran my finger along its rough paddle.

"That blade needs smoothing," Early said, handing me a square of sandpaper. Of course it wouldn't be called a paddle. That would be too common—and make too much sense. I began sanding. There was something reassuring about the rough splinters giving way to a fresh smoothness underneath.

"Maybe her real name was Billie Holiday all along but she had to earn it. Just like Pi."

I didn't answer, not sure if I wanted to hear more about his imaginary story made up of numbers.

"Remember that part, Jackie? The part where Pi wants to go explore and his mother says to keep his eye on the stars? Remember that? And she names the North Star after him. Polaris. Remember?"

"Yeah, I remember," I said, still sanding. "But he hadn't earned his name yet."

"Right. So, you want to hear what happens next?"

"No. That mathematician Mr. Blane knows of—Dr. Stanton—he's going to present his theory next month about pi ending. He says one number has already disappeared and eventually pi will die out."

"Stop that! You don't know what you're talking about." Early moved quickly to sit on his cot. He grabbed a jar of jelly beans off the shelf, poured them out onto his bed, and started sorting them by color. I guess he did that to calm himself down. But at one point he just quit sorting. His hands lay at his sides, and he stared off into space. His eyes blinked and fluttered a few times. I wouldn't have called it a full-blown fit, but I knew he was having one of those seizures the boys talked about. Just as I started to think that maybe I should go for help, he came out of it.

"I know where he is," Early said, as if nothing had happened.

"Where who is?" I was confused.

"Pi. That professor says pi ends, but I know where he is."

"He's not talking about your *character*. It's the *number* that will end." But I could see that for Early, they were one and the same.

"Sometimes he's hard to find for a while, but he always comes back. I always find him." Early kept sorting the jelly beans into neat groups of red, orange, yellow, green, blue.

Billie Holiday's voice trailed off, one song ending and

65

another one beginning. Early replaced the jelly beans in the jar, then flipped his chalkboard around, revealing rows of numbers. "See, it's right here that he gets in his boat. These numbers, see how they look wavy, like the ocean?"

. . . 3285345768 . . .

"No, they don't look wavy. They're just numbers. And you're making up a story to go along with them. I get it. It's pretty creative."

Early balled his fists again. "They're not just numbers. And I'm not making up a story. The story *is* in the numbers. Look at them! The numbers have colors—blues of the ocean and sky, green grass, a bright-yellow sun. The numbers have texture and landscape—mountains and waves and sand and storms. And words—about Pi and about his journey. The *numbers* tell a story. And you don't deserve to hear it."

Early moved the record-player needle, cutting off Billie Holiday in the middle of a heartfelt song. He set it back down on the crackling empty space and sat on his cot with his back to me.

I stared at his back for a minute. He was right. I probably didn't deserve to hear it. But I didn't want to go back to the dorm, and the lonely sound of the record crackling in the empty space made my heart ache as if it had been rowing hard for a long time.

"So, these numbers . . . the wavy ones. What do they say?"

Early didn't turn around. His voice was quiet.

"That's where the sea gets rough."

Student of the Ocean

THE YOUNG NAVIGATOR had set off by the light of the stars. But they were soon covered by clouds, and the sea grew rough.

Pi had lived his entire life next to the sea, and he knew it well. He knew its moods and whims. Its tides and swells. The sound of its playful splash and spray lapping at the sandy shore, as well as that of its waves crashing against the rocks. The salt and brine had worked their way into every pore of his skin. He knew the sea. Or so he thought. But as his voyage began, Pi realized he knew only what the ocean had let him know. What it had deemed necessary for him to know. But now—now that the ocean had allowed him in, it enveloped him with the fury and passion of a master teacher. And Pi had much to learn.

The sea tossed him to and fro, making him cling to his little boat while he retched and heaved and shivered. Until finally the sea dashed Pi's boat against jagged rocks and spit him out on the shore of a distant island. But Pi was angry and turned his back on the ocean. He didn't need a teacher. He would learn the lessons he wanted to learn. And he did learn—that eating all your provisions in a day will leave you hungry the next, and starving the next after that. That yelling at the stars through the night and sleeping through the day will produce a sore throat and scorched skin. And that kicking a wrecked boat will not fix it.

But eventually his anger and pride subsided as fatigue set in, and he lay on the beach, ready to learn. The ocean washed over his dry, burnt body, rousing him from his delirium, teaching him to look for fresh water in hollow stalks and to use the sap from plants to soothe his skin.

The sea withheld food, teaching Pi to search the beach for crabs, hunt boar, and learn the sweet taste of a good berry over the bitter taste of the bad.

The ocean, in its cycle of wind and rain, pelted Pi, encouraging him to build a lean-to of reeds and leaves to keep himself dry.

Over time, Pi's muscles grew strong and his mind stronger. He knew to find shelter when the colorful island birds ceased their chatter. A storm was coming. He knew that fish were easiest to catch in the calm of low tide. And he knew that a boat left wrecked on the beach will not fix itself.

Rebuilding his boat brought new discoveries for the young navigator. He had a keen eye for the craft—carving, bending, lashing—and he found pleasure in the work. The way the wood of a fallen tree would take shape in his hands. The feel of running a rough sandstone over the wood to make it smooth. Through his labor, he discovered that a thumb is best not left under a falling hammer. And that sweat and aching muscles bring satisfaction and restful sleep. Finally, after Pi had learned much in the way of survival, as well as humility, the sea allowed him back.

But Pi was still learning his place in the world. And he had not yet earned his name.

10

In the last days of August and beginning weeks of September, I went to class and worked on the boat with Early. The other boys continued to have crew practice, and I told Mr. Blane I'd catch up as soon as my boat was ready. He didn't seem to mind that I hadn't shown up yet. Maybe he felt responsible for my initial humiliation and didn't want a recurrence of me falling in the bay. I still saw the other boys in class and around the dorm, but ever since that night in Sam and Robbie Dean's dorm room and the talk of the Fish, the awkwardness lingered like the empty space on one of Early's records. It whirled in circles, making it hard to jump back in.

Those after-school hours blended together to the sounds of Frank Sinatra, Glenn Miller, Louis Armstrong, Mozart, and Billie Holiday, depending on the day and the weather. Sometimes Early and I listened to shows on the radio. *The Lone Ranger*, *Buck Rogers*, *Jungle Jim*, and *Captain Midnight*.

There was also local news of the roamings of the great bear still terrorizing wayfarers on the Appalachian Trail. The bounty was up to $750.

One night, we listened in reverent silence as the voice on the radio crackled over the airwaves, announcing the official surrender of Japan on the USS *Missouri*. The war was over. We could hear whoops and hollers from boys outside, but Early and I continued our work without speaking, filled with our own thoughts about the war.

In fact, I think Early and I both enjoyed those times of quiet, when we worked in silence, listening only to the croaking of Bucky the frog and our own thoughts.

I thought I knew a thing or two about woodworking. I even bragged to Early about having built a soap box car before, but Early was much more skilled. As the afternoon light spilled in through the basement windows, we worked at disassembling the *Sweetie Pie*, stripping layers of varnish and repairing splits. Early showed me how to mix in matching sawdust with resin to give a more uniform color under the varnish.

We spent several days on the oars, repairing cracks in the blades, painting them blue with white stripes, and sanding the wooden shaft and handle for a smooth finish.

The bones of the *Sweetie Pie* were sound, but after we'd knocked off all the rotten parts and rough edges, the bones were about all that was left. The only wood we had available was whatever we could find in the workshop or in the boathouse. There were hodgepodge pieces of maple and oak and a little mahogany for the trim.

The Morton Hill Regatta was four weeks away. I had

pretended that I wasn't interested. After all, rowing a boat wasn't a real sport. But as the days went by and my hands sanded, carved, bent, caulked, glued, and fastened every inch of the *Sweetie Pie*, I felt the stirrings of something familiar—the spirit of competition.

Back home we competed over everything. There was always some contest of strength, speed, endurance, or will. There were the usuals—baseball, running, swimming—although the contest didn't have to be a real sport. We'd spar over who could climb the fastest, hit the hardest, hide the longest, and spit the farthest.

But ever since that day in July by the creek, the last day my mom had frizzy hair, I'd lost interest. I gave up my spot on the baseball team, quit going swimming, and pretty much left it up to somebody else to do the climbing, hiding, and spitting. Unfortunately, I found I was still pretty good at hitting.

Melvin Trumboldt and I were tired and sweaty after a day of baling hay at his grandpa's farm. All he'd said was that he was hungry and couldn't wait to get home and have some of his mom's homemade biscuits and gravy. But how could he talk so casually about his mom when I no longer had one? I'm not proud of it, but I hauled off and hit him right in the face. The worst was when he said he'd deserved it. I'm ashamed to say I almost cried. I wished I'd apologized before I left.

But here it was, September, and something had come over me. I think it started the day I ran that portion of the Steeplechase. Once my legs and arms started pumping, something else in me started pumping too. I wasn't sure if it came from sadness or anger or the need to punch someone in the face, but now, with the *Sweetie Pie* looking pretty sweet, I knew I wanted to compete in the regatta. And I wanted to win.

Early talked a lot while we were in the workshop.

Most of what he said began with *Did you know . . . ?*

Did you know that the regatta was originally a gondola race on the canals of Venice?

Did you know that Maine is the only state name with one syllable?

Did you know that hippopotamus milk is pink?

Interesting but exhausting.

He'd also explain things about boat building. The proper positioning of the wooden seat in relation to the clogs, to give enough room for someone my height to take a full stroke without straining his back. The importance of keeping the oars level and positioned at the proper angle.

He spent a good deal of time working out equations on the chalkboard to figure the best ratio for this and the appropriate span for that.

It was the end of September, two weeks before the regatta, and Early was perfecting the lubricant for greasing the tracks.

"The regatta is the kickoff for fall-break week, Jackie. October starts to get cold in the mornings. I got castor oil from the infirmary so the seat tracks can slide easily in the cooler air."

I watched as he used a clean rag, applying the oil to the tracks below the eight-wheeled seat. "Try it," he said.

I took my place on the seat, put my feet in the laced clogs, and pumped back and forth a few times. "Smooth," I said. "Let's take her out for a test run."

Early and I carried the boat up the stairs and out into the open air. She was surprisingly light. My last venture in the *Sweetie Pie* had been such a failure that I was a little nervous about trying again—until we lowered her onto the water. The shiny wooden hull barely made a ripple as it settled to rest, sleek and fine, by the dock. Yes, the *Sweetie Pie* looked as yar as they came, and she seemed to enjoy her own reflection in the glassy water.

"Get in the boat, Jackie."

I got in the boat.

"Start rowing."

I started rowing. And rowing. And rowing. That day. The next day. And the day after that. I was on the water before sunrise, until the bell rang for morning chapel. Then I was on again after school, until sunset. My muscles ached all over again, at first rebelling with every stroke, keeping me awake at night and screaming at my audacity to want to do ordinary things like walk or sit. I wandered around in a perpetual fog of Early's smelly ointment.

As the days went by and the pain subsided, Early praised my strong, smooth strokes that propelled me through the water. But navigating was a problem. I couldn't row a straight course.

"You need a coxswain."

"*Coxsen?*" I repeated the word as he'd pronounced it.

"The person who guides and navigates the boat. The *Sweetie Pie* is a double, and since we took out one of the seats for you to row it as a single, we can fit in a coxswain seat instead. You need someone to give you direction."

My pride bristled a little, but maybe he was right. I had not proven myself an able oarsman yet, and much as I would have liked to be in control of my own race, I knew I was still a little wobbly on the water.

Early went to the Nook, then returned with a small leather seat that he attached to the back of the boat. We had to do some jury-rigging to get the coxswain seat to sit right in the *Sweetie Pie*, but Early eventually settled his little body on board, and we started out again.

This time, he called out directions like "FIRM UP!"—meaning "Apply more pressure where needed"—and "PICK IT!"—meaning "Use only the arms to make a turn."

One thing I learned about Early was that he never doubted his authority as he called, "SQUARE ON THE READY! CHECK IT DOWN! POWER TEN! SLOW THE SLIDE! WEIGH ENOUGH!"

It took time to learn what the commands meant, and even longer to respond to them. But eventually I followed his direction and began to stay on course.

Out on the bay, when the sun would inch lower upon the western woods, Early, in a quieter voice, would give the command "Let it run," meaning, *Stop rowing, oars out of the water, and glide to a stop*. Here we would rest, taking in the last warmth of the day. And Early would tell me his number story. The story of Pi and his adventures.

Sometimes I worried a little about that strangest of boys. If he could let go of even a little of his strangeness, he might not be such an outsider. But then, who was I to talk? I remembered the headmaster's advice to me when I'd first arrived at Morton Hill Academy. *If you want to sit with a group in the lunchroom, they'll probably let you. If you want to go off and sit by yourself, they'll probably let you do that, too.*

I had positioned myself apart from the table, apart from the group, and I let myself drift away as Early told his story.

Citizen of the World

As Pi CONTINUED HIS JOURNEY, he respected the power of the sea and always kept the Great Bear in his sight to guide him. His journey took him to many distant shores, where he encountered the people of the world.

The members of the light-skinned tribe on the cold, rocky shore were small and meek. They set out baskets of food in front of their huts of animal hide but would not look at him.

On the shores of the bluest waters, he found houses built of clay and brick instead of branches and leaves. The villagers wore tunics and sandals and engaged him in great dialogues and debates. They asked him questions he had never thought of: What is more important, the soul or the mind? Are we responsible for each other or only ourselves? Is there such a thing as mystery, or only that which is not yet understood? Pi enjoyed his time with these great philosophers—the Thinkers, he called them—but the food was not good, and after a time, his head began to ache. He was relieved to say his farewells and enjoy the solitude of his boat.

His shortest stay was on an island in the choppy waters to the west, where the sun beat down on hot sand and left so little moisture that nothing could grow. Pi realized that water must be essential not only for life but for happiness as well, because while he was met with open arms, those arms were throwing spears and rocks. He made a hasty retreat and took away only bruises and cuts as mementos of his visit.

His favorite people were those of the lush region off the calm coastal waters. They were big, loud, and boisterous, and after welcoming him into their village with a banquet of savory meats, sweet fruits, and spiced ales, they celebrated his friendship for weeks and nearly refused to let him leave.

But he did leave. After all, he was not looking for a new home. He already had a home. He was a voyager. A navigator. One who keeps plotting a course and finding his way. He was still finding his way.

1 1

One night in the workshop, as we were making some final adjustments to the seat track and rigger bolts, Early said, "I'm going on a trip for fall break. Do you want to come with me, Jackie?"

I was surprised. He *never* went anywhere and seemed to enjoy being alone. On days when all the boys were given day passes to go into town, Early never went along. For the most part, he did what he wanted at school, and I figured that, since he showed up for meals and Sunday chapel, no one really felt the need to keep tabs on him. I couldn't figure out who he would be taking a trip with, but I didn't have any interest in going along.

"Um, sorry, my dad's taking shore leave, and he's coming to visit." I hadn't realized until I said it how much I'd been looking forward to seeing my dad. Maybe he was missing me too. "He's coming to watch the fall regatta, and then we're going to Portland."

"Okay," said Early.

"Where are you going?"

"I'm going on a quest."

"Oh, you are?" I said, humoring him like he was a little kid instead of a boy the same age as me. "A quest for what?"

"For Pi. That Professor Stanton thinks he's dead, but he's just missing. I'm going to find him, and then Professor Stanton will quit saying he's dead. He's *not* dead."

I didn't know what to say. I knew that Early had his story of Pi and that it upset him to hear the mathematician's claims. But how could a story change the outcome of the mathematician's theory?

"Early, I think Professor Stanton is just talking about the *number* pi. He's not saying that the character Pi is dead. He's just saying the numbers end."

"THE NUMBERS DON'T END. PI IS NOT DEAD!" Early spoke with the same authority he used in calling out his coxswain directions. He grabbed his jar of jelly beans, spilled them out on the workbench, and started sorting. Green, blue, yellow, red, orange. His breathing was short and fast.

I just needed to calm him down. "Early, let's not worry about it right now. I'm sure Pi is fine. He's probably had another mishap on his boat. But if *we* can fix the *Sweetie Pie*, surely *he* can get his boat up and running again. What was happening the last time we saw him?"

"He was in danger." Early's breathing slowed a bit as we heard a pitter-pattering on the window. It was raining. I reached for a particular record and placed it on the turntable. A swell of music broke the tension, and Early began his story, this time with no numbers on a chalkboard. He knew the story by heart.

And in the background of Early's story was *her* voice. Her soul. Her sadness and longing. Because when it's raining, it's always Billie Holiday.

Plights and Perils

PI FACED MANY DANGERS. Sharks stalking him for days, their fins gliding alongside his boat. Perhaps waiting for him to fall overboard. Perhaps hoping to drive him mad enough to jump in.

But the bugs were more likely to drive him crazy. On a windless stretch of water, he encountered a swarm of stinging, buzzing insects so thick, the sky was darkened all around him. They hovered and burrowed while he slapped and scratched. By the time a breeze picked up, allowing him to sail away, he was so swollen that he could barely see or breathe, and the welts on his skin oozed and itched for days.

One of his moments of greatest peril occurred in the balmy season, when the winds could whip up into gale force in minutes. His boat was sturdy and strong, and small enough that he could maneuver it quickly, tacking this way and that to steer himself clear of rough waters. But this time it was different. There seemed to be no end to the howling wind and roiling water. Hours turned into days, until suddenly he found himself in an eerie calm. The waters were still. Too still. The wind had died down so quickly, it seemed to have sucked the very breath out of him. He had never experienced such a deathly quiet. Then, as quickly as it had come, the eye of calm was gone. Again he was blown and battered by the storm.

Finally, his strength gave out and he was swept into the sea.

His body floated amid the churning waves, and his mind floated between dream and reality. Was it really a whale that looked him in the eye? He had heard stories of people being swallowed by whales. One voyager even stayed alive for days before being spit out. Did this whale really swim beneath him, keeping him afloat? Would a whale nudge a body safely to shore? Had he really looked into the deep, somber eye of a big white whale? This was the memory Pi was left with when he found himself sprawled on yet another beach, surrounded by mangled driftwood, weeds, and the carcasses of fish that had not fared as well as he during the storm.

The image of a benevolent whale was a pleasant one, but it was quickly shoved aside when he stood and raised his eyes to a great mountain with plumes of smoke and bursts of molten rock spewing from its gaping mouth.

He recalled an expression from his village: *Out of the kettle and into the fire.*

He wasn't in the fire yet, but a glowing stream of it was on its way.

12

The morning of the regatta, I got two messages under my door. One was a notice that, due to an anticipated storm midday on Saturday, the opening race would start at eight a.m. instead of nine. No problem. I'd just have to find Early and tell him about the eight o'clock start time. I knew he wouldn't have received a notice, as I was the registered rower. All the other boys were racing as singles. I'd been allowed to have a coxswain because I was a beginner, but with the extra weight of another person in my boat, no one expected me to win.

Early was probably in the workshop. The night before, he'd said he was going to get up early and polish the brass nameplate. The one engraved with the words *Sweetie Pie*; the one that we'd taken off the boat before we rebuilt her. He wanted to screw it back on the boat before the race. Anyway, we would have plenty of time to get the *Sweetie Pie* from the Nook, nameplate and all, and get her into starting position by race time. Dad would be there for the sunrise breakfast and could get settled to watch with the other parents.

I put down the first message and picked up the other. It was from the telegraph office in town. I tore open the envelope.

The note was typewritten and read:

```
Jack,
     Inclement weather STOP Shore leave
postponed STOP Unable to join you for
scheduled meeting STOP Will contact you
when next possible STOP
                        Capt. Baker
```

I couldn't believe it. He wouldn't be here for the regatta. He wouldn't be here at all. *Unable to join you for scheduled meeting.* Was that the way he thought of it? A meeting? An obligation? For some reason the image of me punching Melvin Trumboldt in the face came to mind. Only this time there was no one to hit.

I looked down at the note once more, then tore it into little pieces and threw it in the trash can. So what if he wasn't coming? I didn't need him to be there.

What happened next might not have been what happened next if I hadn't run into Preston Townsend as I opened my door to go find Early.

"Hey, Baker. You know they upped the race time to eight o'clock, right?"

"Yeah, I heard."

"Good, because I'd hate for you to miss me winning." That wasn't it. That was just the usual banter that goes on before any race. It was what he said next.

"And don't forget your babysitter," he called over his shoulder as he went on his way.

My jaw clenched. My *babysitter*. My coxswain. Early. I didn't need him—I could win that race on my own. My arms were strong and ready. My legs felt like they could outpump anyone. And the last few times I'd been on the water, I'd rowed straight as an arrow. I could do this by myself.

All by myself. It was at that moment that I decided to do something worse than hit someone in the face. I crumpled the note with the earlier start time in my sweaty fist. Then I ran to the Nook and removed the coxswain seat from its place on my boat.

Seven boats were lined up in the starting position. Dark clouds lurked in the distance, but for the time being, the bay water was smooth as glass. Proud parents lined the shore, waving blue-and-white pennants, and all were treated to cups of hot chocolate in anticipation of the opening race. The eighth-grade competition would start the regatta, followed by the races of the freshmen, sophomores, juniors, then seniors. The regatta would end with awards and a big lunch in the cafeteria, with sandwiches, clam chowder, biscuits, coleslaw, and blueberry pie.

As I lowered myself onto the rowing seat, I felt a twinge of guilt at having ditched Early. But I didn't imagine my father felt too guilty about having ditched me, so I strapped on the leather clogs and took hold of the oars. I knew that Preston Townsend was to my right, and that Sam Feeney and Robbie Dean were in the two boats to my left, but I stared straight ahead, trying to get my bearings.

Mr. Blane yelled for the opening ceremony of the regatta to begin. Headmaster Conrady led the opening prayer over the crackling loudspeaker. I wasn't paying too much attention at first, but heard his closing scripture reading.

"'Therefore, since we are surrounded by such a great cloud of witnesses, let us throw off every weight that slows us down and the sin that so easily entangles, and let us run with perseverance the race marked out for us.'"

Mostly what I heard was the part about *throwing off every weight that slows us down*. See, there was even a Bible verse to justify what I'd done. Wasn't Early extra weight on the boat?

I barely heard the starting command, and even as I took my first stroke, I knew I had made a huge mistake. But I kept rowing.

The regatta course began near the dock and went straight across the bay, around a buoy, and back to where the starting line became the finish line. I started off okay, and my strokes were strong and confident. Until I neared the buoy for the turnaround.

I could see the flags waving onshore, parents and students cheering. I found myself scanning the faces. I knew the captain wasn't there. Still, I couldn't help looking for someone in a navy uniform. But the colors all blurred together.

By the time I glanced back over my shoulder, I had lost

sight of the buoy. The other boats had already made their turn and were heading back toward the finish line. I must have overshot. I attempted to make my turn. But without Early there to call the commands—*PICK IT! FIRM UP! EVEN IT OUT!*—I could only heave and wobble with little control and even less direction. The *Sweetie Pie* made a wide arc that steered it dangerously close to the rocky shore on the far side of Wabenaki Bay. I bore down on the starboard oar but only managed to leave the whole port side of the boat vulnerable to the jagged rocks, and before I could get back on course, I heard a horrible grating sound.

A great black rock jutted out from the shore. It had probably been there for a millennium, but it seemed to have been lying in wait for this very moment as it tore through the side of the *Sweetie Pie*.

The maple and oak were strong. There was even some mahogany. I thought maybe the boat could withstand the assault, but water had already started pooling around my feet. I had finally completed my turn and, looking back over my shoulder, I saw the other boats halfway toward the finish line that seemed miles away. I was strong, and all that was left was a straight line. I could get there. But the water kept coming.

I tried to conjure up Early's voice in my head. *POWER TEN! POWER TWENTY!* I checked over my shoulder again. The finish line was in sight, but my feet were completely underwater. Another few strokes and the boat would be sunk. Every muscle in my body was strained to the point of breaking. My arms, back, and legs nearly screamed with every stroke. I was the last boat to near the finish, and my mind was in a panic. The thought of sinking my boat in front of this crowd was unimaginable. I couldn't think. Could barely breathe. But Early's voice stayed clear in my head. *SETTLE! SETTLE. EVEN IT UP. EVEN IT UP. EASY. EASY OARS.*

I came to a stop next to the dock and heaved my shaking body out of the boat. Some eyes were on me and the sinking *Sweetie Pie*, but many had already moved on to congratulate the boys who had finished with boats still intact. Others were gearing up for the next race. Somehow I'd been saved from an embarrassment beyond recovery. I looked down at my soggy shoes, and on the dock, I saw a little brass plate engraved with the words *Sweetie Pie*. It was the brass nameplate that Early had polished and planned to put back on the racing boat.

Mr. Blane was on hand to help me pull the ragged boat from the water. "Tough race, Baker. We'll work on those turns after break. Looks like the storm's moving fast. You'd better get packed to go," he said as the sky opened up and the rain sent everyone running for shelter. I nodded but wasn't really listening. I looked around, scanning the faces for just one: Early Auden's. Holding the nameplate, rain soaking through my clothes, I realized I hadn't been imagining Early's voice out there in the boat. He had been calling commands to me from the dock. But he was gone.

I hung my head, knowing that I had hit Early as surely as I had hit Melvin. Right in the face.

By nightfall, the dormitory was eerily quiet. After the eighth-grade race, the storm had moved in, and with the wind whipping and the rain pouring down, everyone had run to the cafeteria for a quick lunch. Then suitcases were loaded up and boys bustled into waiting cars. Kids whose families lived too far away were invited to friends' homes. Sam was going with Robbie Dean to Portland, while Preston was going hunting with his father. Even Mr. Blane, the faculty dorm monitor, had gone to Boston to visit family and attend the upcoming Fall Math Institute.

Someone might have invited me home out of pity if they'd known I was going to be alone, but I was supposed to be going to Portland with my dad.

It was dark and cold. I kept the light off in my room as I sat in the window seat, listening to the rain and eating the last of the blueberry pie I'd brought back from lunch. I pulled my blanket around my shoulders and tried to read the clock, but it was too dark. I knew it was late, probably past ten.

As I stared out the window into the moonless night, events of the day swam through my mind. Receiving my dad's message. Preston's taunts. Removing Early's coxswain seat. The rocks gouging the side of the *Sweetie Pie*. Early's commands that guided me back to the dock. Mr. Blane saying "Tough race." But mostly I remembered the feeling of being lost and unable to determine my course. Staring out the window was like looking into a deep, dark ocean, and I imagined myself floating, drifting with no direction under a starless sky.

I hunkered down in the window seat, drowning in my own miserable thoughts. Four months earlier, I'd been a normal Kansas kid enjoying my summer vacation, and now here I was, with nowhere to call home, at a school with no baseball, unable to row a boat straight. My heart squeezed as I tried not to think of the biggest loss of all.

I pushed aside the thoughts of the day. Usually some comforting words of my mom's would come to mind, but just then, I couldn't hear her. Instead, the rest of what Mr. Blane had said floated back to me. *Tough race, Baker. . . . Storm's moving fast. . . . You'd better get packed to go.*

It was that last part, *better get packed to go. . . .* Every student had to have signed permission to leave campus, and I'd been checked off to leave. The telegram from my father had arrived that morning, but I was the only one who had read it. During all the hubbub of kids loading up in the rain, Mr. Blane must have assumed my father had come to collect me, just like all the other parents who had picked up their sons, bustling them off to be with family and friends.

No one knew I was still here. I really was adrift. No tether. No anchor. I saw a sudden burst of lightning, and my pulse quickened. There was something intoxicating about being completely alone and unaccounted for. I could travel to California or Kentucky or Kansas, and no one would even know I was gone until the following Sunday, when everyone would return to school. Of course, I didn't really know how to get to any of those places. That was the nature of being lost. You had the freedom to go anywhere, but you didn't really know where anywhere was.

I thought of the Fish and wondered about him in France before he was killed. Was he alone? Was he lost? Was it dark? The darkness outside seemed to tighten its hold on me. Suddenly being alone didn't feel so intoxicating. It just felt . . . lonely. Again I strained to find my mother's voice. But there was only the spatter of rain and the deafening darkness.

Then I saw a light. It was tiny, insignificant, but I knew from many a game of hide-and-seek on the open prairie that even the smallest light can shine like a beacon. I peered harder through the window and realized it was coming from the basement of the upper school. Early's workshop. I sat up straight, and a wave of relief washed over me. Even though there were no stars to guide me, no landmarks to set a course by, not even my mother's voice to comfort me, I realized I did have some bearings. There were certain things I knew to be true.

It was raining, so I knew that Billie Holiday was singing on the record player. I knew Early's workshop was warm and inviting. I knew there were peanut butter sandwiches at the ready. And I knew Early was there. I wasn't alone.

I pulled on my slicker and headed across campus to the workshop.

13

I had been right about Billie Holiday singing. And the room was warm and toasty. But Early had a few surprises up his sleeve.

I didn't think he'd heard me come in, as he stood with his back to me, wearing his bright-red tartan jacket, putting items near his backpack—matches, a flashlight, a rain poncho, and peanut butter sandwiches, apples, hard-boiled eggs, and canned beans. Not just items but supplies. I'd forgotten about Early's quest and hadn't taken him very seriously about going anywhere. Compass, map, pocketknife, length of rope, canteen—that all made sense for a journey. But then he also packed a jar of honey, a tobacco pouch, a pack of gum, his jar of jelly beans, and a leather journal of pi notations. I was most surprised at the wad of dollar bills that Early took from a jelly jar. He rolled up the bills and put them in an empty can of beans, placing the tin lid on top and securing it with a rubber band. He was definitely packing for a journey of questlike proportions.

Early dumped the jelly beans out of their jar, and this time, instead of sorting them by color, he began counting them. He sectioned them off into rows of ten, as I'd seen the pharmacist at home do, counting out pills or vitamins.

I wish I could say I stayed quiet because I didn't want to interrupt, but the truth was, I was ashamed. I'd dumped Early from the race and ruined the *Sweetie Pie* in the process. Leaving Early to count his jelly beans, I turned to the bulletin board that he had layered with newspaper clippings, graphs, string, maple leaves, maps, and, of course, numbers and equations.

I hadn't really paid much attention to the clippings before. They were such a hodgepodge of news. Everything from articles on D-day and the Normandy invasion to Maine weather conditions to news of the great black bear still stalking the Appalachian Trail. It seemed to be a nonsensical array of information. But then, who could understand the way Early's mind worked? To him it probably all made perfect sense.

One article told of the supposed killing of the Great Appalachian Bear. The picture showed a large black bear, reportedly six hundred pounds, but the article said the paws were too small to be those of the much larger bear still on the loose. The grainy picture must have been taken before the authorities measured the paws, as it showed the hunter standing proudly next to his kill, apparently unaware that he wouldn't be winning any bounty money, and off to the side, a bearded lumberjack who seemed somewhat amused by the whole spectacle.

The bulletin-board collage looked just like what I imagined you might find in Early's mind—a hodgepodge of information, texture, color, clutter, and chaos that only Early could understand. Navigating Early was as challenging as navigating mysterious and uncharted waters.

"I think Billie Holiday and Mozart would have been friends."

I jumped at Early's voice. His back was still to me. Had he known I was here all along?

"They would have liked each other's music."

He didn't say anything about the race. I knew Early was different. Odd. Maybe he didn't feel things like disappointment or the pain of being left out. Maybe he was just simple and unaffected in that way.

"If they were on a boat," said Early, "Billie Holiday would never leave Mozart behind. That's not what friends do."

Scratch that idea.

"Dorothy didn't leave Toto. Ruth didn't leave Naomi. Captain America would never leave Bucky."

I got the point.

"Don't you know the school motto, Jackie? *Semper Fidelis?* That means—"

"I know what it means." I did know. "'Always Faithful.'" And I knew all too well what it meant to be left behind.

"Early, I shouldn't have done that. I'm sorry."

"Okay, Jackie," he said, lifting his frog out of a pondlike terrarium. "Bucky and I need to get going."

Now I knew where he'd come up with the name for his frog. I smiled. And if the frog was Bucky, that made Early . . .

"Listen, Captain America. I know you're really gung ho about heading out on your big quest and all, but you can't go running off into the woods by yourself. You'll get lost or eaten up by that bear that's roaming the trail. Let's just get a good night's sleep, and we'll both be more clearheaded in the morning."

Early's breath became a little rapid and shallow. He knew I was giving him a pat on the head.

"I'm going."

He meant it.

"He's lost, and I have to find him."

I was tired, but the thought of going back to my room in the empty dorm was unbearable. He'd probably only be out for a few hours anyway.

"All right," I said. "I'll go with you. But we'll have to leave Bucky here."

There was a pause. Then Early picked up the frog. "Friends don't leave friends behind, Jackie." He put Bucky in his pocket, then picked up the coxswain seat. "You row and I'll navigate. Let's put this on the boat."

Suddenly I had a knot in my stomach. He planned to go by boat up the Kennebec River. I thought he knew I'd ruined the *Sweetie Pie*. I swallowed hard. "Early, the boat, the *Sweetie Pie*. She's damaged. I ran her against some rocks. You were there. I know you called out commands for me to get back, but I almost sank the whole thing!"

Early picked up two oars, different from the ones I'd used earlier that day. They looked older but were a better make. He wiped them down as if he hadn't heard a thing I'd said. I had to make him understand. I grabbed one of the oars.

"Early, there is no boat." I waited for his reaction. Would he cry? Would he hit me? Would he put on the empty space of a record and retreat into himself? I prayed he'd hit me.

But he just handed me the other oar and said, "Not *that* boat." He stepped into the hall and pulled a tarp from a mound I must've walked right past when I'd entered his workshop.

Early didn't say *voilà!* But he might as well have. Because, like a magician, he revealed the last thing in the world I expected to see.

The *Maine*.

In my shock, I glanced around, fearing we'd be caught red-handed, having stolen the holy grail from the Nook. Even in the dim light, the *Maine* gleamed almost with a light of her own. The rich alternating woods of mahogany and oak were cut and honed and painted with a beauty that made the *Maine* seemed like a work of art rather than a racing boat.

"Early," I breathed, "you can't take *that* boat. It shouldn't even be down here. Don't you know this is like the treasure of all treasures at Morton Hill?" I couldn't believe I was having to explain this. He'd been here for years. I'd been here only two months, and I knew the significance of the *Maine*. "You might as well have brought the *Mona Lisa* down here. Or the Ark of the Covenant or . . . or . . . the Statue of Liberty!"

Early busied himself folding up the tarp.

"How'd you get it here?" I asked. "You couldn't have carried it by yourself."

"Mr. Wallace helped me on the condition that I don't tell anyone he took more than a few swalleys during the storm this morning. He doesn't like storms. They make him nervous."

I didn't care how many swalleys Mr. Wallace had taken. "Early, don't you know whose boat this is?" I spoke to him kind of slow, as if he were a simpleton. "It belonged to someone who is a legend at this school. He was a student here and then went off to war. Surely you've heard of him. They call him the Fish."

Early stood looking straight into my eyes, as if he couldn't understand what I was so intent on getting across to him. Finally, he spoke.

"I know who he is. His name is Fisher. He's my brother."

To say you could have knocked me over with a feather would be putting it mildly. This didn't make sense. Heroes and legends didn't have brothers, did they? No one ever talks about Sir Galahad's brother. Superman had two sets of parents, but, as far as I knew, he didn't have a brother. The Lone Ranger had Tonto but no brother.

Uh-oh. I was starting to think like Early.

Then I realized something—this was coming from a kid who had conjured up a whole story out of a number. He probably knew full well who the Fish was and had created this fantasy world in which they were brothers.

I put my arm on Early's shoulder. "Okay, let's say he *is*

your brother. That doesn't mean you can just make off with his boat, does it?"

"It's not just his boat, it's *our* boat. We built it together." Early took a wooden seat from inside the boat and fixed it into position toward the stern of the *Maine*. It went in as nice and easy as you please and fit perfectly. We'd had to do some heavy-duty finagling to get the coxswain seat to sit right on the *Sweetie Pie* because it hadn't been designed for one. But the *Maine* seemed to have been designed to hold not just any seat, but this very one.

If it was true that Early and the Fish were brothers, why hadn't any of the other boys mentioned it? There had been plenty of talk of Morton Hill's greatest athlete and fallen war hero. Why hadn't they said anything? I already knew the answer to that.

Because they didn't want to believe it. I knew how they felt about Early—he was strange, he lived in a cluttered old workshop, and he rarely showed up for class. They had cast him aside, and they didn't want to acknowledge that the Fish could possibly have had a brother who was such an oddity, such a misfit. They ignored Early, students and faculty alike. They ignored him into nothingness, to the point where his name could be called during roll and nobody noticed or cared that he never answered. Or that he lived in the basement.

And apparently nobody cared that he was still at school when nearly everyone else had left. Mr. Wallace, the custodian, was still around, but he was a bit of a loner himself and would probably not be aware of Early's comings and goings throughout the break.

Early stepped back into the workshop and headed toward his bulletin board, with its display of papers and leaves. He reached up high, to the upper right corner, and removed something. A chain—with two silver-colored metal pieces. He handed them to me. *Dog tags.* A soldier's identity tags, worn around the neck. I touched the raised letters on metal that spelled out a name, serial number, and hometown:

FISHER AUDEN

37887466

BETHEL, MAINE

Then he handed me a small, crisply folded piece of paper. A letter with the words typed so sharply, I could feel them, raised, on the other side, so that forward or backward you'd get the same message.

It is with deep regret that I write to inform you of the death of your brother, Lieutenant Fisher Auden.

The message was clear. *Your brother, Lieutenant Fisher Auden.* This must be what Mr. Blane meant by *proof by contradiction.* Because those dog tags contradicted everything in my head that said Fisher could not be Early's brother. The typed words went on.

Eight members of Bodie Company were on a mission to destroy the Gaston Bridge along the Allier River in central France. Their

position came under heavy fire. An enemy
tank destroyed their barn shelter with a
direct hit. There were no survivors. The
remains were buried on site.

I held the tags and remembered the clothes Early had
loaned me after the incident in the pool. Clothes that were
too big for Early. Fisher's clothes. I felt my heart break for
Early. His brother was dead as surely as my mother was
dead. But somehow Early had maintained a sense of direction. He knew who he was and where he was going.

I did not.

By then the rain had slowed so that it no longer tapped
on the window but only ran in teary streaks down the glass.
The only sound left was Billie Holiday's voice. That grainy
sound of the record playing, and her words, filled with sadness and heartache.

The song wound its way around me with echoes of
gloom and sadness and ghosts of yesterday. A yesterday that
was gone and wasn't coming back.

A restlessness rose in me. I didn't want to be left alone
with the gloom and the rain and the ghosts from the past. I
knew then that I would follow Early, wherever he was
headed. *He may get us both lost, but that would be better than
being lost and alone.* That was what I thought, anyway.

I turned around and handed Fisher's dog tags to Early
just as Billie Holiday finished her song and the needle
shifted into the crackly empty space. Early handed me a
backpack and indicated a drawer where I could find a few
things to pack for myself. Among the items I threw in were

a pair of extra socks, another flashlight, and my own Swiss Army knife, which I'd left there a few days earlier. Then, together, Early and I hoisted the *Maine* onto our shoulders and carried it to the mouth of the Kennebec River. The rain had stopped.

"READY ALL, ROW!" Early called the command that was the rowing equivalent of "LOAD 'EM UP AND MOVE 'EM OUT!" His voice was a little flat and a little too loud. And it was clear and true. Right now, his was the only voice I could hear. And the only one I could trust. With that knowledge, I dipped the oars in the water and began rowing into the night with Early as my guide. If I still had any doubt about Fisher being Early's brother, it was dispelled when the moon broke through the clouds and I saw a name carved into the handle of each oar: *Early* on one and *Fisher* on the other.

I knew it was crazy to be searching for a fictional character who existed only in numbers, but Pi's journey struck a chord in me. He was a voyager, Early had said. A navigator. *One who keeps plotting a course and finding his way.*

"Early," I said, working my arms and legs in smooth, efficient strokes as he had taught me, "don't you think you'd better fill me in on how Pi got lost?"

Early crouched in his seat, letting me row on my own without calls or direction. "Well, it all started back at the part where every number shows up in a row except one."

473906528 . . .

Bound for Home

THE SUN SET, and darkness covered the small island. But no darkness could smother the bright red and orange that spread like a blanket down the mountain. Pi was stranded. He had no boat. His skin prickled, and beads of sweat formed on his body as the heat oozed closer. Which way should he go? The lava shifted direction with no regard for what was in its path. Trees toppled. Rocks were smothered. He could run up the shore or down, but either way he might find himself with burning lava licking at his heels.

How was it that he could survive a great storm and be saved by a whale, only to die on this tiny island? He knew that this time there would be no whale to escort him to safety. The very sight of the volcano nearly seared his eyes. He looked to the heavens, longing for a moment of calm like the one he had experienced in the storm. And then he saw it: the Great Bear, pointing the way to his star. Polaris. It had guided him this far. His mother had said the Great Bear was a mother herself. And a mother's love is fierce. He would trust her. He would follow her. But she was pointing him out to sea, and he had no boat.

He would trust her. A piece of flat driftwood lay nearby. He took it up, gave it a shake, and set it on the water. It was small. It was thin. But it stayed afloat. Pressing his chest to the wood, he lowered himself into the water and paddled. When he could no longer paddle, he kicked. When he could no longer kick, he let the sea cradle him while he slept. Always he knew the Great Bear was watching him, beckoning him.

A mother's love is fierce. After many months and many trials, he felt he had earned his name. And he wanted to hear it in his mother's voice. It was time for the young voyager to go home.

To be called by name. To be known. To be loved. He was almost home. Floating on the driftwood, his mind wandered back over the many adventures of his journey. Learning the ways of the sea. Meeting strange people in even stranger lands. Surviving storms and sharks and bugs. What adventures he had to tell. As his body and mind floated, aimless and adrift, he felt a shadow pass over his face. But even more, he felt eyes upon him.

It was a ship with a group of men, blurred by his sun-drenched vision, staring at him from the deck. He squinted, and just as his eyesight cleared he was hoisted aboard. Who would believe it? He'd been saved by a rough and ragged band of men, scarred and maimed from many a sea skirmish, always at the ready to steal goods, treasure, or kegs of rum from any vessel within their scope.

They plopped Pi's exhausted body on a pile of ropes and

called for a jug of rum. A woman, the Haggard and Homely Wench by name, came forward with the rum and a jigger. She appeared to be the only feminine presence on board but was treated with such ill temper and vulgarity by the men that she could do little to soften their rough edges.

The wrinkled, weathered, and one-eyed captain stepped forward, giving the order to administer the spirits to loosen the young man's tongue. One of the crew grabbed Pi by the hair and poured a jigger of rum down his throat to rouse him enough to talk. Pi sputtered and coughed out words of searching and wandering and home. When the pirates realized he had nothing of value for them to steal, no buried treasure to lead them to, they prepared to throw him back into the ocean, until he dared them to go ahead. He told them he'd been hunted by sharks and nearly eaten by giant insects. He'd been attacked by an angry tribe of parched natives and outrun a river of molten lava. And he'd stared a whale right in the eye. "Go ahead," he dared them. "Throw me into the ocean."

The pirates looked at each other, puzzled. Who was this young man who could not only escape death time and time again, but could tell the tale of it with such delight?

"Tell us about your travels," the captain said. "We have been long at sea and want to hear more."

So night after night, he regaled them with stories of his travels and adventures, the Haggard and Homely Wench filling their mugs with ale and rum. They threw him back in the brig at sunrise, but each night the pirates drank their rum and let Pi's stories take them to distant lands and exotic peoples.

Sometimes the head pirate, Darius, would tell stories of his own. Stories that Pi was sure were greatly exaggerated. Heroic tales of finding buried treasure and sinking entire fleets. Darius told of winning the pale and homely servant maid in a game of dice with a powerful witch doctor in the South Seas. The witch doctor had put a curse on the girl so that she would always appear the way others told her she looked. That was why she was always referred to as the Haggard and Homely Wench.

Pi convinced the captain that he needed a better name—a pirate name. Darius was too plain. He called him Darius the Dreadful to his face, but to the servant girl, the Haggard and Homely Wench, who brought Pi fresh water and fruit and whose real name was Pauline, he called him Darius the Disagreeable. The two laughed about it. Pi looked at the girl and, gently tucking a strand of hair behind her ear, he told her she had a pretty smile. And suddenly she did. After a time, Pauline wasn't so haggard and homely after all. In fact, she had turned into a beautiful girl. But always Captain Darius would call her from the deck by her Haggard and Homely name, and her hair would turn haggard and her face would turn homely.

Pauline told Pi of the words the witch doctor had said would break the spell.

Let go of your bondage,
Step out of your chains.
No longer be captive,
Your beauty remains.

But to break the spell, the chant had to be spoken by the one who held claim to her. And she knew Darius would rather be thrown into the sea than speak the words that would release her. She said he kept her ugly so that she would be so hideous, she would never run off in some port of call.

As weeks went by, Pi dropped hints of calm waters filled with fish, and sandy beaches sprinkled with gold dust. He pretended to be drunk with ale when he told them of sailing into the north and around the Cape of Fortune, past the Blue Island Archipelago. Darius plotted a new course and steadily steered Pi closer to home.

Finally, one night when Pi knew they were within safe distance of an inhabited island, he told Darius a story of a great and daring sea captain who had learned of a secret treasure buried in a rocky cave. But a sea witch had hexed the treasure with many spells and incantations.

Darius pulled a knife from his pocket, demanding that Pi draw a map with the location of the treasure. Pi agreed but told Darius that without the proper words, he would find only a chest of rusted coins and jewels that had turned to dust.

"Write it down," he said. Pi did as he was told. Darius's eyes glimmered. He raised his glass in a toast but found it empty. "Haggard and Homely Wench," he called, "bring me more rum." As she poured the liquor into his glass, he read the words from the treasure map.

"Let go of your bondage,
Step out of your chains.

No longer be captive,
Your beauty remains."

His eyes still on the map, Darius didn't notice Pauline's features turn back to their beautiful state.

That same night, while Darius and his men slept, Pi assisted Pauline into a side boat and rowed her to the safety of that nearby shore.

The perils of the sea were great. The small and rickety side boat was not a safe means of travel for a young woman. So, after leaving her in the care of a kind tavern owner and his wife, with assurances of love and a hasty return, Pi again set off alone, but this time he set a course for home. The journey was short and his heart light.

But when he finally reached the shores of his youth, he found that his village had been attacked. There was great destruction, and his people were dead.

He walked amid the ruins of his village. Some huts were burned to the ground, while other dwellings remained intact. The hut of his family was still standing, but most of the possessions had either been taken or smashed. In a corner, on the ground, he saw something. A great sadness pierced his heart as he reached to pick up the shell necklace his mother had made for him. She had wanted him to be able to hear the sea lapping on his home shore. She had wanted him to come home. But he'd left it behind. *Too late*—he remembered the words he had called out to her as he left. *When I return.* But he had been absent when this great destruction happened. He had returned too late.

He placed the string of shells around his neck and felt

their weight—the loss that they now symbolized. His family, his home, and the sound of the sea lapping the shores that he would not return to again.

Despite his confusion and grief, he found a small fishing boat and once again took to the sea. But he did not look to the sky for guidance. Many days he sailed without direction, letting the wind steer his course. The moon waxed and waned and waxed again. Eventually, he could see past his tears, and once more he looked to the sky for guidance. To the Great Bear.

But he couldn't find her. At first there were only clouds and darkness. And even when the sky cleared, he found no Great Bear to lead the way. Perhaps his sadness had confused him. It was as if the stars had changed places in the sky and he could no longer distinguish which star was which. There was no longer a crab, a hunter, a fish. There was only a jumble of lights that seemed to flicker and fade.

He thought of his mother—remembering the boy he was, standing next to her, cradled in her arms. But now she was gone, and he realized he had yet to earn his name. Pi drifted alone, with no direction, no bearing, no stars to guide him. He disappeared over the southern horizon and was lost.

14

We glided along in silence for a long time, each of us lost in our own thoughts. The river had a few turns that Early guided me through, and even though we were heading upstream, the current was slow. I took nice, easy strokes, and we settled into our assigned stations—me rowing, him calling out an occasional command. It felt good to be the brawn of our duo and let Early set the course.

I couldn't begin to guess what was going on in Early's mind, and every once in a while, he would lapse into his absent stare. It usually only lasted ten or fifteen seconds, and then he'd be back. Always as if nothing had happened.

My mind meandered this way and that, to Pi and Fisher and Mom—and Early, that strangest of boys. And yet here I sat, heading into the wilderness, rowing backward, facing Early. I didn't know for sure that Early really knew where he was going, but I was in it for the long haul.

. . .

After what might have been a few hours, Early took the length of rope from his pack and began making intricate knots. The sun was rising, shedding light on the folly of our trip. It was one thing to set off in the middle of the night. It had seemed more like a dream. But now, as Early worked his knots, I had a knot of my own forming in my stomach.

I rowed harder, trying to keep ahead of the feeling I'd had since the end of Early's last Pi story.

Early looked up from his knots. "That's sad about Pi's mom, isn't it?"

"Yeah," I said, my voice catching in my throat.

"You're thinking about *your* mom, aren't you?"

"No," I lied, nearly losing hold of an oar.

"Yes, you are."

"No, I'm not."

"What was she like?"

I looked up at Early. I'd never had to describe her before. Everyone I knew also knew my mom. "She was just a normal mom," I answered, not giving Early's question its due. Then I remembered he didn't have a mom. "She was pretty, and smart, I guess. She knew how to take off a bandage without pulling off the scab. She didn't mind putting worms on a fishing hook. And she was good with words. Her high school teacher entered one of her poems in a contest. She didn't win but said it was nice to be considered."

"What happened to her?"

"She died, that's all," I said, surprised to hear myself say it. And then I realized, not only had I never had to describe my mom, I'd also never had to explain what had happened to her. I hadn't really spoken of her since she died. People had whispered their condolences at the funeral, but I hadn't been required to give a response other than *Thank you for coming.* Early, however, was not a guest at a funeral.

"But what happened?" he persisted.

"I don't know!" All I could do was keep rowing to stay ahead of myself.

Early was quiet, but I knew he was waiting for an answer.

"We'd been talking down by the creek," I said, leaving out the part about getting lost during the Scout campout. "She said she had a headache and was going to bed early. But no one dies of a headache. The doctors said she had a brain aneurysm. That she died in her sleep." I lifted the oars out of the water and let the boat glide. "But I wouldn't know, because I wasn't there."

I was absent, I thought, recalling the words in Early's Pi story. *I was absent, and I returned too late.*

"I was supposed to be in charge. I was supposed to take care of my mom. But I wasn't even there. I was sleeping in the barn because it was cool there." And because I was mad. "When I went into the house the next morning for breakfast, it was still dark; her chipped teacup with the little red flowers was hanging on the hook by the sink. She hadn't touched it. I went to her room and found her in her bed. It shouldn't have happened that way."

"You're right," Early said. "Those are two different things."

"What are?" I asked, surprised that he thought I was right about *anything*.

"Dying and sleeping. A person should be able to do one without the other one sneaking up on him."

I tried to imagine those words coming from my mom. Tried recalling her voice. I realized I couldn't hear her saying it. Her voice was gone.

I tried to focus instead on how many strokes of the oars I took, and how many times I pumped my legs forward and backward, and how many breaths I took. Eventually, I guess I wore myself out with counting and pushing and breathing. Then I noticed Early pulling items out of his backpack. Honey, tobacco, lavender-scented ointment, jelly beans.

"What's all that stuff for?" I asked, trying to get my mind off my clenched gut and aching muscles.

"They're called *provisions*—things you need on a trip. But you can also call them *victuals, provender, necessaries, staples*. In the army, provisions can be called *rations*, but my favorite is *foodstuffs*."

"I know what provisions are, but all that stuff you brought—the honey, tobacco, jelly beans? What's all that for?"

"Tobacco is for ringworm and poison ivy," he said, taking Bucky from his pocket. He poured a handful of water on the frog to moisten his skin.

"And the jelly beans?"

"They're for Bucky. He likes jelly beans." Early held one out to the frog, who gave only a halfhearted croak. "And the honey and lavender ointment are for snakebites."

"Oh, yeah," I said. "The rattlesnakes."

"Timber rattlesnakes," Early clarified.

"Everybody else seems to think there are no timber rattlesnakes in Maine. How come you're so sure there are?"

I knew my mistake the minute I asked the question.

"Lots of reasons. First, it's a matter of statistics and odds. There were seven sightings of timber rattlesnakes last year in eastern New Hampshire, and twelve in southern Canada. The odds of the timber rattlesnake not going past the Maine border are very low."

"Uh-huh," I responded, with limited enthusiasm.

"And timber rattlesnakes like quiet, remote areas, especially deciduous forests with rough terrain. They find a comfortable habitat in open, rocky ledges where temperatures are higher, but they also like cool, thick woods with a dense forest canopy. Maine has both. Not to mention the migratory patterns of the timber rattlesnake, which indicate that . . ."

"Fascinating," I muttered as Early wrapped up his informative segment on the timber rattlesnake. I yawned but tuned in again just in time to hear his closing argument.

"Bucky gets nervous when there are snakes around, especially timber rattlesnakes." He stroked Bucky's head.

Bucky didn't look particularly nervous. In fact, he looked a little lethargic from the journey so far and hadn't touched the jelly bean that Early still held in his outstretched hand. I thought about suggesting again that Early let the frog go but didn't want another lecture on fidelity.

I continued rowing in silence.

We'd stopped a couple of times throughout the day, but it was near dusk, and we were both exhausted and hungry. Early's peanut butter sandwiches, apples, hard-boiled eggs, and canned beans were running out fast.

We pulled the *Maine* out of the water and hid her in a patch of trees along the riverbank. There was a fairly decent clearing of grass and fallen leaves that would make for a nice campsite.

The night air was clear, and the temperature dropped quickly with the setting sun. I rubbed my hands together, trying to warm them with my breath. As my stomach growled and my cheeks grew cold, I wondered how I'd gotten into this mess of a quest with Early.

"Let's get a fire going," I said, thinking maybe I should have just stayed back at school and been miserable for a week. At least I'd have had a warm bed to sleep in.

"Superman could build a fire with his X-ray vision," said Early.

But then I would have missed out on this encyclopedia of comic-book information.

"Yeah, well, Captain America would have to do it the old-fashioned way, and so do we. Help me gather up some twigs and grass."

As I placed dry leaves and grass in a pile and shaped a twig pyramid above it, I was glad I had learned to build a fire, even though my road to being an Eagle Scout had taken a detour when most of the troop dads went to war. Not to mention the fact that I'd gotten lost on the first survival outing. Only Jimmy Arnold's dad was left, and that was because he got a ranking of 4-F, which meant he was unfit for service on account of his vision. He was a banker and didn't know a mulberry from a whistleberry. The troop nearly fell apart when we were on a campout and he reached down to pet the "nice doggy" and had his hand bitten by a badger. Later we thought he'd gotten rabies, but it turned out he'd just developed a nervous twitch.

I pulled out my Swiss Army knife, with its built-in can opener, and cranked the lids off the two cans of beans. We didn't have a bowl, so I set the cans in the dirt and warmed them near the fire.

We divvied up the hard-boiled eggs and waited for the beans to warm.

My mind went to Fisher Auden. I remembered his happy-go-lucky face in the picture in the trophy case as he held his championship cup. I wanted to ask Early about his brother but thought it might upset him, and there was no record here to soothe him with its empty space.

Plus, it was late and we were both tired. The beans went down good, and with full stomachs and the warmth radiating from the campfire, we stretched out in silence, Early on one side of the fire and me on the other. It reminded me of the painful, awkward silence after my mom's death. All the boys from the baseball team signed a card, but no one said anything. No one came over. No one even looked me in the eye. It was as if I had something contagious—as if somehow what had happened to me could happen to them. Except for Melvin Trumboldt. He came to the house and found me picking cucumbers out of Mom's garden. He was the first person my age to drop by or even speak to me. And he said, "I'm real sorry about your mom." That meant a lot to me.

The fire had burned down to glowing embers when I finally worked up the courage to speak. "I'm sorry, Early, about your brother."

Early rolled over and said, "That's okay. We'll find him."

I found that a bit confusing. "You mean you don't know where he's buried?"

"He's not dead, Jackie. He's just lost."

I sat up. "What do you mean, he's not dead?"

"Just like Pi. Haven't you noticed how Fisher and Pi have been on the same journey?" Early reached for his backpack and took out the leather journal. "Remember when Pi first set off on his journey but the sea knew he wasn't ready? Pi had a lot he needed to learn first. Well, look." Early held out a postcard from Dover, England. "Fisher did the same thing. See, he says they were teaching him all kinds of things he would need to know, like how to eat on the run, run in his sleep, and sleep standing up. I bet Pi didn't even know how to do that," said Early, with the pride of a little brother.

"Well, yeah, it's called boot camp, Early. All soldiers have to do that."

"And see here," Early continued, as if I hadn't spoken. "After Pi built himself a boat, he set off on a great voyage."

"Let me guess. Fisher boarded a troop ship and sailed off into the sunset."

"It wasn't sunset. I saw it in a newsreel at the Anchor

Theater. It was really early in the morning—still dark, and they set sail on boats that could move in water and on land. See here. It was on June sixth. Summer before last."

"You mean D-day? That was the invasion of Normandy. But that's not the same thing as—"

"And remember when Pi landed on that one shore and the people were unfriendly? Remember how they threw sticks and arrows at him? Well, look at this."

Early handed me a worn newspaper article from the Portland *Press Herald* that read:

ALLIED FORCES STORM
THE BEACHES AT NORMANDY
Germans answer with Deadly Force
HEAVY CASUALTIES IN FIRST DAY

"*Heavy casualties*, Jackie. That means those Germans killed a lot of them. But not Fisher. They missed him."

I couldn't believe what I was hearing. Early was shaping the Pi story to match what he knew of his brother's life in the army.

I wanted to smack him, but my heart was breaking for him at the same time.

I tried reminding him of the facts. "But the dog tags. The letter."

"They tried to tell me he was dead. They must not have known he said he'd come back. That's what he told me before he left. And now he's looking for the Great Bear, just like Pi. And when he finds him, he won't be lost anymore."

The Great Bear. Now it was clear. The Great Appalachian Bear.

"Early, you need to listen to me very carefully. Are you listening?"

"Yes, Jackie, I'm listening."

"They all say they're coming back. Every soldier says that. And they mean it. They want to believe it. It's just that . . . not all of them make it back."

"I know that some of the soldiers die. But Fisher is still alive. And he's coming back. See here?" Early said, pulling more newspaper clippings and notes from his backpack. "His squad was supposed to blow up the Gaston Bridge along the Allier River in central France. With the direction of the current and the fact that there was a full moon that night—"

But I didn't care anymore about protecting Early's theories or his feelings. I'd had enough. "He isn't coming back!" I yelled.

"Yes, he is."

"No, he isn't."

"Yes, he is."

"Early, Fisher is dead!"

"No, he isn't."

Criminy! This could go on all night.

"Look. You've got his dog tags. You've got a letter from the army. Just like every other family in that squad got dog tags and a letter. What makes you think you're so special that your brother should come home when the rest of them aren't?"

"BECAUSE PI ISN'T DEAD, AND IF PI ISN'T DEAD, THEN NEITHER IS FISHER!" Early hugged his knees and began rocking back and forth.

"Ohhh," I breathed. That was why Early was so intent on proving that the Pi of his number story was still alive. That was why it upset him so much to have Professor Stanton suggest that the number pi would end. Early had said he wasn't making up the story of Pi, he was just reading it. But I didn't believe him. I thought Early *was* making up a story.

Until now.

It was partly in the way that Early told the story, in words that didn't seem to be his own. But mostly it was in his inability to *control* the story. If Early needed Pi to be alive in order for Fisher to be alive, why didn't he just create the story that way? Because he couldn't. The story was not his to create. He was only retelling it, translating the story he read in the numbers.

Early needed the numbers to continue, the *story* to continue, and he needed Pi to stay alive. Because in his strange, convoluted, and amazing mind, if Pi was dead, that meant that Fisher was dead also. I knew it made no sense. I knew it was crazy, but how could I argue with him? Part of me wished I had some crazy story that would make me think my mom was still alive and that she would eventually come back. But my brain didn't work that way.

I lay back, my heart pounding. As I stared up at the stars, it became clear to me that in joining Early in this quest, I'd certainly gotten into more than I'd bargained for. But I knew I wasn't ready to turn back. Don't get me wrong.

I wasn't continuing out of any sense of fidelity, duty, honor, or any other of those words that Early liked to throw around. It was just curiosity, and maybe a little fear of getting lost on my own. I had no need to stick it out or complete the quest. No, Early was the one who couldn't leave a frog behind. I would have cut Bucky loose in a heartbeat.

And in this case, that would have been a better idea, because by the next morning, Bucky was dead.

15

In the gray of early dawn, I kicked some dirt over the fire, which had long since died out, and we packed up our stuff without a word. The *without a word* part was fine, as I was sure that enough had been said the night before. Besides, Early was in mourning.

He laid Bucky on a sturdy maple leaf and set him adrift on the river. The current carried him out of sight, so at least the poor kid didn't have to see his frog get swallowed up by a fifteen-pound trout.

A big old *I told you so* was on the tip of my tongue. My mom used to say, *Don't pour salt in the wound, or you'll never get the taste out of your mouth.* So I kept my mouth shut.

I was ready to get going, but Early said we needed a song for the funeral. I let out a sigh and waited for him to start up with "Amazing Grace" or maybe "Rock of Ages." But once he started singing a heartfelt and very off-key rendition of "Up a Lazy River," I realized it was Monday. That meant Louis Armstrong.

It did provide a nice sendoff for old Bucky, and with that, we lowered the *Maine* onto the water and took up our positions. My arms and legs, cold and stiff from sleeping on the hard ground, practically moaned as I took the first few strokes through the morning fog. We hadn't brought along any of the wax, honey, and vinegar concoction. But Early was apparently taking a moment to primp a bit as he put on some kind of ointment or lotion that he had in a flat, round canister. His meticulous attention to covering every area of exposed skin grated on my nerves. First the nose and ears, then neck, cheeks, hands, and ankles. When he reapplied it to the ears, I'd had enough.

"What is that stuff?" I grumbled. "It smells like shoe polish."

"It's made out of Mentholatum, lemon juice, and saddle soap. It keeps the bugs away."

"Bugs? What bugs?" As soon as I asked it, I had a feeling I knew what was coming.

"Remember that part where Pi runs into a swarm of biting insects? They can't be too far off, and I don't like to get bitten by bugs."

I did remember that part. In fact, I must have listened more closely to the story of Pi than I thought. The bugs, the sharks, the hurricane. I remembered it all.

I smiled at Early. The kind of smile you give to a little kid who still believes in the Tooth Fairy. "Well, you be sure to lather up real good, then. Sit tight and don't let the bedbugs bite." If I'd been sitting closer, I might have ruffled his hair.

I rowed on as the fog thickened around us, and then— "Ouch!" I slapped at the back of my neck. Then again at my hand and my ankle. It wasn't fog; it was a cloud of mosquitoes or biting gnats or maybe tsetse flies. Early sat calmly, apparently unaffected by the bugs.

"Ouch!" I said, again, swatting at my cheek. "Kind of late in the season for mosquitoes, isn't it?"

"It's been a warmer-than-usual fall," Early said, looking over the side of the boat. "It's called an Indian summer. That's the opposite of a blackberry winter."

"Quick! Give me that stuff. I'm being eaten alive!"

Early tossed me the tin as he concentrated, staring intently into the water, first on the starboard side of the boat, then the port. "Shh," he whispered, with a finger to his lips.

"What? Do you think my talking is going to attract more bugs? I think we're already in the thick of it."

"Not bugs," he whispered, still gazing into the water. "Sharks."

I stared at him. I even opened my mouth to explain to him that sharks did not live in freshwater rivers. But after swatting another insect, I clamped my mouth shut, grabbed the dragging oars, and began rowing with a vengeance.

The Kennebec River stretched out for miles in front of us. Once I'd gotten Early's bug repellent on, the insects left me alone, and we eventually rowed out of the swarm. By nine o'clock, the clouds had lifted, and the air around us was crisp and clear. I always loved October at home, with its morning chill in the air, the afternoon sun warming the wooden planks of the front porch, bowls of steaming chili, and of course, baseball. I could feel a familiar ache coming back again, and I didn't want it. I needed something to distract me.

"So, Early, why don't you fill me in on the latest installment of Pi? What's been going on in his world lately?"

"There are only a few numbers left that I know, and I don't have those memorized. Some parts I can tell from memory, and other parts—I need to read the numbers. After that I have to figure out more numbers, but it takes a lot of calculating."

That made me wonder, how *did* Early read those numbers? It was clear to me now that he was not making up a story and pretending that it came from the numbers. I should have known Early was not one to play make-believe. He may have thought some crazy, unbelievable things, but he *believed* them.

"Can you teach me to read numbers?" I asked.

"I don't think it's something you can learn. Nobody taught me. I've just always seen numbers differently than most people. Fisher says it's a gift. He says when he sees the numbers that start with 3.14, it's just a bunch of figures that don't mean anything more than numbers. That made me sad for him. For *me*, they are blue and purple and sand and ocean and rough and smooth and loud and whispering, all at the same time." He paused for a breath.

I wished I could see what he saw—color and landscape, texture and voice.

We passed under a rain cloud that shed a few sprinkles

on us. It made me think of Billie Holiday, her rich voice. She could just hum with no words and you could hear the sadness, the pain, the feeling. That made me think.

"Maybe it's like listening to music," I said. "How it can make you feel things without any words. There was a song at my mother's funeral. It was all in Latin, and I didn't understand a word of it, but the way the sounds blended together and the music rose and fell, well, it could make a person cry—if they were prone to that sort of thing." I blinked hard.

"How come Kansas doesn't have any color?"

"We have color."

"No, you don't."

"Yes, we—" Oh, not that again. "What makes you think we don't have color?"

"Because in *The Wizard of Oz*, Kansas is all in black and white and grays. There's no color until Dorothy gets to Oz."

"Oh." I laughed. "That's only in the movies. Kansas has plenty of color. Especially in the fall." I allowed the memory of it to draw me back. "The sky is a beautiful blue."

"Like the ocean?"

"Kind of. My mom says if the world ever got turned upside down, you could just dive right into the sky and swim in it. And the wheat just before harvest is a golden blanket of waves and ripples."

"That's nice. What does it sound like?"

"It's just waving wheat. It doesn't make any noise." But then I thought about it. "Well, I guess if you listen really hard, it makes a *shoosh*ing sound."

"What if you listened harder?"

"If I listened harder"—I closed my eyes as I kept rowing—"I suppose it would sound kind of happy and full, like Benny Goodman and his band playing 'In the Mood.' It would be music you'd want to dance to." I kept my eyes closed, trusting Early to guide me if I started rowing off course. "And then there's all the fall produce in my mom's garden and the Bentley orchards." I could practically feel the dirt under my hands. "The pumpkins are bright orange, there are sweet red apples and yellow squash, and of course, there's plenty of green. And all that ends up sounding like *mmmmmm*. Pumpkin pie, meaty stews, and cinnamon-apple cobbler. And the trees—"

"Yeah, the trees," said Early.

I opened my eyes. I'd always liked the brilliance of leaves changing color at home, but here—I'd never been *surrounded* by trees like this, their leaves all turning color, to bright oranges, deep yellows, and flaming reds. Whole forests of trees that looked like they were on fire.

I eased up on the rowing, grateful for the rest and the moment to soak it all up. Early had given me a glimpse into what he saw and heard and felt through his numbers. And there was a beauty in it that was warm and real. "I suppose if color could be sound," I said, "these trees would be playing a whole symphony."

"A Mozart symphony," Early answered, "if it were Sunday."

We rowed along in a contented quiet, listening to the sounds of all the colors around us, when a barge emerged from a little side stream and pulled up alongside our boat. There were seven or eight bearded and weathered faces staring down at us.

These faces belonged to a ragged band that leaned over their ship's railing with arms crossed. They smelled a little rank even from a distance and looked like they'd been apart from civilization for some time.

They just stared, and I wondered if they were waiting for us to speak first. Then the group parted, and a large man stepped forward. He put his hands on the rail of the barge and peered down at us. Dense trees reached out over the Kennebec River, allowing brief flashes of light to shine through the branches and leaves as we floated underneath. It was in those flashes that I could see the man's face—it was scarred on one side, and a black patch covered his left eye.

"That's a fine-looking boat you have there, lads." His face pulled into a contorted smile. "You look like you've had a long stretch of rowing. How about we tether your boat behind ours, and we'll motor you upstream a ways?"

Early caught his breath. His eyes opened wide. I stopped rowing, and our boat lagged just a bit behind their barge. It was enough distance for Early to whisper what was on his mind.

"Pirates!"

16

Quicker than we could say *Jolly Roger*, we were pulled on board the barge, and the *Maine* was tied to a rope to be towed behind. One of the men with bulgy eyes took a firm hold on the back of Early's jacket and plopped him in the corner of the barge, next to two slobbering bloodhounds. One of the dogs didn't even look up; the other gave Early a passing glance and continued licking himself in what my mom would have called an unseemly manner. Then the man deposited me in the corner next to Early, and both dogs gave low warning growls.

The bulgy-eyed man rummaged through Early's backpack and took out an apple, then pulled a dirty knife from his pocket and wiped it on his pants. He sliced a piece out of the apple and chewed it right in front of us.

Granted, it was rude to eat with your mouth open and not even offer us a bite, but if that was the definition of a pirate, my uncle Max would be a card-carrying member, complete with a peg leg and a parrot perched on his shoulder.

No, these were just scruffy woodsmen giving us a lift upstream. Still, the scruffy woodsman with the apple was eyeing us pretty closely and seemed intent on us not moving a muscle. He rummaged through our packs some more and seemed to take a liking to Early's compass. He admired its shiny case, shoved it in his pocket, and dumped the backpacks at our feet.

The barge chugged along, gasping and sputtering, sending occasional plumes of smoke into our faces. I thought about asking if we could move to the other side of the boat, away from the engine, but thought better of it. Early piped up instead.

"Do you have any rum?" he asked.

The man didn't answer. He just continued eating the apple. I nudged Early, trying to shush him, but he went on. "Pirates like rum. I've never had any, but I heard it puts a fire in your belly. Does it do that to you?" Still no answer. "Sometimes I get a fire in my belly, but it's usually just gas. It doesn't feel good, so I don't think I'd like rum. Do you think you'd like rum, Jackie?"

"No. Now be quiet and let the man eat in peace," I whispered.

"But that's our last apple."

"Then let him eat our last apple in peace."

Early finally quieted down as we slowly made our way upriver. I don't know if it was the fumes or just fatigue, but my eyelids grew heavy, and the next thing I knew, it was almost dark. The barge's engine was off, and I could hear the side butting up against what sounded like a wooden dock.

"Early," I whispered. His breathing was deep, and he was slumped against me. "Early," I said again, shaking him. I grabbed the backpacks. "Let's get out of here."

Early stirred, but just as we stood up, we heard a voice yell, "Olson, go get those boys!" It was a wiry fellow whose shoes clomped as loud as a peg leg. "Have 'em haul up those barrels and put 'em in the truck."

Olson was the man who'd been watching us. He came back and pointed to a stack of medium-sized barrels. "Haul up those barrels and put 'em in the truck," he said, as if we hadn't just heard Long John Silver say the same thing.

Early tried to lift one on his own. "These are heavy. What's in them?"

"Never you mind what's in 'em," said Olson. "Just get a move on ya."

"I bet it's rum. Pirates like rum."

One by one, Early and I lugged the barrels and set them in the back of a flatbed truck that was waiting at the end of the dock. The night was dark, and with only a gas lantern propped on the dock railing, we couldn't make out any labels on the barrels. I hoped it didn't matter whether they were going in right side up or upside down, because we couldn't tell top from bottom. Besides, those barrels were likely to fall out, as the bed of the truck was full of holes and rotted boards.

Of course Early, who had more curiosity than what

killed the cat, climbed right up in the truck with the lantern, poking around, his bright-red tartan jacket popping up here and there among the barrels until Olson caught him.

"Get out of there, kid," he snarled.

"Okay," said Early. "But I'm here to tell you, whoever sold you your rum is having a good laugh. It's all dried up."

"Is that so?" said Olson, raising a flask to his lips. "Then it's a good thing I got some good and wet right here."

"Are you three sheets to the wind?" asked Early. "That means drunk. You can also say *tipsy*, *pickled*, or *schnockered*. But my favorite is *goosed*. The custodian at school has a little too much to drink on weekends. He calls it *having the whirligigs*. Have you ever had the whirligigs?"

Olson just stared at Early, his flask half-raised. Whirligigged or not, this seemed like a good opportunity to hightail it out of there. "We'd like our boat now, and we'll be on our way," I said, even though I figured it wasn't going to be that easy.

"Well, that's fine and dandy. Why don't you go on up to the Bear Knuckle"—he pointed to the shack up the hill—"and tell that to the boss. I'm sure he'll hand it right over."

"What's his name?" asked Early.

"The boss? MacScott."

"But what's his pirate name?" Early said, with no small amount of disappointment.

"Oh, I get it," said Olson. "Eye patch. Pirate. You're funny, kid. He can be pretty nasty, but I don't think he's got his pirate name yet."

Olson climbed in the truck and started up the engine,

grinding it into gear. He pulled away from the dock and started the slow climb up the mountain, hitting every rut and rock along the way. Early and I were left in darkness.

"Mangled MacScott," Early breathed with satisfaction. "That's a good pirate name. I bet his first name is Darius. What do you think would be a good pirate name for Olson?"

I didn't care what his pirate name would be, but I thought Early might move quicker if I answered him. "Sir Drinks-a-Lot," I said.

"Sir Drinks-a-Lot." Early pondered the name. "I like it."

"Now let's get moving," I said, trying to figure out a way to get the *Maine* back without having to face MacScott again.

"But we're getting closer, Jackie."

"Closer to what? Having our heads chopped off in a guillotine?"

"No, Jackie. Pirates don't do that. They might hang you by the neck, or cut out your insides, or slit your throat, or string you up and let birds pluck your eyes out, or feed you to sharks, or cut out your tongue, or—"

"All right, Early." I stopped him before he could come up with a hundred and ten other gruesome types of death and torture.

"Let's go find the pirate MacScott," said Early. "Maybe he knows something about the Great Bear."

There seemed nothing else for it but to do just as Olson had suggested: go find MacScott and see about getting our boat back.

Early and I walked up the hill about fifty feet. We came to what might have been a road but turned out to be just a dried-up creek bed that allowed a couple of mangy trucks and a beat-up old motorcycle to somehow ease their way up to a ramshackle building.

In the moonlit night, we got our first glimpse of the Bear Knuckle Inn. When Early and I walked in, MacScott and two of his men sat at the bar, and a thin, pitiful-looking girl stood behind it. Animal heads loomed on every wall—moose, deer, elk. A ferocious bear head, its teeth showing in an angry snarl, seemed to be leaping from a place of distinction just above the bar.

Of course, two kids walking into any drinking establishment would draw some attention, but Early and I walking into this one seemed to stop everyone in their whiskey-filled tracks.

I started to tug on Early's sleeve, which everyone knows is the unwritten code for *Let's get out of here!* Everyone but Early, that is.

"That's a nice bear you got there." Early pointed to the bear head on the wall. "Have any of you seen a different bear around here?" he asked in his too-loud voice. "We're looking for the bear we read about in the newspaper."

That was news to me, but I could piece together Early's thinking. Pi was always trying to keep the constellation of the Great Bear in his sights. It was his guiding light. So it made sense, in an Early kind of way, that he would follow the Great Appalachian Bear to find Pi.

The burly men in their heavy jackets looked at each other while the girl behind the bar wiped out a glass with a dirty rag.

"Early, come on." I tugged on his sleeve.

"It probably looks like that one you've got there, only bigger."

MacScott laughed, a smoky wheeze, his weathered fingers cradling a mug of ale. Keeping his gaze on his drink, not turning to face us, he said, "He's twice as big as that one."

"So you've seen him?" said Early. "Is he still alive?"

MacScott's shoulders hunched. His hand trembled slightly, making the liquid slosh in his glass. "Alive?" He raised his eye patch and turned to face us.

I flinched as if I'd been slapped. In the dim light of dusk, when MacScott and his men had overtaken our boat, his face had been somewhat shadowed. Now, in the light of the bar, I could see the horrible scars on the side of his face—his eye was missing, and the socket was pulled into a misshapen divot. How old he was, I couldn't be sure. Old enough to be a grandpa, although I couldn't imagine him being one.

"Alive?" He repeated the question as if he couldn't make up his mind. "Like most demons, it's more dead than alive."

"Did the bear do that to your face?" Early asked.

The man took a drink. "Yeah." Then he smiled, his skin pulling tight and shiny. "But not before I killed her cub and got off a round in her. Took out her left eye, so tit for tat, you might say." He placed a hand on the lever of his rifle, propped against the bar. "I plan to finish her off and collect the bounty. Folks are getting so scared, it'll be up to a thousand dollars before long." He pounded back the rest of his drink and set down his glass. "Another," he said, turning his back to us.

The girl looked up from her task of scraping something off the bar top with her fingernail, then poured him another drink, peering at Early and me through her stringy red hair.

I wanted to leave. There was a hardness in this place. I'd been around people who drank before, but it was usually a festive kind of drinking among friends at a wedding dance or Fourth of July picnic. These were not festive people. These men preferred to drink alone, inside, with their coats on.

"Is your name Darius?" Early asked. "I think your name is Darius."

"I think my name is none of your business," MacScott growled.

We had to get out of there before Early drove a half-crazy man all the way crazy. "If we can have our boat back, we'll be going now," I said.

MacScott slammed down his glass, splashing his drink onto the bar top. "That boat is *my* boat now." He kept his back to us while nodding at the two men sitting at the bar. "Take care of them."

The burly men stood and grabbed Early and me by our coats. They didn't seem to be interpreting MacScott's instructions to mean they should draw warm baths for Early and me, give us mugs of hot apple cider, and tuck us into fluffy feather beds for a cozy night's sleep. Just as I was envisioning a pit of hissing vipers, Early spoke up.

"You want to hear a story?" Early nudged me and whispered in a voice that everyone could hear, "Remember, Jackie, how pirates like stories?" He addressed MacScott again. "I know someone who's looking for the Great Bear, and he'll find her before you do."

MacScott hoisted himself from his stool and stepped toward us. He put his face up close to ours so that we could see every scar, hear every wheeze. "If someone's crazy enough to go looking for that bear, they'll need to have a better reason than the bounty. That animal is a killer." Still, there was an uneasiness in his voice at the mention of someone else looking for the bear.

"Come on, Early," I said more firmly. "We need to get out of here."

"He's just trying to scare us," said Early as I pulled him away from MacScott.

"Yeah, well, he's doing a pretty good job."

"The someone I know that's looking, he'd always kept his eye on the Great Bear," Early continued. "But then he got lost."

"I figured's much." MacScott's words were slurred. "It takes some doin' to track that bear. She'll lead you deep into the woods, only to double back and come up behind you." MacScott held his glass of ale in front of him, gazing deep into the cloudy liquid as if he might find the Great Bear within his murky sights.

"Pi, that's his name," he explained to MacScott and his men. "He got lost. But he remembered a story about an ancient burial ground—big, watery caves where people went to bury their dark secrets and accidental treasures."

MacScott stared at Early, his interest suddenly piqued and his eyes smoldering. "Go on," he said. "Tell me about this cave. This place of buried secrets and treasures."

He motioned to the barmaid, who set about preparing sandwiches and hot soup and refilling the men's glasses with ale and whiskey.

Early continued his story, starting from a place I hadn't heard before.

Land of Lost Souls

PI WAS LOST. He sailed under stars he did not recognize. The Great Bear eluded him. He knew he had traveled far to the south, and in that strange sky, there was a group of stars that formed what looked like a cross or perhaps a spear. But what did it matter? There was nowhere to go. No one to find. The shell necklace his mother made had become a heavy burden—a weight he could no longer bear around his neck. He removed the string of shells and placed it in a pouch with a strap that he slung across his shoulder.

But he remembered a story he'd heard from the Thinkers. They told of an ancient burial ground. A place of great, cavernous tombs. Catacombs, they called them, where the dead were laid to rest. But not all of the dead rested.

Many brought their burdens of life and roamed the catacombs, trying to shed these burdens. From one soul to the next, they tried to fix the unfixable. These souls roamed the halls of rock tombs, uttering words they wished they had said or grasping to take back words they wished had been left unspoken. They turned this way and that, trying to retrace steps from the road gone bad or searching for the path not taken.

When Pi had first heard of this place, it had sounded horrible. A place where desperate souls tried to find meaning for the random happenings of life. He shuddered to think of it and wanted never to go to such a miserable place. But now, the caves, the darkness, the souls—they beckoned him to join their ranks, to wander in their world of loss and regret. He would find this place. He would join those souls, these kindred spirits who had no direction and no hope. He would carry his own burdens to this place.

After many months of sailing with no real direction, the ocean currents somehow landed his boat on a rocky shore. It felt good to have his feet on solid ground. No more rocking and listing on the waves. So he left his boat behind and set off. He walked and walked. And as he made his way inland, the trees grew large and thick around him, buffering him on all sides. The dense foliage dimmed the bright sunlight. Fallen leaves muffled the sounds around him, so that he could hear the rhythm of his own breathing—and he thought if he strained hard enough to listen, he might hear his own heartbeat. It felt as if the world were growing smaller around him. But the feeling was strangely comforting.

Then he realized he was not alone. At first it was just a movement, a flutter of leaves or a branch twitching back and forth. Then a glimpse of something passing just out of sight. Eventually he saw them. Real people, but *not* real too. Pi could see them, but there was a transparency to them, as if one could see them but see through them at the same time.

Other than that, this translucence, they were just men and women going about normal daily tasks of chopping wood, washing clothes, honing tools. They lived near one another but separately, in tents and huts. They spoke to one another, but only words of necessity.

Pi eventually took his place among them, set up his own tent and his own work. But still he wondered, *Who are these people, and why are they here?* As he watched them from a distance, he considered them a group apart from himself. Until one day, as he placed twigs together to make a fire, he noticed his own hands—the thin sheerness of them, their translucence—and suddenly he saw everything clearly.

I am one of them.

He saw it in his hands as clearly as he saw it in their faces. The grief, the loss, the pain. This was a land of lost souls. Human beings who had weathered great storms in life, had suffered unspeakable loss, had been put to painful tests of existence, and still remained standing—but just barely. These people, like Pi, had been drawn to this place by shifting currents and fickle winds and had all ended up here for the same reason: to bury their dark secrets and accidental treasures.

17

Dark secrets and accidental treasures. The words drifted their way into my drowsy head. The heat from the hearth had warmed me through, and with a couple of corned beef sandwiches in my stomach, my eyelids drooped and I shifted in my seat, trying to stay awake. MacScott's men were full of ale and heavy with sleep, but MacScott's eye remained open, glowering, as Early continued his story. MacScott traced his finger over the wooden grain of the gun stock, almost in a caress. Early had captured the pirate's attention in a way that was both admirable and frightening.

I heard Early in a distant, far-off way. It was as if I were on a boat, floating in the middle of a lazy stream, with wakefulness on one bank and sleep on the other.

Dream took over, and I felt myself floating in the world of Pi, translucent, among the lost souls. I saw the faces of the men and women going about their chores, but I realized that the things they were doing didn't lead to anything, didn't accomplish any task. A young man in overalls placed kindling in a campfire but cooked no food. A bearded man cut down a tree but left it where it fell. A woman wearing an apron hung little-boy denims on a line to dry, but . . . there was no little boy to wear them. I wanted to move on. To row away from this place. But I had no oars. I clutched the sides of the boat. My hands were light and sheer. Translucent. *I am one of them*, I said, rousing from my dream.

My heart was pounding. MacScott's chin rested on his chest, his rifle cradled in his arms. He and his men slept soundly, but I couldn't hear Early. He wasn't sitting at the hearth. I clutched the arms of the easy chair, glancing at my hands to make sure they were solid. But still my heart pounded. I *was* one of them. I was lost. I'd felt this way before. At the regatta. I had been trying to row my way back to the dock in a sinking boat. Early had called out his commands that guided me back. Where was Early now?

I recalled Early's telling of Pi being hauled aboard the pirate ship. And yes, Pi's nighttime storytelling on the ship kept him alive, but still he was thrown into the brig every morning. I didn't know if there was a brig at the Bear Knuckle Inn, but I didn't want to wait around to find out.

Then I saw him. Early stood at the counter as the young barmaid cleaned mugs and whiskey glasses. She kept her head lowered, her eyes on the hot, sudsy water as she washed one glass after another.

I moved to the bar. "Come on, Early. We need to get out of here before everyone wakes up."

But Early paid me no mind. He just looked at the girl as if he knew her from somewhere.

"Is your name Pauline?"

Pauline? I recognized the name. She was the Haggard and Homely Wench, from the pirate vessel.

The girl shook her head, a limp strand of hair hanging in her face.

"Are you sure? Maybe it was and you don't remember."

"I think I know my own name," she mumbled.

"Come on, Early. Let's go."

Then Early did something I'll never forget. He reached across the bar and gently took that strand of stringy hair and tucked it behind the girl's ear.

She looked up, startled.

"You have a very pretty smile."

"What?"

"You have a very pretty smile. You just don't remember."

She touched a soapy hand to her face. She still wasn't smiling, not with her mouth, anyway, but something had changed in her green eyes. The dullness was gone, and something light and alive had taken its place. With that and the bubbles of soap clinging to her hair, there was something . . . well . . . pretty about her.

But before she could say anything else, there was a terrible explosion outside that shook the whole place, rattled the windows, and nearly made the bear's head come off the wall.

It was enough to wake everyone in the Bear Knuckle Inn, and we all streamed out to see what had happened.

MacScott, his men, Early and I, we all looked to the top

of the mountain that Olson had driven up earlier. The explosion had shot a great blaze of fire into the air. And creeping down the mountain was a trail of fire shooting its way left, then right, in a winding blaze of yellow and orange and heat.

"Get up there and put out that fire before it hits the trees!" yelled MacScott. "Bring a truck round, and we'll go up the back side."

Men were scurrying every which way. And I couldn't take my eyes off the blazing spectacle.

"Early," I said.

"Yeah, Jackie."

"What *was* in those barrels?" Those barrels that were right side up and upside down on the rickety truck with gaps in the bed.

"Nothing but dried-up rum. It was all turned to black powder."

Black powder. Explosive powder.

It must have been pouring out of the kegs all the winding way up the mountain. I didn't know if it was the gas lantern or maybe a stray cigarette that had set off the explosion, but it didn't matter. Early needed no explanation as he looked up the mountain in awe.

"I've never seen a volcano before."

18

This was our chance to retrieve the *Maine* and make a clean break from MacScott and his band of not-so-merry men. Early and I made our way down the hill from the Bear Knuckle Inn to the river, where the *Maine* was still tethered to the pirate ship, or rather, the logger's boat. But as we slipped and slid down the wooded slope, dodging branches and twigs, we came to a sudden halt—partly because we reached the bottom with a thump, but mostly because of what we saw. Even with all the fire and noise and hubbub, Long John Silver staggered his way ahead of us, down to the dock, and clambered aboard the logging boat.

What he was doing, I couldn't say, but it involved a lot of banging, clanging, pitching, hurling, and cussing. And even if we had dared to sneak down to the dock to untie the boat, it was too late, as the barge suddenly came to life with a cough and a sputter and slowly puttered away from the dock. There was nothing for it but to watch as the boat chugged off with the *Maine* in tow.

It was a pathetic sight—the legendary rowing boat of Morton Hill Academy's fallen hero being led upstream into the wilderness like some great king being held captive and taken away in bondage.

It was painful to watch, but we did, Early and I. We watched like some kind of honor guard, waiting until the *Maine* rounded a bend and drifted out of sight.

"Now what do we do?" I said, not really expecting Early to have an answer.

"Let's go, Jackie. We have to walk now."

Part of me wanted to argue. To say *We can't just head off into the dark.* But I could already hear how that conversation would play out. *Yes, we can. No, we can't. Yes, we can.* And as always, Early would have the last word. Still, I opened my mouth to argue.

The words never came out. Instead, up the hill at the Bear Knuckle Inn, we heard the unmistakable sound of a lever-action rifle being readied for firing.

"Let's go," I said, and we headed into the darkness.

We'd lost some of the supplies that we'd left on the *Maine*, but Early and I each had our packs on our backs, which meant that we still had the essentials—the map, matches, our blankets, a flashlight, tobacco, extra socks, and lots of jelly beans. So in the orange glow of the burning mountain, we walked. It wasn't so bad, traveling at night. The air was still, there was a three-quarter moon, and so far, we had encountered no bugs, sharks, pirates, or volcanoes. What more could a couple of travelers ask for?

Then I heard a twig snap. I stopped and held my breath, straining to hear what manner of creature might go bump, or snap, or hiss or growl, for that matter, in the night. But the lions and tigers and bears remained silent. Oh, my. *That could be worse. They could be lying in wait.* My mind was playing all kinds of tricks on me when Early broke the loud silence.

"Jackie, did you know the Appalachian Trail—"

"Yes," I answered, hoping to avoid the list of facts that was sure to be coming my way. "I do happen to know that the Appalachian Trail is the nation's longest man-made trail, stretching through fourteen states, from Maine to Georgia," I said, quoting a nature journal I'd read in the school library. "It's roughly two thousand one hundred and seventy-eight miles long, and very few people have hiked the trail all the way through."

I paused, pleased with my knowledge, and waited for Early's reaction. Unfortunately, it was a little too dark to see his face, but I imagined him looking a little deflated that I had stolen his thunder. "See," I said, "even a kid from Kansas knows a thing or two about the Appalachian Trail."

"So you already know about the hiker who got stuck in a bog and had to be pulled out by a couple of horses. And that the horses got spooked and nearly tore him in two."

Now I was the one who was deflated. His trail knowledge was much more colorful than my own.

"And," he continued, "did you know that a logger went missing on the trail a few years ago?"

"Uh, no, I didn't know that." I racked my brain for some equally interesting and disturbing tidbit about the trail, or Maine, or Kansas, or anything, but only stumbled on a tree root. "What happened to him? The logger, I mean."

"They don't know, but if he wasn't killed by some wild animal, or crushed by a falling tree, or drowned in the river—well, then he's probably lost his mind in the woods. People do that, you know. Go crazy when they're lost. They call it *going mad*, only it doesn't mean *mad* like you're angry but *mad* like *cuckoo*." Early drew circles around one ear to emphasize his meaning. "You can also say *nuts* or *cracked* or *bonkers* or *bananas*. *Batty* is my favorite. That's British for *crazy*. Which would you rather be, Jackie? Angry mad or crazy mad? I think I'd rather be crazy mad, because you can be crazy and still happy. Mozart may have been a little crazy, but his music . . ."

Great, I thought as I stopped listening to Early. Not only did we have to worry about bugs, sharks, pirates, and volcanoes, not to mention a ferocious bear that slashed people's eyeballs out, but apparently there was also the possibility of a crazed logger on the loose. Or the possibility of us stumbling over a slashed, mauled, half-eaten logger's body. Either way, this trip was filled with the strange and dangerous. We walked in silence, but I couldn't shake the feeling that we were being watched. Somehow I suspected that we had not seen the last of MacScott.

After some time, when we could no longer see the fire and smelled only a hint of smoke, we figured we were far enough from the Bear Knuckle Inn and the volcanic mountain that we could take a rest. We stretched out under our blankets, using our backpacks as pillows, and I could soon tell from his heavy breathing and slight snoring that Early had fallen fast asleep. I was tired too. Exhausted, in fact. But for me, sleep did not come so fast.

I lay awake, pondering how I'd gotten there. How did a normal kid from Kansas end up in the middle of the woods with a strange kid like Early? I looked up at the stars and found myself asking the same question Pi asked when heading out on his journey.

Why?

Why did everything get turned upside down? Why did my mom have to die? Why am I following Early, with his endless stories of Pi, on a crazy bear hunt?

With these questions swirling in my head, I wished Early was awake to tell me one of his stories. But Early still breathed the breath of deep sleep.

Maybe I could try remembering something pleasant on my own. My mom was a great one for working up a raucous tale on a cool October evening just like this one. I closed my eyes tight and imagined myself when I was younger, snuggled up next to her on the porch swing while she sipped hot tea from her white teacup with the little red flowers. Or, more recently, just sitting beside her, holding a skein of yarn while she rolled it into a ball.

I tried to hear her voice, but she remained silent. My eyelids grew heavy. Just as the questions started to swirl around in my head in a dreamy way, Early—not as asleep as I'd thought—said, "The numbers are running out."

19

We didn't say much to each other the next morning as we packed up our things. It was Tuesday morning. We'd been gone two days, and Early showed no signs of turning back. I kicked some dirt over the campfire, and we started out.

Just a little ways from our camp, I noticed a pile of cracked walnut shells on the ground. Looking up, I studied a tall oak tree that might have been home to a hungry squirrel who'd been spying on us during the night. That was probably it. Still, I couldn't help feeling that someone else had been watching us.

The sky was cloudy and gray, and a soft mist surrounded us. We knew we'd have to venture farther north into the woods to actually be on the Appalachian Trail, and from what I'd heard, it wasn't that easy to find. I'd read that trees on the trail were marked with an occasional white swatch of paint, and that there were supposed to be warming huts and campsites for hikers. So far, we hadn't seen anything like that. Just lots of wilderness, with an emphasis on *wilder*. In fact, we'd *wildered* around so much, I'd have sworn we were lost. Since Olson had pilfered Early's compass, we were relying on our wits, and mine were getting dimmer by the minute.

But Early seemed to still have his bearings. He had a map but never checked it. I didn't know how he even knew which way was north, since the clouds were thick and dark. A storm was brewing.

I was just getting ready to dig in my heels. We were heading back. And if Early wouldn't go, then I'd head back without him. I hoped he wouldn't call my bluff, though, because I didn't know how I would find my way.

I squared my shoulders, turned to face Early, even held up my hand to tell him to stop. Then we heard the dogs.

They were a fair distance behind us, but we heard them, barking and bellowing after whatever they were tracking. I couldn't be positive they were after us, but even Early sensed the need to pick up our pace.

We veered to the right, and the barking followed us.

"Early, I think those dogs are following our scent."

"Why would they do that? We don't have any food left except the jelly beans."

"Maybe they're not looking for food. Maybe they're looking for us."

"Maybe they're looking for the bear."

"Could be," I said. Early had made it clear that we were looking for the Great Appalachian Bear. Maybe MacScott wanted to make sure we didn't find it before him. Still, I couldn't help thinking there was more to it than that. The barking was getting louder.

"Either way, don't you think we'd better cross that river?"

"There's no bridge. We'll get wet. I don't want to get wet," said Early.

"But if we cross the river, the dogs will lose our scent. Then we can find the bear first." I didn't really care who found the bear first, and I didn't know what Early planned to do if he did find it, but this seemed to be enough to get Early moving.

"Okay, but where can we cross? The river is moving fast. It could be dangerous."

"Dangerous?" I repeated. "That's a funny word coming from someone who didn't think twice about heading off into the woods in search of a seven-hundred-pound bear. Come on, it looks like the river narrows a bit up here, and there are some logs jammed out toward those rocks in the middle. Maybe we can work our way across there."

I could tell Early didn't want to give in. But the dogs were getting louder, their bellowing and high-pitched yelping competing with the roaring of the river.

"Early," I shouted, "we need to cross!"

"Let's find a bridge. I don't want to get wet."

Just then, the dark clouds let loose, and what had been a fine mist turned into a downpour.

"There," I said, "you're already wet. Now can we cross?"

Early tried to blink the raindrops out of his eyes. "We can cross."

As I looked at the swiftly moving current and how it

glossed over the wet logs jammed haphazardly against each other and a few large rocks, I realized that getting Early on board would be the easy part of crossing the river.

I knew I should go first, since it was my idea, but my hand was itching to do rock-paper-scissors. Then Early saved me the embarrassment.

"I'll go first," he said, and stepped out onto the closest log. For someone not very athletic, Early was surprisingly nimble and sure-footed. After a time watching him, I realized I shouldn't have been surprised at all. He was very sure about most things—whether they were true or not. He was sure that the number pi held within it a great story. That, contrary to the theory of a renowned mathematician, the number pi and the story it told would never end. That his brother, who had been killed in the war, was still alive, and that a great bear would lead us to him. And that I was a person he wanted to be friends with.

With that thought in mind, I again put one foot in front of the other and followed Early Auden.

He was halfway across by the time I got started. The logs seemed firmly jammed one against the other, and I worked at keeping my eyes straight ahead. My feet kept slipping on the wet bark of the logs. I extended my arms to keep my balance, but my backpack shifted left and right, nearly pulling me into the rushing water.

Early reached the boulder in the middle of the river, which seemed to be the reason for the tie-up of logs. He turned around and motioned to me to keep going before he continued on. I figured it was late in the logging season; otherwise, the entire width of the river would have been congested with logs. These must have been the last few stragglers that had gotten snagged against each other.

My heart was racing as I neared the boulder marking the halfway point. I stepped onto the rock. *I made it!* Halfway, at least. Here I was, standing on a wet rock in the middle of a swiftly moving river. *I can do this*, I thought. Then I made a big mistake. I looked around—and *saw* that I was standing on a wet rock in the middle of a swiftly moving river. Suddenly I was back on Dinosaur Log, frozen with fear.

"Come on, Jackie." Early, almost to shore, turned around, urging me to follow.

I looked behind me, wondering if it would be better to go back in the direction I'd come from, but the first of the hound dogs had already arrived and was yapping and snarling. The dog whined and panted, dipping his paws into the water, only to back up and start howling again. Even he knew better than to take on this powerful river.

I turned to face Early and carefully stepped out onto the next log. It was slimy with moss, but I mustered another couple of steps. Then my foot slipped, getting wedged between two logs. I cried out in pain as the rough bark tore at the skin on my ankle. The logs shifted slightly, clamping my foot in a painful vise. I tugged and pulled but couldn't budge.

"I'm stuck!" I called out.

Early began retracing his steps, heading back toward me. I used my free foot to stomp on one of the logs, and it moved. I was almost free. Just one more shove and—

The logs gave way, freed from their jam. The world slid out from under me and I was swept away.

· · ·

The next minutes, or years—I'm not sure which—were a blur of icy water and logs, bumps and gashes, and short gasps of air. I tried to grab hold of a log, but every time I grasped at it, the log would bob and roll away as if this were some kind of game.

The current was strong, and my body grew cold and weak. It was a game I wasn't going to win. I tried to stretch out my body and float as best I could. Maybe I could get one more bit of air. A log was rushing straight at me. It struck me. I felt a sharp pain in my forehead.

Then I saw something and knew I must be slipping into unconsciousness. At first I could see only its color and great size as it floated alongside me, just as in the story of Pi. Then I tried to take another breath, and as my lungs took in more water than air, I looked into its eyes.

The deep, somber eyes of a big white whale.

20

I was sure I'd dreamed the whole thing. After all, there are no whales in freshwater rivers. Still, the memory of it was so clear. The whale's skin was smooth, and the water rolled cleanly over its folds and creases. I felt its buoyancy as it floated along beside me, gently guiding me out of the rushing current. I could still see those eyes, dark and mysterious as the ocean.

But gradually, the dream receded. Try as I might to hold on to it, to the feeling of being lifted and held and cared for, almost loved, I became aware of sounds and smells and a whopping headache that were not in my dream. Against my wishes, my eyelids fluttered open. I jerked awake as I stared into a pair of glassy, unseeing eyes that held me fixed in their gaze. My heart raced; then, as my vision cleared, I realized it was just a pair of wire-rimmed spectacles perched on a nightstand next to a large bed. A very large bed that made me feel very small.

Goldilocks came to mind, but the ache in my head cut that story short. I'd have to tell Early—

Where *was* Early? Had he fallen in the river too? What was this place? I bolted upright. My head pounded with the shift in position. I touched the throbbing lump on my temple and felt the stickiness of blood in my hair. I must have gotten a pretty good bump from a log or rock and passed out. And my ankle felt raw from being scraped against the rough bark.

But somehow I'd gotten from the stream to this place—a room with wooden beams in the ceiling and logs for walls. I ran my hands over the patchwork quilt covering the bed. Pots clanked in the next room, and my mouth watered from the smell of simmering meat. I was drawn to it like, well, like a kid who hadn't eaten in some time.

Standing on the cold wooden floorboards, I was relieved to find that my foot didn't seem to be broken. My ankle was a little tender, but I could walk on it. I shivered in my still-damp T-shirt and shorts, and not knowing who might be in the next room, I padded over to peek through the door. Peering out, I felt as if I were in some kind of exotic jungle, but hanging from above, instead of leaves and vines, there were animal furs and snowshoes; hooks, nets, and fishing lures; wooden bird decoys, mounted fish, and maps. A bearskin lay on the floor, its teeth bared, its eyes looking straight at me.

I scanned the room for a glimpse of Early's tartan red jacket, then noticed something out of the corner of my eye. As I turned my head to the right, I jumped back a bit at the gleaming knife stuck right in the wall, not two inches from my face. It was an eerie sight and could have been a good indication that some crazy woodsman lived there, but I couldn't just stay put. I had to find Early. And there was simmering meat. But mostly I had to find Early.

I heard footsteps. Not small, padded steps like Early would make. Big, lumbering footsteps like a giant would make. That must have been what it was, in fact, as a huge shadow passed over the side wall, darkening everything in its path.

Now I felt less like Goldilocks and more like that other boy named Jack after he'd climbed up the magic beanstalk. I waited for the deep voice of a giant to bellow *Fe, fi, fo, fum*.

Then I heard Early, his voice clear and a little too loud, filling me with relief.

"You got a lot of stuffed animals in here. Do you have any timber rattlesnakes?"

"No," the man answered.

"Elephants?"

"No."

"Do you think it's true that elephants can't jump?"

I listened, wondering if the man had already had enough of Early's questions.

"I cannot say I have seen it for myself," answered the man. "But if one had good reason to, he might figure out a way, no?" He spoke with an accent, and his words bobbed up and down like a whale skimming above and below the surface of the water. His voice was clear and full of feeling. What the feeling was, I couldn't say. It reminded me of the church bells you'd hear from a distance back home and how sometimes those bells could call you to a funeral just as surely as a wedding. Sadness or joy—strange how those bells could toll for both.

"Good reason like what?" Early asked.

"If he wanted something that was just out of reach. If he wanted it, you think he jump for it?"

I couldn't be sure where the man was from—he said *dat* for *that* and *tink* for *think*—but whoever he was, he had a way with Early. I don't know if the strange boy from Morton Hill had ever been asked what he thought.

Early pondered the question. "If he wanted it bad enough."

"Oh, yeah."

"Did you know that the largemouth bass isn't large-mouthed or a bass? It's a sunfish," Early said.

"You don't say. I never hear such a thing in all my life."

My curiosity got the better of me. I ventured out of the back room, drawn to the warmth, the smells, the voices.

There, by a great stone fireplace, sitting on a very sturdy wooden crate, sat the biggest, baldest bare-chested man I'd ever seen. He looked up and met me with the somber eyes I recognized from the river.

"Land sakes, little man, you give us a scare," the man said.

"Yeah, Jackie," Early piped in. "You shouldn't have gone in the river like that. It's dangerous. If Gunnar hadn't been nearby, you'd have drowned. Plus, your clothes are still wet." He gestured to my denims, shirt, and soggy backpack hanging near the fireplace. The man's—Gunnar's—much larger shirt hung drying on the other side.

"It is true," Gunnar said. "But today you do me a great favor."

"I do?" I said, wondering how his saving my life could have done him a favor.

"Oh, yes. I catch many fish in my life, but the Lord, he say, 'Follow me and become fishers of men.' Today I go out and catch me one!" His shoulders shook with a rumble of laughter.

I must have looked as dumbfounded as I was, because the great bald man stood, his head nearly brushing the ceiling and his width blocking almost the whole of the fireplace, and stretched out a massive hand to me, taking my small one in his. "Hello, young Mr. Jack. I am Gunnar Skoglund."

"*Skoglund?*" Early repeated the last name, apparently hearing it for the first time. "What kind of name is that?"

I thought it was a strange name too, but I wouldn't have pointed it out. Still, I waited for Mr. Skoglund's explanation.

"I come from Norway. A village near Oslo."

"Are you a Viking?" asked Early. "Or do you know any?"

"I suppose every Norseman is a Viking. We are boat people. Voyagers. Seafarers. It is how I come to America. I work the docks in Portland. But that life is no longer for me," he said, with a note of regret. "Come on over here, and let's have a look at that cut." I winced a little as he moved my hair to check the gash. "Oh, yes. It need a stitch or two. It could have been a far sight worse, I give you that."

He motioned for me to sit on a smaller crate. I did. Then Gunnar Skoglund moved around the cluttered cabin like a great bull but somehow managed to disturb nothing. He came back to the fireplace with a jug, probably of whiskey, and a needle and thread.

My fingernails dug into both sides of the wooden crate. *Stitches,* he'd said.

"Don't you worry," said Gunnar. "I had stitches once before, on my knee, but the doctor, he give me an anesthetic that numbs the skin and I barely feel a thing."

Gunnar popped the cork out of the jug. Maybe he planned to get me so liquored up that I wouldn't feel the pain. But instead of pouring me a jigger, he took a clean rag and soaked a corner in the liquid. Of course I knew what was coming next. He put that rag right on the gash on my forehead. It hurt like a son of a gun. I pressed my lips together and only yelped a little.

All this was being done to a running stream of questions and commentary from Early.

"What are you doing with that needle, Gunnar? Are you going to sew up Jackie's head? I had a hole in my pants one time and I sewed them up, but then I couldn't get them zipped anymore. Do you think if I brought you my pants, you could fix them?"

Gunnar remained silent, leaving Early's questions unanswered as he placed the needle in a pair of tongs and held it to the fire. The sight of it nearly made me pass out all over again. "Now then," he said, "I do believe I need my glasses."

The glasses on the nightstand. "I'll get them!" I jumped up and made a beeline.

"While you are there, could you check the bookshelf? There is a medical journal that should have instruction for the proper conferment of stitches."

Was he kidding? I tried to gauge his tone, listening for a hint of a smile or smirk to let me know he was just pulling my leg. The glowing needle had burned its image in my mind, and I was in no hurry to see it again, so I scanned the bookshelves, looking for any type of medical guide. *"Proper conferment of stitches?" Who talks like that?*

I studied the titles, and the answer came to me: people who read Plato's dialogues. Philo of Alexandria. Dante's *Inferno*. Aesop's *Fables*.

I recognized some of the titles from my mother's book collection at home, and others I'd seen in the library at Morton Hill. Still, this display of books reminded me of something else. I took one off the shelf, then another, touching their embossed covers and smelling their pages. *Robin Hood*. I'd read that one. *The Confessions of St. Augustine*. I hadn't read that one. *Romeo and Juliet*. That was a love story; I would *never* read that one.

They were all hardbound volumes, old and worn but lining the shelves like trophies. That was it! Like the *National Geographic* said, you can tell a lot about people by what they enshrine. This was Gunnar's shrine, and it reminded me of the trophy case at Morton Hill. These books, with their tales of valor, love, sacrifice, and mystery—these books were special and important.

"Do you find it?" Gunnar called. "It is on the second shelf, right next to *Frankenstein*."

A shudder ran down my spine. There it was, the *Alford Medical Manual*, right next to Mary Shelley's *Frankenstein*. Frankie Daniels had been Frankenstein's monster last Halloween. His mother had drawn a huge scar with ragged stitches across his forehead. Hopefully, the medical manual would provide better instructions for the "proper conferment of stitches" than the ones Frankenstein used.

But it was the small rose-colored volume two books down from *Frankenstein* that caught my attention. It stuck out at an angle, just begging to be looked at. I pulled it from the shelf—*The Journal of Poetry by Young Americans*. *Figures*, I thought. *What else is a pink book going to be?*

I'm not a fan of poetry unless it's the kind that starts with *There once was a man from Nantucket*, so I gave it only a brief flipping through. There was an inscription on the inside cover. *To Gunnar—Love, Emmaline*. This was getting gushier by the minute. Then I noticed a paper peeking out from the pages. I knew it was snooping, but I opened the folded sheet. It was a handwritten letter dated June 5, 1938.

Dear Emmaline,

I have strength to move mountains but cannot move time from present to past. I wish I could speak the words you have read to me in the books. Words of love and regret and of things lost. But I wish even more that I could hear your gentle voice. Instead I have comforted myself in reading the books you would have read with me. Filling my mind and heart with the tales of adventurers, thoughts of great thinkers, and poems of

the stars. You have given me a great gift, this love of
words, and for that I am

Gratefully yours,
Gunnar

"The needle, it gets hotter!" Gunnar called, startling me from the then and there and returning me to the here and now.

Returning the rose-colored book to its place on the shelf, I reached for the black and more masculine-looking *Alford Medical Manual* and headed reluctantly back to the main room.

Gunnar placed the glasses on his nose and thumbed through the pages.

"Oh, yes. Here we are." He moved his lips and muttered words like *incision* and *laceration* and *coagulation*. Then he placed the book facedown in his lap, as if he might need to refer to it again during the procedure.

"Have you ever done this before?" I asked, my eyes growing wide as Gunnar took up the needle.

"Oh, you bet. I make the stitches one other time. Of course, I was much younger then. Just a boy myself." He threaded the needle. "It was another boy, his name is Lars. He start a fight with me, saying all manner of mean things, and I punch him in the mouth. His lip, it start to bleeding all over, so I stitch him up good. He never say those mean things again. In fact, I don't recall him saying *anything* again, his lips sewn up so good."

I pulled my head back but caught Gunnar giving Early a wink as he set to work on my forehead. I winced and grimaced. If I'd had a bullet to bite on, I might have bitten clear through it. But with a few steady strokes, Gunnar had stitched me up good. The wound was throbbing. Early reached into his backpack and unscrewed the lid of a small tin. It was some kind of lavender-scented salve that he gently dabbed on my new stitches. "It will ease the pain," said Early. "It's really for snakebites, but it should work on stitches too."

"Now it is the time to eat lunch." Gunnar cleared away the stitching supplies and washed up while Early made himself completely at home and stirred the simmering stew.

Gunnar took three wooden bowls from a cabinet and spooned out generous helpings. We all sat on stools around the fire and ate for a time in silence. The stew was hot and filled with flavors and spices.

I was just pondering what might be in it when Early said, "Jack, did you know Gunnar's missing a toe?" I gagged a little on the stew. "Gunnar, tell Jackie about that time when you went fishing and you caught that sea bass, but when you pulled him out, it was a shark instead, and he bit your toe right off. Remember that?"

I looked at both of them, Early and Gunnar, with my mouth hanging open. It was only lunchtime. How could Early have learned so much of Gunnar's life?

"Yes, I remember. But we'll save that story for later. I'd like to hear how young Mr. Jack is feeling after having drink half the Kennebec River."

"A little shaky," I answered, partly because of the stitches and partly because I had bitten down on something

166

I hoped was a carrot. I still had not heard the fate of Gunnar's toe, and my imagination was running wild.

"That's right. Go on now, eat your supper."

I was hungry enough, and the meaty broth was so good, I decided to take my chances.

"So," Gunnar continued, "Mr. Early tells me you are on a quest." He finished his stew and set the bowl aside.

"It's really Early's quest," I said, trying to distance myself from Early's crazy notions. "I'm just going along."

"I see." Gunnar picked up a rabbit skin and, using a curved white bone, started scraping the inside of the pelt. "Just going along? That is what you are doing in the river too—just going along." He puckered his lips out. "You might consider taking a more active role in your pursuits." There was something between a challenge and a chastisement in his voice. "Leastways, if you end up in the river again, you'll have the comfort of knowing you played some part in getting yourself there."

My face flushed a little at being called out. "Yes, sir," I said. I knew what he meant. My mom used to say, *If you get caught with your hand in the cookie jar, don't pretend like somebody else reached it in there for you.*

"What is it you do here, exactly?" I asked, trying to change the subject. Plus, the cabin, with its array of animal skins and gear, begged for an explanation.

"I am a veterinarian" came his answer. I felt my insides ball up again. *He can't be a very good one,* I thought, looking at the stuffed badger in the corner with his mouth pulled open in an angry snarl. And the raccoon hides that hung from the ceiling. Yes, every doctor loses a patient now and

167

then. But how many doctors hang their dead clients from the rafters or have them stuffed and on display in the corners of their homes?

Gunnar let out a slow laugh. "I am only fooling with you. I am what they call an *outfitter*. I have the gear you need for the hunting, fishing, trapping, and the like."

"What about tracking?" Early asked, without mentioning the Great Bear.

"Well, now"—Gunnar pursed his lips together—"that can be dangerous. You never know when what you are tracking might be tracking you."

"Will you outfit us?" Early asked. "We can pay you." He reached into his nearly empty backpack, most of our provisions having already been eaten or lost to the pirates. But somewhere in a zippered pocket that Olson had overlooked was Early's bean tin with his wad of money.

"Oh, Lord. You two are greener than a couple of cucumbers. You make a big mistake just now, waving money around like that for anyone to steal. And what business do you have wandering around up here in these woods?" He squinted at us.

I was afraid Early might say too much. "We're just on a nature hike," I said.

"Oh, sure." Gunnar peered over his glasses at me. "Well, I suppose it would be better that you are prepared, or you might end up, how shall we say—floating up Runamuck River without the paddle. Too many folks roaming around looking for the wrong thing, that's what I think."

"What do you mean?" I asked. "If someone's going to come out here, maybe even spend a lot of money on equipment, seems like they'd be pretty sure what they're looking for."

"And that is where you would be wrong. The ones who are most consumed with their hunt—desperate, you might say—for what they think they are after, it is often a far cry from what they are really after. It is a fact, too, that sometime, they not really looking for anything at all but are running *away* from something instead." His voice was clear and full, as if it came from the vast glacial waters where the great whales roam.

"Like dogs?" Early asked in his off-the-wall way.

"Maybe." Gunnar breathed in deeply, so deeply that I wondered if he had a blowhole in the top of his head and could hold his breath for long periods of time. But eventually he let the air out in a slow, measured breath.

"Maybe," he repeated. "But sometime, what they run from, it just follow them until there is no place left to run." Then, as if wanting to change the subject, he turned his back to us to stamp out the smoldering embers in the fireplace. That's when I saw that Gunnar himself had run from something. And that *something* had followed him, leaving him restless and unsettled. I had seen it first in his dark, somber eyes. I had read it in his letter to Emmaline. And just then, as he stamped out the embers, I saw it most clearly in the thick, angry scars that marred his back. He had run from something, but it clung to him and would not let loose.

21

Gunnar must have heard my little gasp behind him, because his shoulders stiffened, and he quickly reached for the white shirt beside the fireplace, pulling it on over his scars. Early had seen it just as I had. I was sure he would ask where Gunnar's scars had come from. Early *always* asked. He always said whatever was on his mind. But this time, for some reason, Early said nothing. He just reached out, slipping his small, pale hand into Gunnar's great, weathered one.

I felt strangely on the outside looking in, but eventually, Gunnar said, "Come. The stew will not keep you full for long, and it is time for your first lesson in survival skills. The Lord say, *Put out into the deep and lower your nets for a catch*." Gunnar reached beside the cabin door for a long, slender rod. "But that is only because the Lord, He never been fly-fishing!"

It was afternoon as we made our way down to the river, accompanied by a running commentary by Early about whether or not the Lord had actually been fly-fishing.

"Jesus did have lots of friends who were fishermen," said Early. "Maybe after Peter fell into the Sea of Galilee, he decided to give up deep-sea fishing and take up fly-fishing in the river Jordan. Jesus and Peter were friends, so they might have gone together. And besides, Jesus wouldn't have even needed waders, because he could walk on water. . . ."

By the time we reached the river and Early had exhausted all his reasons for why fly-fishing might have been a New Testament pastime, the sun was high, casting warmth and shimmering light across the river. Gunnar had his waders on and gave Early and me each a pair, insisting we join him.

"Fly-fishing is the sport of the thinkers and the dreamers," Gunnar said. "It is the contemplative man's recreation."

If that was so, I thought Jesus a likely candidate for fly-fishing, but—not wanting to reignite the discussion— I took up my waders and kept quiet.

The rods were longer than regular rods and had a lot more give to them. The line hung loose, with a bit of colored feather on the end. Gunnar waded into the water and began a long, slow motion with the rod, sending the string and the colored lure gliding through the air and glancing off the water.

"You see, it is a fluid motion," Gunnar said. "No herky-jerky of the rod and the reel. The line—it is an extension of yourself. Come," he said, his arms spread out wide in a gesture of invitation.

I held the big rubber pants in front of me and felt a tremor of fear as I eyeballed the coursing river. *Put your big-boy pants on,* my mom would say when I was reluctant or afraid to try something new. The waders reached clear to my chest. These were definitely big-boy pants. *I'd better get them on so Early won't be afraid to do the same. Poor kid has probably never been chest-deep in a river, and he'll be swallowed up in the waders.* I sat down on a rock and pushed and pulled, trying to get the rubbery bottoms on.

"It's okay, Early," I called over my shoulder. "You can stay in the shallow part right by the side. See there—" I grunted, struggling to stand up, only to topple over side-ways onto the pebbly bank. I rolled to the left and then to the right, trying to gather enough momentum to hoist my-self up. Another couple of tries and I'd be standing.

"Hang on, Early. I'll help you as soon as—" I turned to face the river, and there was Early, in full gear, already out in the middle of the stream, casting his lure with the ease and grace of a ballerina. My mouth fell open.

"Come on in, Jackie," Early called. Gunnar must have given him a smaller pair of waders, as they seemed to be an appropriate size for Early's height.

"What—how—" I sputtered, finally getting to my feet and taking baby steps to make my way into the current.

"Very good, Mr. Early. You have a fine cast," called Gunnar.

"I know. My brother taught me before he went to the

war." Early swished his line back and forth. The motion seemed to take him away somewhere.

Gunnar's expression registered what he knew, what we all knew, of the fate of so many of those brothers who went to war. He looked at me, asking the question he didn't want to say out loud. *Did Early's brother make it back?*

I shook my head in answer. No, Fisher was dead.

Gunnar allowed the quiet to take over as Early moved farther out into the water and into his own thoughts.

Finally, Gunnar spoke, his voice so fluid and moving, it could have come from the river itself. "I once hear a poem about angling. It say when you send out your line, it is like you cast out your troubles to let the current carry them away. I keep casting."

I liked the sound of that. The river pressed and nudged, each of us responding to it in different ways, allowing it to move us apart and into our own place within it.

We fished for a couple of hours, the fresh air and cold water easing my aches and pains. Gunnar and Early each had a catch. Then we spent the rest of the afternoon on several more lessons in survival skills and wilderness training: How to start a fire using a mirror and the sun. How to set a trap for an unsuspecting rabbit or squirrel. And, most important, how to track a bear.

Early and I were eager students and tried our best, but Gunnar frequently shook his head in dismay. Like when I burned a hole in my pants with my fire-starting mirror. Like when Early fell out of a tree in the "What to Do If a Bear Is Chasing You" lesson. And just when I was sure I'd found some bear droppings to track, Gunnar merely popped them in his mouth and said they tasted strangely like black-berries.

Eventually, I got the feeling that Gunnar's plan all along was to convince us that we were not ready for a true wilderness adventure. Unfortunately, he was probably right. He finally gave us a reprieve, and just as my stomach was beginning to growl, the stew a distant memory, two beautiful bass were simmering on a spit above the open fire along the river. We ate every bit of them, down to the last shred of meat, leaving barely more than bones and eyeballs.

Our bellies full, Gunnar, Early, and I sat by the fire as the first stars shone in the night sky.

"O look at all the fire-folk sitting in the air," said Gunnar in a dreamy voice.

"Fire-folk?" I asked, looking around.

"Yes, have you not heard of the fire-folk? That is what a famous poet—Hopkins, it was—called the stars. *Look at the stars! he says. Look up at the skies! O look at all the fire-folk sitting in the air!*" His accent was rich and full, lifting each word as if sending it off to float in the night sky.

I followed Gunnar's gaze to the stars. "I can name them all. There are the Pleiades." I pointed to a cluster of bluish stars. "And Orion, the Hunter, is over there. And those five stars that look like a *W*—that's Cassiopeia." I was showing off.

"How do you know those names?" asked Early.

"Learned them when I was a little kid. Just picked it up,

I guess. My mother wasn't much into knowing the names of the stars and the constellations."

Gunnar grunted, clearly unimpressed with my astronomical knowledge. "No one say anything about *knowing* the *names* of the stars. No, the sky, it is not a contest or an exam. The only question is, can you look up? Can you take it all in? As for names of constellations, they are not the be-all and the end-all. The stars, they are not bound one to another. They are meant to be gazed upon. Admired, enjoyed. It is like the fly-fishing. Fly-fishing is not about catching the fish. It is about enjoying the water, the breeze, the fish swimming all around. If you catch one, good. If you don't . . . that is even better. That mean you come out and get to try all over again!"

If Gunnar hadn't been a big, bald barrel of a man with a strange accent, I'd have thought it was my mother talking.

Early piped up. "You mean looking at the stars is like looking at clouds? You can come up with different constellations every night?"

"Ahh, yes. Look up at the skies. What do you see?" asked Gunnar.

Early scanned the sky. "I see something! Over there." He pointed. "A boat! Just like the *Maine*."

I followed his finger. There was a cluster of stars that, if you squinted, did look a little like a boat.

"Oh, sure. Now, let me see," Gunnar said, rubbing his chin as he looked up. "I see a beaver just there . . . and a largemouth bass over there, with a very small mouth." He grinned. "And there"—his voice grew soft and wistful—

"those two twinkling stars. I have seen them before. I call those Emmaline's Eyes."

I saw the stars he had pointed to, bright and shining. The sky seemed to draw me in, and I recalled the feeling of fly-fishing in the river earlier that day. The sounds, the pull of the current, the light sparkling on the water like—stars.

Gazing into Emmaline's Eyes, I could imagine Gunnar casting his line. I thought of the letter to Emmaline and the scars on Gunnar's back, visible now beneath his thin white undershirt. I was pretty sure that he had tried to cast his troubles into the river, but things were too jammed up inside and they couldn't break free.

"And what do you see, Mr. Jack?"

I looked at the sky. Searching—for what, I wasn't sure. Then I saw a cluster of stars in the shape of a circle. Like a ring. It twinkled and shimmered elusively. I pointed to it but couldn't find it anymore. There one moment and gone the next. Just like my dad.

I looked harder, for something else. Wanting to see something other than scars and logjams and navigator rings. "I don't see anything," I said. But I felt as I had that day in the Nook, when I'd placed my hand on the *Maine* and been unable to come up with a real wish. Once again, I was left lost and adrift. The silence ended our little star game.

Early sat next to Gunnar, and without even glancing sideways, he reached over and touched Gunnar's wide back. Gunnar caught his breath as if something had shocked him. It had probably been a long time since anyone had touched those scars.

"What happened, Gunnar?" asked Early.

As Gunnar breathed out, it was as if Early's touch somehow caused that logjam inside him to shift, and the words began to flow.

"I was a fighter. A tough kid, sixteen years old, fresh from Norway. I work the docks in Portland, build up strong muscles, and could fell a grown man in three blows. Eventually, I get paid for it. Men make wagers on me. Mr. Benedict, he make me *his* fighter. He say he pay me good as long as I keep up the winning. That is how I grow up, the only life I know for years. Until I meet Emmaline.

"I used to see her pass by on her way to the library where she worked. So I start going to the library. She recommend the books, and I take them home so I can bring them back and see her again. It don't take her long to figure out what's what." Gunnar smiled.

"One day I bring a book for the return. *Huckleberry Finn*. She ask me, 'How do you like it?' I say, 'Oh, I like it just fine.' She say, 'That Mr. Twain, he got some imagination. Whoever hear of a dog named Huckleberry?' I nod and say, 'Yes, but that Huckleberry, he is a rascal of a dog.'

"She give me a stern look and say, 'Gunnar, Huckleberry Finn is a boy, not a dog. I believe you cannot read.'

"Well, I want to walk out of that library and never come back, but she say, 'There's nothing to be embarrassed about. I'll teach you.'

"And she does. Hours and hours we spend in the park, in the library, she read to me, I read to her. She love the poems of Hopkins. I find a book of his poems in a used bookstore and give it to her. Her favorite is 'The Starlight

Night.' There is nothing for me to do but fall in love with her. But she will have none of the fighting."

Gunnar shook his head. "She say fighting is for people who don't know their own worth. She say I got a good mind and I should use it instead of my fists.

"So one night, I tell Mr. Benedict this is my last fight. I tell him I save up enough money and I am going to the college. I am to get married. He smile a mean smile and say he own me and I do what *he* say.

"That night, I know something is different. There is a buzz in the room I don't understand. Until the bell rings. And suddenly there are *two* men in the ring with me. Brothers. Mr. Benedict nods from the side rail. I can tell he has bet a lot of money on me this night.

"They come at me. One punching here, another punching there. I stagger back, then my eyes go red. All of my hate pours out, all of my shame. Hitting whatever comes in front of me. Until one of them does not get up. He is dead.

"The brother look at me, in a rage at what I have taken from him. He look at Mr. Benedict, who give a nod. Two men hold my arms, and the brother beat me. But I almost laugh. The two men are wasting their time holding on to me. I don't fight. I don't struggle to get away. I let him beat me. Because I am ashamed. We hear police sirens. A raid, they call it. They drop me to the floor. I am barely conscious. The room clears as everyone scatters. Bottles are smashed. Whiskey spills everywhere. I smell the fumes. I hear the match. But my vision is blurred and my mind cloudy. I stir at the smell of smoke and my own burning skin. Then I know I must get out or die. I get out. But part of me dies anyway."

The campfire had dwindled to embers, and the sky was alive with stars.

"How did you end up all the way out here?" I asked.

Gunnar leaned back against a rock near the fire pit and looked into the sky. "I crawl in the back of a truck and it heads north. The truck belong to a veterinarian, and I wake up at his place. He puts ointment on my burns and lets me stay in the barn for a couple of days, but then I have to move on." Gunnar ran his hands over his eyes, as if trying to wipe the memories away. But it didn't seem to work.

"Everything had changed," he continued. "I could not go back to Portland. I could not face Emmaline again, after what I had done. Looking like this. I want to go far away. To hide my scars. The ones on the outside as well as the ones on the inside. So I come here. To the end of the world . . ." His words trailed off.

The end of the world. I'd landed there myself. And I knew that it was a hard place to find your way back from. Was that what I was doing out here with Early? Trying to find my way back? Or was I just running away? Maybe Gunnar and I were alike—both strangers in a strange place, both stuck outside our own lives, unable to jump back in. In fact, after our fly-fishing excursion that day, I felt very much like that tiny fly, glancing off the water time and time again, never quite able to break the surface.

"But what about Emmaline?" Early's too-loud voice interrupted my thoughts.

179

"I told you. Emmaline would have none of it. She would never want me back."

"I bet she knows you feel bad. You didn't mean to kill that man," Early said.

I thought of the letter to Emmaline tucked away in the poetry journal and wondered how many times Gunnar had tried to put words on paper without being able to send them off.

"Maybe you could send her a letter," I said.

Gunnar looked up, startled. I couldn't see the redness of his face in the dim firelight, but I felt it. I was pretty sure I'd given away the fact that I'd snooped through his books. He settled back on his rock. "I don't know. I suppose I lack the courage to do what you say. As long as I am away, as long as I do not write to her, there is still a chance. But what if I get a letter back and she say, *Do not write to me again?* Or what if a reply never comes?" Gunnar shook his head. "I wish I had not killed that man."

"But it was two against one," I said. "You were just trying to protect yourself."

"If that is what it take to protect myself, to keep living, I think I rather it have been me who was laid flat in the ring that night."

The conversation died out, and Gunnar shoveled sand onto the dying fire.

We trudged our way back to Gunnar's cabin, tired and sore from the day's happenings, our steps making hardly a sound on the soft, damp leaves underfoot. It was in that quiet that we heard the sound of dogs panting and yelping, along with that of men grumbling and milling about, while we were still some distance away from the cabin.

Don't go putting your hand in a honeypot till you make sure it's not really a bees' nest.

That was one of my mom's sayings that was plenty clear.

Now that we were close enough to see into the clearing near Gunnar's cabin, we got a full-on view of MacScott and his sidekicks Olson and Long John Silver. The dogs were in an excited state, having caught our scent again. It was clear the honeypot *was* a bees' nest. And the bees were buzzing mad.

22

Gunnar put a finger to his lips, motioning for Early and me to wait as he raised his lantern and walked into the clearing. We quickly found a better spot behind a large oak tree, where we could see but were still hidden.

"Greetings to you, gentlemen." Gunnar's voice boomed out of the darkness, startling the three pirates. "Might I offer you some beef jerky or a cool glass of water on this fine evening?"

MacScott spun around, startled. He stared hard as the giant Norwegian stepped into the lamplight, Gunnar's undershirt unable to conceal his scarred back and arms. MacScott seemed stunned by the sight. Could he be that repulsed by one man's scars when he wore his own plain as day?

Finally, MacScott grabbed a large walking stick. "What you can do is tell us if you've seen a couple of boys hiking along this trail," he said, clanging the stick against some hanging camping pots, as if Early and I might fall out of one of them. "My dogs seem fairly sure they've been here."

Gunnar splashed his face with water from a bucket on the porch. "Well, no telling who might have been here while I was away. Two boys, you say? And what do they look like?" He casually took a canister of shaving cream and rubbed foam over his stubbly face. He drew a razor from beside the bucket and proceeded to shave as if he were getting ready to go to church—and looking as if he didn't have the slightest concern about MacScott and his dogs.

Olson and Long John tried to create a description.

"Well, the little one was kind of skinny."

"The bigger one was skinny too, just taller."

"But the shorter one was real chatty."

Finally, MacScott interrupted the two. "What difference does it make what they look like? There can't be too many pairs of boys wandering around these woods. Have you seen them or not?"

"Now, there's no call for the harsh words," said Gunnar, rubbing the remaining foam off his face. He patted his pockets and offered beef jerky to the whimpering dogs, scratching them behind the ears. "But as I have not seen any two boys of late, like you say, it really makes no difference what they might look like."

MacScott raised the rifle he'd been cradling in his arm but hung back outside the circle of lamplight. "You think you're being funny?" He motioned to Olson. "Go look inside."

Gunnar stood straight, the muscles in his arms twitching. "I think unless you're looking for some beaver traps, fish bait, or maybe a fine hunting knife, I am unable to help you gentlemen this evening."

MacScott rubbed a finger over the gleaming gun barrel. He turned the mauled side of his face into Gunnar's lamplight. His scars took on an even more mangled look in the flickering light. "Do I look like someone who needs beaver traps or fish bait?"

Olson emerged from the house. "No one there, boss." Even the dogs seemed to understand, as they gave up their panting and whining.

MacScott kept his eyes fixed on Gunnar. "You may be unable to help us this evening, but we'll check back." He placed the gun in its sling.

MacScott and his men gathered up their packs and headed in the opposite direction from where we were hiding. Early and I waited a while longer before giving up our safe spot.

Early was the first to speak, of course. "Gunnar, who do you think would win in a fight between Captain America and Captain MacScott? MacScott has a gun, but Captain America's shield would protect him from bullets."

"It's too late to make a guess, little man. They won't be coming back tonight, I don't think. You two go to bed, and we iron it all out in the morning."

"But the dogs," I said. "They'll smell us."

"They'll be smelling nothing but menthol for a while." He held up his hands, giving us a whiff of the shaving cream he had applied generously to his hands and apparently to the dogs' noses as well.

Early and I crawled into the big bed I'd occupied earlier that day. Gunnar clanked and rummaged around in the cabin while Early and I made our plans. Finally, we heard Gunnar shove a wooden plank against the front door to bar it shut.

When everything was locked up tight, he lowered an extra quilt over Early and me as we pretended to sleep, both of us knowing we would be gone before Gunnar woke up the next morning.

Early and I knew we had to leave. The pirates were looking for us, and we had no business bringing our troubles on Gunnar. The farther away we got from the outfitter's cabin, the safer he would be. Early and I found our packs, crawled out the bedroom window, and walked away in the dark of night.

It was overcast, so we set off in what we thought was a northerly direction. I had taken only a few steps behind Early when I felt something crunching underfoot. Walnut shells, again.

"Jackie," Early said once we were far enough from the cabin that Gunnar couldn't hear, "those pirates really want that bear, and they must think we're getting close."

I'd been thinking that myself. But I also remembered Early telling his story of Pi. "I guess so. But MacScott got real interested when you mentioned the part in Pi's story about caves and buried treasure. Maybe he thinks we know where there's a secret treasure and he's going to follow us until he finds it."

"It doesn't say *treasure* is buried in the caves. It says that's where people go to bury their dark secrets and *accidental* treasures."

"Who knows? Maybe he's got his own dark secrets buried somewhere."

"Maybe," Early breathed.

We stopped for a short break to rest our legs and eat a piece of beef jerky. Reaching into my backpack, I found some extra items that had not been in there the night before—a pouch of nuts, dry matches, some chocolate bars, and two apples—and a new flashlight to replace the one that had gotten soaked in the river. I flicked it on and off. It worked.

"Look," I said, giving Early a chocolate bar. "Gunnar knew we'd run out of food and supplies. I guess we didn't fool him into thinking we were experienced travelers." But it was what I found next that left me bewildered.

"What's that?" Early asked as I pulled out the small rose-colored volume. Gunnar had also known that I'd seen the book.

"It's a book of poetry. And"—I removed the delicate envelope that was now sealed—"a letter to Emmaline. Why would Gunnar put this in my backpack?" I wondered out loud.

"He wants you to mail it," Early said in his characteristically straightforward way, which left no room for doubt or rebuttal.

Early took out a fresh box of matches and lit one to shed some light on the book and the letter. The envelope now showed a complete address—*Emmaline Bellefleur, Portland Public Library, Portland, Maine.*

"Why wouldn't he just mail it himself?" I asked.

"He needs a proxy." Early blew out the match. "You know, someone who can act in another person's place." I could hear the string of synonyms coming from Early, the walking thesaurus, even before it began. "A deputy, a second, a substitute, a surrogate, a representative, an emissary—"

"I get it," I interrupted.

"Like, if Captain America needed to keep a Nazi spy from discovering war secrets and keep Red Skull from assassinating the president of the United States at the same time, he could send Bucky as his proxy for one or the other. Probably he'd send Bucky after the spy."

I studied the letter. "So, Gunnar wants me to be his sidekick."

Early's eyes lit up. "Yes, a sidekick. I like that one the best."

I tucked the envelope and book back in my pack. "Well, that's a bone best chewed on another day." Early didn't seem quite sure what to make of that. "That just means we'll worry about it later. For now, we'd better keep moving," I said.

We walked a ways in silence. Early looked up at the night sky as the clouds cleared and found the constellation Ursa Major, the Great Bear. We followed it into the darkness, in search of another great bear—this one on the Appalachian Trail. My feet were heavy, and the woods closed in around us. There was only darkness and danger in front of us. And now there were dogs and pirates behind us. Early's quest had gone on long enough. It was time to turn back. I opened my mouth to say so, but Early spoke first.

"Jackie?" Early said again.

"Yes, Early."

"Thank you for coming with me."

For a moment I didn't know how to answer him. I could be honest and say, *I think you're crazy and we're both crazy for looking for this stupid bear*. Or maybe, *I know you want your brother to be alive, but he's just not, and nothing is going to bring him back*. Or, *I only came because my dad didn't show up and I didn't want to be alone*.

Then the moment passed, my feet kept moving, and all I said was "You're welcome."

23

The dawn was just beginning to cast a purple hue all around, and we could see puffs of air coming from our mouths as we breathed. We were getting tired. You'd think we'd have figured out that it was best to sleep at night and walk during the day, but with dread pirates following us, what worked best and what was safest were two different things.

Eventually the sun peeked out, stretching into the day around us. We came to one of those covered bridges that New England is famous for. It seemed a little strange to me, why anyone needed a covered bridge. Even in the horse-and-buggy days, when travelers were more at the mercy of the elements, that bridge would keep them covered for only the minute or two it took to cross the bridge. Then they'd be out in the rain or snow again. Our neighbor back home, Mr. Kloster, who—according to my mom—was as cheap as the day is long, would call that a poor use of good lumber. But even Mr. Kloster couldn't argue with the fact that that covered bridge spanning the banks of the Kennebec River and nestled among countless maple, ash, and birch trees, with their red, gold, and orange leaves, was a pretty sight.

Seeing that bridge gave us a sense of direction. After all, a bridge is meant to be crossed, isn't it? Bridges are a means of getting somewhere. They give you safe passage to wherever it is you need to go. So we went.

Once we set foot on the shaded wooden planks, it felt like we were stepping back in time. Our shoes clopped along, echoing like horses' hooves in the cavernous structure.

"HELLOOOOO!" I shouted, expecting to hear an echo.

"HELLOOOOO!" came the reply. But it was only Early.

"Very funny," I said. "I was waiting for an echo."

"Oh, do it again."

"EARRRLLLLLYYY."

"WHAAAAAT?"

I just shook my head.

"CAPTAIN AMERICAAAAA," he called.

"TO THE RESCUUUUUUUE," I answered.

We ran the rest of the way across the bridge and into the warm sunlight on the other side, where the path forked. I was just getting ready to ask Early which way we should go, when I caught sight of something red on the path to the right.

"Hey, look! Berries!"

And lots of them. They were dark red in color and had that squishy look of berries that are past their prime.

"I think we should stay to the left," Early said.

"What? And miss out on a feast of free berries? Both paths head north. They'll probably end up in the same place eventually. Besides, it's my turn to lead for a while."

I started off to the right, and Early followed a reluctant two paces behind. I don't think he liked me choosing the direction, as he didn't even eat any berries.

Suit yourself, I thought, popping one berry after another into my mouth as we walked. They glistened with dew and had a moist taste that was both bitter and sweet.

I don't know if it was the berries or having decided on a course, but I felt relieved and sort of relaxed. I had chosen a path and could let go for a while, just let it take us where it would.

"Does Billie Holiday have any good hiking songs?" I asked.

"No. Besides, it's not raining."

"How about Benny Goodman?"

"Nope."

"Sinatra?"

"No."

I popped another berry in my mouth, thinking, *I guess good singers don't make good hikers.* But I recalled my grandpa Henry's favorite walking song.

*"Camptown ladies sing this song
Doo-dah, doo-dah . . ."*

I paused for Early to join in.

"We're going the wrong way," he said.

"Don't be a spoilsport. Just enjoy the scenery."

He was grumpier than I'd thought. But that was okay. I let my eyes take in the soft shades of some evergreen trees. And the reds of the berries, a few here and a few farther down the trail. Just enough to keep me moving along, beckoning me. It felt good to get drawn into the intoxicating colors, scents, and flavors of the path.

"The Camptown racetrack's five miles long,
Oh, doo-dah day."

And so we went along, me feeling like a sleek racehorse moving at a brisk clip, and Early—well, Early was more like a mule, being slow and stubborn.

"Goin' to run all night
Goin' to run all day
I bet my money on a bob-tailed nag
Somebody bet on the bay."

Even as I sang that last line, I could tell that my voice sounded unusually loud in the dense woods. It seemed that while I was betting on the bob-tailed nag, the woods had grown dark around us, lining our narrowing path with thorns and brambles. Then I started to feel a little queasy, the berries in my belly turning sour.

Pretty soon our path was nothing more than a narrow opening between branches that tore at our clothes and roots that caught our feet.

"I told you we shouldn't have gone this way," said Early.

"Oh, all right, Mr. Know-It-All. So maybe we got a little off track. All we have to do is turn around and find our way back out."

But backing up was more perilous than walking forward, as there wasn't much room to maneuver without getting further scratched and poked. And the path that had been there seemed to veer and split in unexpected directions, leading us in circles and to dead ends.

Because we'd turned around, Early was now a few paces ahead of me and back in the lead position. And since he'd been so sure about where *not* to go before, I thought it only fair to ask him, "So, you think we should have gone left back at the bridge?"

He didn't answer. Instead, he looked around, getting a feel for our surroundings.

"This must be where the numbers start going in circles," Early said.

"You mean the pi numbers?" I knew that he saw things in a different way than most people. And a lot of what he saw, he somehow related to the story of Pi. But MacScott wasn't really a pirate. The explosion on the mountain wasn't really a volcano. The barmaid wasn't really the Haggard and Homely Wench. Of course, there had been strange similarities and connections, but Early had a way of making them fit the story as if he were making jigsaw pieces fit into a puzzle just because he needed them to. I rolled my eyes at the ridiculousness of it but couldn't help asking, "You're the one with the crystal ball. What happens when the numbers start going in circles?"

"You don't want to know."

I tugged at a branch that was clinging to my ear. "Would it be a place called LOST?"

"Sort of. It's part of the story I haven't told you yet."

"What part is that?" I asked, my voice skeptical.

"The part where Pi gets lost. For a while."

"Lost how?"

"The same way we got lost. In a maze."

"A maze," I said, staring. "You mean like in England, where you enter a section of bushes and tall hedges, then wander around until you come out the other side?"

"Yes, but the maze he was in started with one two three. Easy enough at the beginning. Then it turned into four six four seven four eight. Very tricky. But it's where he ended up that was really strange. . . ." Early's voice trailed off, as if the ending were something really amazing.

"What? Where did he end up?"

"Well, it ended with three six seven seven seven seven. The place of the Ancient One."

The Ancient One

PI WANDERED IN THE MAZE FOR HOURS, maybe days. He'd turn left, only to find himself blocked on three sides, in a dead end. Then he'd backtrack and this time take a right, only to find his way blocked again a little farther on. His mind began playing tricks on him as shadows grew longer, and the path of the maze seemed to toy with him, leading him the wrong way time and time again.

As he became more lost, wandering in the tangled woods, it seemed that the maze was more in control of his journey than *he* was. It led him deeper and deeper into its twists and turns, until eventually Pi was paralyzed by his inability to set a course and move according to it.

He lay down, overcome by exhaustion, and closed his eyes. Maybe if he could sleep, he thought, he might wake with a clearer head and a better sense of the workings of the maze. Just as he felt his body give in to the watery, floating sensation of sleep, he was awakened by a sound. A bell.

It rang with a clarity that drew him to it. Then he saw her. She must have been the oldest person in the world, with flowing white hair cascading over her thin shoulders, pale and wrinkled skin, and eyes that held the memories of centuries.

Something in Pi held him back, but the ancient woman saw him and beckoned him forward. She placed a mantle around his shoulders and took his hand in hers. "Come," she said. "You belong here. You need to be here."

It was the word *need* that struck him. And he knew that hers was greater than his. But he followed her. She took him to her home and fed him savory meats and delicious fruits. She gave him warm clothes made of soft and colorful fabrics. She spoke to him words of comfort and solace.

Once he suggested that it was time for him to leave, but she only explained to him that this was his home. She tried helping him recall stories and events that were at first unfamiliar to him. But the more she described them in great and wonderful detail, the more they became his own stories, his own experiences. Swimming in the stream as a boy. Fashioning toy animals from twigs. Picking flowers for her in the meadow. Her memories washed over him, making him think they were his memories.

She called him by another name. Filius. It must have been a nickname he'd forgotten he had. Soon he forgot about a world outside this ancient one encased in a maze. As time passed, he no longer thought of leaving. He grew comfortable in the home of the ancient woman. Until one night.

It was late. He was just finishing drawing water from the well before bedtime when a dark, shadowy form crossed his line of vision. He couldn't quite make out what it was at first, so he followed it into the trees. A few steps. Then a few steps more. The moon shone bright in the sky and revealed a clearing, where he saw the dark form before him. A bear. Something shook loose within him. Maybe it was the way that great black bear held him in his gaze. Maybe it was the way the breeze ruffled his hair as he gazed back.

He remembered something. Something apart from the memories of the Ancient One. A memory that was his own. It was of a different woman who spoke words of comfort and solace. A woman who ruffled his hair while she told him stories. A woman who told him to keep his eyes on the Great Bear, *because the Great Bear is a mother bear. And a mother's love is fierce.*

There was a great rending within Pi as he realized he had been lulled, just as he had been upon entering the maze, and drawn into a life that did not belong to him. Returning to the house, he took one last look at the Ancient One as she slept in a chair by the fire. He placed an extra shawl around her shoulders, tucked it under her chin, and kissed her on the cheek. That night, under cover of darkness, he turned his attention from the Ancient One, who had mesmerized him with her comforts and stories, back to the Great Bear, whom he had lost sight of for so long.

The maze did its best to divert and distract, but Pi no longer looked to the path to lead the way. He kept his sight on the Great Bear to guide his steps. And just as the sky was growing light, he made his way clear of the maze, its brambles and bushes, its twists and turns, and found himself once again facing the ocean. It beckoned him. But he was so alone. And he had lost so much. So he turned away from the ocean and set out on foot once more. In which direction, he couldn't say and didn't care.

24

Early had a way with his story of Pi. He was so convinced that we were following in Pi's footsteps that I found myself cocking my ear in anticipation of hearing a faint chime or ringing in the distance, just like the bell sound Pi heard when he was lost in the maze. But I heard nothing more than the sprinkling of rain, which was beginning to fall on the trees and leaves around us. My face was hot. How could I have fallen for this craziness and let Early sucker me in with his story?

"So Pi heard a bell that led him out of the maze? Well, lucky for him," I said, pulling the rain poncho from my pack and putting it on over my already-damp clothes. "I don't hear anything but the sound of us getting wet. We'd better keep moving."

Early didn't respond. He seemed lost in his musings about Pi as he put on his own rain poncho.

That was okay; I didn't want to talk anyway. And pretty

soon we were trudging along in a steady rain that soaked our shoes and chilled us to our bones. I wished I had the wide-brimmed Stetson that I could still see hanging on the hat stand in our mudroom back home. I hadn't brought it to Maine, because who needs a cowboy hat in Maine? But just then, it would have provided some protection for my rain-spattered and scowling face.

I narrowed my eyes so that they were open only a slit and tried to let the sounds of the wet forest guide me. It's amazing what you can hear when you're not distracted by seeing. A few squirrels and birds chattered and squawked, first to my left, then to my right, as if playing some sort of forest game of hide-and-seek.

But as we continued on and the day grew darker with more clouds and trees, the noises grew darker as well. The wet leaves gave a sucking sound beneath my feet, as if trying to pull me into the ground. The rain lost its pitter-patter as it grew heavier, seeming more like a heavy sigh now. The whole forest exhaled an ancient breath that it must have held since its great trees were saplings. I felt as if I were being drawn deeper and deeper into the mystery of the woods. I knew that inside each tree, etched into its core, were circles, each ring telling the story of a year in the life of that tree and this forest. *What kinds of scars and jagged lines would someone find in the life of a tree?* I wondered.

Did people have telltale lines like that? What would mine look like? I didn't need to see them. I knew they had been severed last summer. A gash had been cut into me, so deep that I felt I was at that tipping point, when the lumberjack is just about to yell "Timber!" But somehow I remained poised, in precarious balance, not sure which way I might fall.

As I let my thoughts ramble, the sound of the rain changed, becoming tinnier, like the pinging of water off a metal roof. Maybe there was a barn or shed nearby.

I veered toward the sound, not because I was trying to find its source, but because that was the only way the narrow path would let us go. The pinging got louder and more rhythmic. It reminded me of my mother's laughter, light and musical. *The forest must be playing tricks on me*, I thought. I could almost hear her calling my name.

Jackie, Jackie. Time for supper.

My steps quickened, even though I knew it wasn't real. It was probably just the wind rushing through the trees.

"Do you hear that?" Early said, drawing me out of my reverie.

"No," I said, not wanting to let on that my imagination had run away like a bee-stung horse. Besides, what could I say? *Hear what? That woman calling out from the middle of nowhere?* He'd think I was crazy.

"Hear what?" I said.

"That woman calling out," he answered, plain as day.

Then we heard it again, closer. The rhythmic sound. *Ting, ting, ting. Ting, ting, ting.*

Without warning, the trees opened onto a tiny clearing, where there was a rusted-out Model T providing a rain break for a raccoon lounging underneath; a worn-out, old log cabin; and an even older-looking woman with a long gray braid that hung past her waist. The braid swung back and forth as she worked a metal rod around the inside of a triangle, making the rhythmic clanging sound.

"Martin," she called. "Time for supper."

Early and I watched her long braid swing to and fro. I wondered if she had one twist in her braid for every year of her life, just as a tree had one line in its core for every year of its life. If she did, she'd be over a hundred. And she looked it.

"She's old," I whispered to Early.

He shook his head. "She's ancient."

I hung back under cover of the trees, still clearing my head of my mom's voice calling me, realizing it was just this old woman calling someone named Martin. But Early had his own plans, as usual.

"Go on." He gave me a shove, pushing me out into the clearing. "She said it's suppertime."

The woman stopped ringing her dinner triangle, leaving the clanging rod in midair.

She'd spotted me.

"Well, *there* you are," she said. "Come in out of that rain—you'll catch your death."

25

I looked around to see who she might be talking to, but somehow I already knew. She was talking to me. It was the way she'd said *Well*, there *you are* that struck me. She didn't say, *Who are you?* or *Who have we here?* or even *Look what the cat dragged in.*

No, it was *There you are,* as if she'd been calling me, looking for me, waiting for me, for a long time.

"Come on," she beckoned. "And bring your friend. Is that Archibald with you? I saw him come by today. I think he got a new gun too, and wanted to show it off. I told him I expected you home any minute, but he said he couldn't stay. You know you're supposed to be back before supper." She stepped out into the rain and put her shawl around my shoulders, guiding me into the cabin, every step, every movement showing her age.

"You too, young man," she said to Early, slowly reaching for another blanket from the porch and wrapping it around him. "Usually, Martin brings home stray cats and dogs, and occasionally a stray boy. Let's do our introductions, shall we. I'm Eustasia Johannsen." She held out her hand, spotted and wrinkled.

Early took it in his. "My name is Early Auden. I'm on a quest."

"Well, isn't that splendid. My Martin's been on a quest too. He wanted to try out his new gun. Did you shoot a rabbit for supper?" she asked, putting her arm around me. "No matter," she said before I could reply. "I've got plenty of soup simmering in the pot. And your favorite jam, and biscuits." She winked at Early. "Now, you boys go get changed and wash up for dinner. Early, you can change in Martin's room. He'll have extra clothes for you to wear until yours are dry. Don't be dillydallying."

She handed Early an oil lamp and steered us toward a back bedroom where we could change, then busied herself over a white enamel cook pot on the stove.

Before I could close the door, Early said in his too-loud voice, "Is that your grandma?" Then, before I could answer, he followed it up with "I didn't know your real name was Martin."

Then I shut the door with a thud. "She's not my grandma, Early. And I'm not Martin. She's mistaking me for someone else."

"I'm cold, Jackie. Can I borrow some of your clothes?" Early began opening drawers.

"They're not *my* clothes, Early. That's what I'm trying to tell you—"

Early already had his wet clothes in a pile and was pulling a neatly folded pair of pants and a shirt out of a drawer.

Suddenly I realized I was shivering. "Give me some clothes," I said, exasperated. "At least we can dry off until she figures out we're not who she thinks we are. She's old, and she probably has a great-great-grandson who lives nearby."

Early was looking at the articles in the room. "Then why are his clothes here?" I glanced around. There was a wooden bed, neatly made, with a red-and-blue flannel blanket on top. Several books lay open on a small desk next to the window. A McGuffey reader. *The Odyssey*. Quackenbos's *Practical Arithmetic*. Their pages were a little yellowed, but otherwise, everything was clean and tidy.

I picked up a pencil and a sheet of paper that had several math problems written out. The last problem was unfinished, as if the student working on it had decided there was much more fun to be had outside and set his pencil down right then and there.

"These are really old textbooks," I commented. "You don't think—" I put the paper and pencil down, considering my unfinished question.

Early put on a pair of socks, of course carefully making sure the seam was placed evenly across his toes, while I put on a pair of pants that felt a little stiff and old-fashioned. Then I picked up a Sears Roebuck catalog lying on the nightstand next to the bed and thumbed through it, looking at old pictures of hammers, stoves, sewing machines, fishing rods—all manner of necessities.

"What's your favorite jam?" Early asked.

"What?" I said, distracted with the catalog.

"Your grandma said she made your favorite jam. Is it blueberry or strawberry? I like both. I just hope it's not raspberry. One reason is because the raspberries got a lot of rain this year, and the newspaper said they're more tart than usual. And another reason is because I don't like raspberries."

One thing I'd learned about Early was that once he got something in his head, right or wrong, it was very hard to convince him otherwise. His mind was like one of the lobster traps I had seen hanging in the boathouse at Morton Hill. The lobster can find his way in through a small opening but is unable to make his way back out. So it went with Early's ideas.

"Besides, raspberries also look kind of hairy, and they have those little seeds that get caught in your teeth. . . ."

I stopped listening to Early as I looked at a particular picture circled in the catalog. *1894 Winchester Short-Barrel Carbine Rifle. $17.50. Initials engraved for an extra fifty cents.*

This was the "new" rifle that Eustasia Johannsen had mentioned. I looked at the front of the catalog. *1894.* I tried to figure things out in my head, but I couldn't even formulate the question.

"Early?"

"Yes."

"I have a question for you."

"You still haven't answered *my* question."

"Blueberry," I answered.

"Good, I like blueberry."

"Now is it my turn?"

"Yes."

"Okay. It's kind of like a story problem in math class. If Martin Johannsen bought a new 1894 Winchester rifle, wears old-fashioned clothes that fit you and me, and has unfinished homework from an eighth-grade primer, how old would he be?"

"It depends. When he bought the rifle new, it would have been in 1894, and if he was in eighth grade, he'd have been around thirteen. So he'd have been born in 1881, and if he was still alive today, he'd be sixty-four."

"Yeah, but wouldn't he have bigger clothes by now? And Mrs. Johannsen said he'd gone off hunting this morning with his new rifle. There's no gun in this room, and I didn't see one when we came in."

Eustasia Johannsen called from the other room. "Martin Johannsen, you better find your way out here. And don't try to fool me into thinking you're finishing your lessons. I wasn't born yesterday."

Early and I stared at each other. He went over to the desk and picked up the sheet of math problems. The look on his face registered confusion. At least he was realizing that something very strange was going on.

"What do you think?" I asked.

"I didn't think you had any homework over the break. And you missed number four. It's *negative* six."

I couldn't believe he still didn't get it. The solution to the story problem was finally taking shape in my head.

Eustasia Johannsen didn't think I was her grandson or her great-grandson. She thought I was her *son*, Martin Johannsen.

"Let's go eat." Early was out the door before I could utter another word.

The cabin was warm and cozy but showed signs of age in every corner. The tapestry-covered sofa was threadbare. The braided rug was frayed and faded. The enamel pots and china dishes were chipped. Even the gingham curtains were faded and worn. Eustasia Johannsen was still the most ancient of all. Her body curved over on itself like a morning glory that is well into nighttime. But her pale cheeks had gained a little color, and her eyes were a sparkling blue.

The bizarre scene played out with Early and me sitting at the little white kitchen table, eating chicken-and-dumpling soup and, strangely enough, blueberry jam on biscuits. I hadn't seen any chickens in the yard, and considering how old and frail Mrs. Johannsen was, and how secluded her home was in the overgrown maze of bush and bramble, I couldn't imagine how she kept herself from starving. But she didn't offer any explanation. And of course, Early led the conversation.

"We're looking for a bear. Have you seen any around here?"

"Oh, I can't say that I have. But Martin here is a fine one for tracking. Now that he has his shiny new rifle, he goes out for hours and hours." Her face grew a little drawn. "All the neighbors have been so worried. They kept trying to tell me that something must have happened to Martin because he'd been gone so long. They told me I needed to face the facts—that he wasn't coming back. But I said *no*."

She looked at me with tears in her eyes and gently touched my hand. "I knew you'd come back, Martin. I told them. I said, 'He'll come back, and I need to have supper ready when he does.'" Her voice shook just a little, and she caught her breath. "And here you are."

That was shocking enough—being thought to be the long-lost son of a very old woman. But what she said next was even worse.

"Now, finish up your supper, and the two of you can go out and start digging."

"Digging?" Early said. "For what? Fossils? Arrowheads?"

"No. You're not digging to find something. I've been ready to let go of this life for a good long while. Neighbors and kin have been telling me, *Eustasia, you've got to let go.* But I couldn't. Not until my Martin came home. Now that he's back, I'm ready to die. We haven't had a hard freeze yet, and it doesn't have to be all that deep. Just a couple feet is fine."

"Are you sure?" said Early. "You don't want some animal digging you back up."

I choked and spit some soup back into the bowl.

"Well, maybe you're right." Eustasia Johannsen sighed. "I guess we'd better make sure I stay put."

For the umpteenth time in recent months, I asked my-self how I'd ended up where I was. These two, Early Auden and Eustasia Johannsen, seemed made for each other. Why hadn't she mistaken *Early* for her son? They were a match made in crazy heaven and could have been very happy together. At least until Eustasia Johannsen began her eternal rest in her newly dug, two-foot-deep grave.

"Are you planning on being dead before you get in it?" I muttered, not intending for anyone to hear my question.

Eustasia and Early exchanged amused glances, as if I had just asked the most ridiculous question they'd ever heard.

"Of course, dear," said Eustasia.

"Did you think she was just going to lie down in it and wait?" Early said much too loudly.

"This worn-out old body has been hanging on for some time. I've had to will it every day to keep going. Keep waiting. Keep watching." She laid her hands in her lap, one on top of the other, and looked at me. "No, this body's done the work of living, I expect it can do the work of dying, too. Now that I'm ready."

Early slathered a little more blueberry jam on the last of his biscuit and gulped it down. "Are you ready, Jackie? We need to start digging."

I opened my mouth, but nothing came out. Partly because I couldn't think of a thing to say and partly because Eustasia Johannsen started giving Early instructions on where the shovels were and where she wanted her grave.

"There are two good shovels in the toolshed, and of course, I'd like to be buried next to Martin's father, over by that sycamore tree. He was a Civil War hero, you know."

Well, crazy is as crazy does, and apparently I did whatever crazy thing I was told to, because I got up from that table, put on my—or should I say *Martin's*?—coat and hat, and headed out to the toolshed with Early.

It took a few minutes of rooting in and around the shed to find the shovels amid the mess of chopped wood, rusted-out oil cans, cigarette butts, and broken garden tools. We eventually found two weather-beaten shovels and, as directed, made our way to the old sycamore tree next to a grave marked *Colonel Jacob Johannsen*. The marker was ready and waiting with Eustasia Johannsen's name and date of birth, July 14, 1845. Even I could do the math. She was a hundred years old.

The rain had stopped, and I watched as Early put foot to shovel, driving the blade into the wet ground, clearing out the first chunk of Eustasia Johannsen's grave. I admit I joined in, but only to make it look as if we were both duly occupied, and the work helped warm us up in the cold of the evening. Plus, I hoped the sound of the shovels would drown out what I had to say.

"Early," I said, determined to get his attention. "Early."

"What? Is something wrong with your shovel? Here, you can use this one."

"Yes, there's something wrong with my shovel. It's digging a grave for a woman who's not even dead yet."

"I know she's not dead yet. But she's ready. Her worn-out old body has been hanging on for some time," he said, repeating what he'd heard Eustasia Johannsen say earlier.

"But she's not dead. You can't just decide one day that you're ready to die and have it happen."

Early seemed to think this over, letting the wheels in his brain examine the idea from this way and that. "Maybe not."

Finally, I was getting through.

"But she's not telling her body to *die*; she's just done telling it to keep living. You're back, and that's all she's been living for."

"But, Early, I'm not her son! She's old and confused. I'm probably the same age Martin was back then, and I must look like him, but I have a mother." I caught myself at the use of the word *have*. Present tense. That was wrong. Or was it? When you have a mother and she dies, is she still and always your mother? In the present tense?

The strokes of my shovel grew deeper. The pile of dirt being flung off to the side grew in inverse proportion to the hole Early and I were now standing in, up to our shins. My breathing grew rapid, and sweat dripped down my back.

"But if you're not Martin"—Early steadied his shovel in front of himself—"then she has to go back to waiting again. She'll keep waiting and making her body hang on. Even though she's ready."

I continued digging, now feeling a strange sense of responsibility sinking in as I thought about what Early had said. Eustasia Johannsen was ready. Anyone could see that. Everything about her ancient self gave evidence to it: Her skin, wrinkled and transparent, covering her body like a thin shroud that has been washed and dried more times than it can bear. Her hair, the color of dingy snow in February just waiting to give way to spring. Her remaining teeth, crooked and yellowed, the others gone the way of the old gray goose. But mainly, it was her eyes. They were drawn into her face as if her memories occupied more of her sight than what was actually in front of her.

I shook my head. "I'm not her son. I'm not Martin."

As Early drew his shovel up to his chest, I felt a movement behind me. It was Eustasia Johannsen. I turned around to see her bracing herself against the chill, her shawl hanging loose around her shoulders and her long gray hair being whipped by the cold wind.

She had heard me. I could see it in the way she drew her shawl up around her shoulders, as if adding an extra layer of skin to fortify her body. To muster enough warmth and substance to persuade her body to keep going another day, and then another.

"Mrs. Johannsen, I—"

"Shh." Eustasia Johannsen held up a hand, her attention having already turned back to the woods. She peered into the trees, searching for a glimpse of a boy's jacket or the gleam of a shiny new Winchester. "Martin will be coming home soon. I'd better fix his supper. He's always hungry as a bear when he gets back." She walked a little ways toward the dense maze of trees and shrubs, searching again.

I set my shovel against the sycamore tree, and Early followed suit. Once again, it was time for us to leave. We had to go back to the house to get our packs from the porch. Our clothes and jackets hung by the fireplace, nearly dry, and we changed, neither of us saying a word.

We emerged from the little house ready to resume our journey, but first, Early went to Eustasia Johannsen and did what I did not have the courage to do. He placed an extra shawl around her shoulders, pulling it tight under her chin.

"Thank you, boys. I hope you come back and visit soon. Martin will enjoy making your acquaintance." She turned and walked back to the house.

Somehow, as Early and I forced our way back into the brambly woods, the maze that had drawn us in seemed to loosen its hold, and the path emerged a little clearer than before. We cinched up our packs and hoisted them on our backs, trying to add enough warmth and substance to get ourselves going again, to take another step, and then another.

26

The next day was filled with a sad silence. It was easy to forget that Early felt things. He was normally so focused on one thing or another. The goings-on of Pi or building a boat or the quest of finding the Great Bear. Or even just listening to Billie Holiday on a rainy day. But every once in a while I was reminded that Early wasn't just a mathematical genius, and he wasn't just a kid on a crazy quest. He was a real boy who had real feelings. And right now his were hurt.

"I know you're mad at me," I said, finally.

"I'm not mad at you. It's just that I was wrong about her—the Ancient One from the Pi story. I thought she was a witch or an enchantress. That she was luring Pi away from his real life. But Eustasia Johannsen is just sad because she lost her son. She's waited all these years for him to come back. And just when she thought she could let go, *now* she has to go back to waiting and watching all over again."

Somehow it felt that Early was blaming *me*. As if my not being Martin Johannsen was my fault.

"Well, if that isn't the pot calling the kettle black. If you're so big on letting go and not looking for someone who's not coming back, then why are we looking for a stupid bear on this stupid trail, where supposedly we'll find your brother, who is also not coming back?"

It all came out in such a rush that I barely had time to hear my own words before Early ran at me like a charging bull and knocked me flat. He pinned me to the wet, leafy ground, and his arms went flying, landing punches I could barely feel through my padded jacket.

"Don't you say that, Jackie. Fisher is not dead." His fists punctuated his words. "He's just having trouble finding his way back. And if you say different—"

Suddenly Early's arms stopped flailing. His brow furrowed as he wiped his nose on his sleeve. He was still sitting on me, and I thought he was going into another seizure, but then his eyes got big, and he said, "Holy moly, Jackie! Look at that!"

"I can't look at much of anything until you get off me!"

Early scooted to the side and kept his gaze on the ground. I sat up to see what had become so important that it had stopped Early's tirade.

There it was. Plain as day, right in the wet ground. A paw print the size of a pie pan.

We had learned enough from Gunnar to know what a bear print looked like. Wet as this one was, it must have been fresh. And it was big.

I placed my hand in the giant imprint. "Holy moly," I repeated. Early and I inched forward on our hands and knees to see the next print, which we knew would be just ahead of this one. There it was. We found six paw prints before the point where the bear must have veered off, onto a rocky patch of ground.

I was grateful for the diversion, as it got Early's mind off being mad at me.

"Come on," I said. "Let's see if we can follow him."

Between the two of us, Early and me, we found some broken branches and a tree that had some of its bark scratched off. These telltale signs were leading us farther north and farther off the path, but it was good to feel like we were actually making progress, even if it *was* in search of a ferocious bear. Judging from the spring in Early's step, I could tell that he felt the same way.

And somehow, I was getting caught up in Early's Pi stories—starting to anticipate the ways in which the line between story and real life would blur. We'd been wandering for days, on and off the Appalachian Trail, and now here we were, looking for the Great Bear. And all of it was starting to seem less and less crazy. I was beginning to worry.

According to Professor Stanton, the numbers in pi would eventually run out. What would happen when we found the Great Bear and there was no Pi? And there was no Fisher? My steps grew heavier as I followed Early, knowing he was heading toward a huge disappointment. But then again, at least Early knew what he was looking for, regardless of whether he'd actually find it or not.

Which is more important? I wondered. *The seeking or the finding?* My mom would say the seeking. My dad would say the finding.

"We've run out of tracks," said Early.

"Tell me about it," I grumbled.

"But we know we're heading in the right direction."

I didn't answer.

We walked a ways in silence, listening only to the rustle of leaves and an occasional woodpecker getting his nose out of joint.

"Fisher always says, 'If you don't know where you're going, you'll never get there.'"

"Yeah, well, my mom always said, 'You'll get there eventually, even if you have to go everyplace else first.'" *So there,* I thought.

"Fisher says, 'You'll always find what you're looking for in the last place you look.'"

Typical. Early had to have the last word. Well, not this time. "Mom said, 'No need to look twice under a donkey's tail. You already know what you'll find.'"

"Fisher says, 'Always wear clean underwear, because you never know—'"

"All right, you win! Now can you shut up about Fisher?"

Early did shut up. For too long. He could stay mad, for all I cared. But eventually, the silence got to me.

"So what was Fisher like?" I asked, trying to break the ice between us. "I've seen his picture in the trophy case at school. He seemed like he had the world by the tail."

"I guess."

"I mean, he seemed like he could do anything."

"I guess."

"But," I said, baiting Early into talking, "he probably wouldn't do well on a quest like this. I mean, this isn't a contest that you can win and take home a trophy for."

"Fisher didn't care about trophies. He never got a trophy for being the best underwater swimmer. They don't give out trophies for that kind of thing. But he could hold his breath longer than anyone. That's how come I know he's not dead."

"Because he could hold his breath a long time underwater?"

"Yes. There were nine men in his squad. They were trying to blow up that bridge. The Germans were coming from the north side of the bridge. The shed that was blown up was on the south side. One man had to swim the charges across the river and under the far side of the bridge. Fisher would have volunteered to do it. And he would have taken off his dog tags so they wouldn't make a noise or reflect the moonlight. And he would have swum underwater to avoid being seen."

"How do you even know there was a moon that night?" I knew Early had an answer before he spoke it.

He pulled the leather journal from his backpack, revealing all kinds of handwritten notes and articles on river currents, weather patterns, moon phases, explosives, detonators, waterproof army gear.

"Where'd you get all this?"

"The *Encyclopaedia Britannica,* the *Old Farmer's Almanack.* I even wrote the War Department. I didn't hear back from them, but I guess they're busy."

I looked at the hodgepodge of notes, sketches, letters, articles. It was a confusing jumble of information.

"See here, where it says—"

I had heard enough. "Early, think about it. If he's still alive, where is he? Why does the army say he's dead?"

"Because he's lost," Early said, taking back his journal as if I were an unbeliever and not fit to see the truths it held. "Just like Pi. And we have to find them."

"That's good, then, because Pi made it out of the maze, so I'm sure he'll be okay," I said, not sure why I was encouraging Early's fantasy and at the same time wishing somebody could do the same for me.

"No," Early said, his eyes on the ground, as if the trail would somehow lead us to Fisher and Pi and the Great Bear all at once. "I've figured more numbers, but the story is all jumbled up. And I can't find any more ones. Pi is missing."

"What happened? You said he made it out of the maze."

"He found the catacombs."

Catacombs

Pi DIDN'T REALIZE he was searching for the catacombs until he stumbled across them. He still carried the shell necklace in his pack, and it weighed heavily on him. So much so that when he waded into a stream to cool off and wash the sweat from his face, the pack shifted, putting him off balance. Slipping off the rocks, he plunged into the swiftly moving current, the pack dragging him underwater. He tried to slip the strap over his head but could not get free of it.

Finally, the current swept him over a ledge, and he landed in a deep, watery basin. Kicking and pulling, he struggled to reach the surface, water crashing all around him. When he finally emerged, he grabbed for anything solid he could find and heaved himself out of the water. Dripping and half drowned, he found himself in a small cave. A bit of light came in from behind the falls, but a few steps in, the cave grew dark. Still, his eyes adjusted, and he was able to make out vague wisps of light even within the darkness. Or maybe they were shadows that were just less dark than the cave around them. He knew where he was, and he knew the kindred spirits that roamed these caverns. The damp. The dark. The walls pressed in around him. All of it spoke of a place where people would come to bury their darkest secrets and accidental treasures.

He could hear the voices, the whispers, the sighs, of these souls who were unable to let go of their burdens. They clung to them like precious gems that gave them weight and substance.

Pi understood this need to hold on. To not let go of his pain. It had become such a part of him. Who would he be without it? The thought frightened him. So he wandered the halls of the catacombs like the other souls who were half-dead and half-alive.

But the balance between life and death is precarious. After a time, Pi felt the balance tipping in him. And it made him dizzy. He took another step, and where he expected to touch ground, there was only a dark abyss. Without a sound, without a whisper, he was gone.

27

I stopped walking. "So what does that mean? What happened to Pi?"

"I can't find any ones," Early said, still walking. "There are a lot of zeros. And the numbers are changing color. But let's go. We have to keep looking. The Great Bear is a mother bear, and a mother's love is fierce. She'll find him. So we have to find *her*, and she'll show us the way."

I stood my ground, ready to give up on his story, until something caught my eye. "Look," I said. "More paw prints." I pointed but stopped short.

"What is it?" asked Early. "What do you see?"

I touched my hand to the thick wetness on the ground and rubbed two fingers against my thumb.

"Blood."

I could tell Early was shaken by the red splotches. He reached down and traced one with his own finger.

"It's like the zeros. Liquid and red."

"Come on, Early. We can end this right now. We can head back to school—"

I didn't even get the whole thought out of my mouth.

"No. There are more numbers. There are. I just can't figure them out." Early clutched the sides of his head and rocked back and forth in his squatting position. "There are more numbers. Pi is not dead. Fisher is not dead. We have to keep looking."

"But what if the bear is injured?" I asked. "She could be wounded. She could kill us."

"We'll follow her."

He had already started off, following the tracks. Part of me knew this was foolishness. But something had stirred in me. It had started days before and had been growing in me all along this journey. Was it curiosity? A sense of adventure? It felt more like need. Whatever it was, it was powerful.

I let Early take the lead and followed him down a path that seemed both old and new at the same time. Old enough to have borne the steps of native hunters and warriors, Spanish conquistadors, and English pilgrims. New enough to cushion the footsteps of new explorers trying to find their way. At least, that's what *National Geographic* would have said.

The tracks were clear for a time; then they disappeared again. But we continued in the same direction as best we could and tried to find other signs. The sky had grown cloudy, and what had been a mild blue had suddenly become a sharp shade of gray. The air had a bite in it that crept through our jackets and into our bones.

I followed Early, trying to match his stride and purpose. Just when I thought maybe we'd lost the bear's trail, Early would point out a tree stripped of its bark. I might have suggested that any bear could be responsible for that tree, but then again, not just any bear could reach eight feet off the ground and leave such great scars in the trunk. And there were blood smears on the bark.

Visible puffs of air came out with our every breath, as if to remind us that we were living and breathing. Something that, I was beginning to see, should not be taken for granted.

As our own footsteps grew quieter, and more and more leaves had given up their place of fall glory in the trees, it seemed that all colors and sounds had been stripped away and left behind as well.

Everything in the woods had become muted and still, but we kept following the bear's trail. Every sound, every shadow, tricked and taunted. A hooting owl, a snapping twig, a swaying branch, all seemed stranger and darker. But it was the shadows that played with my imagination the most. A darkness behind a tree. A movement seen from the corner of my eye. Was someone out there?

"Do you hear that?" I finally asked Early. "That crunching noise." I thought of the walnut shells.

We both stopped and listened. Silence.

"Come on," said Early.

I had the horrible realization that, just as we were *following* tracks, we were leaving our own at the same time. Footprints that someone else could see and touch—and follow.

Fear was rising in me and needed to be put down. I

narrowed the gap between Early and me and tried to distract myself. I whistled a few bars of "Old Man River," but it sounded too spooky. Plus, that's not really a song made for whistling.

So I let my mind wander. Big mistake. Early's story of Pi took off in my head and wove its tale of the young navigator entering the Land of Lost Souls, where the people were half-dead and half-alive.

Before long, everything around me started to seem like it was coming straight out of that story. Trees looked half-dead and half-alive, with their bare, gnarled limbs and scratched-off bark.

But nothing spoke more to the lifelessness of these parts than what we saw when we emerged from the trees into an abandoned logging camp. There were a few buildings—shacks, really—that some loggers must have called home for a while. A large fire pit that hadn't warmed a meal in a long time. An assortment of abandoned logs lay about as if they'd fallen off whatever wagon they'd been strapped to and no one had had the wherewithal to hoist them back up.

Early and I stared at this ghost of a camp, looking for any signs of life, half-dead or otherwise.

"This has to be it," said Early. "This is just the way it's described in the numbers. They have to be here. The lost souls."

"There's nobody here, Early. Just look at this place. This must have been abandoned years ago. Maybe they moved the camp farther north, where there are more trees."

But just as I was saying this, there was a noise inside one of the shacks. A soft *plink, plink, plink*ing sound, as if some ghostly person were stirring a metal spoon in a pot. Early and I walked together to the shack, and Early reached out his thin, pale hand and pushed on the door. It gave a creak as it opened, and we walked inside a very cold, nearly empty log cabin. In the center of the room, however, there was a small wooden table with a chair pushed up to it, and a small dish and cup placed just so.

A curtain ruffled in the open window, giving the room a feeling of liveliness, but it was just the breeze. There was the sound again. Early looked around the room, then moved toward the table and lifted the cup a few inches off of it. *Plink, plink, plink.* It was the sound of a tiny drip of rain coming in through the battered roof, of single drops landing in the cup.

The plate, the cup, the curtain. All signs of occupation, maybe even hospitality, extended to a fellow logger or traveler, but the fireplace offered no warmth. The plate served no food. Maybe there were inhabitants, the ghostly kind, that were no longer at the mercy of the elements and no longer needed food or drink.

I wondered, *If a person is half-alive and half-dead, which half of that person needs food and warmth? And does the other half no longer care?*

The rain plinked more rapidly into the cup in Early's hand. The way he stood there, holding it in place to catch the drops, made my heart hurt. He looked like a poor beggar boy pleading for alms and receiving only a few drops of water for his trouble. Was that just the way things were? People held out their hands without ever getting them filled?

I wanted to tell Early, *Put the cup down. You're just going to come up empty.*

And then Early did put the cup down, leaving it to catch the drops. "Let's go," he said.

Maybe he was finally finished with this quest of his. Maybe he'd given up the ghost of Pi and the ghost of his brother.

"You're right," he said.

Unbelievable. I was never right about anything when it came to Early.

"We should probably go farther north. That's what Pi would do. He'd follow the Great Bear."

I didn't even argue. We headed north.

We had been going wherever the bear tracks led us and now were way off the path. There was no way to know if we were anywhere close to the actual Appalachian Trail. As we walked, the terrain got more rugged. Rockier and steeper, and just wet enough from the drizzle to become dangerously slippery.

"We haven't seen any tracks for a while, Early. How do we know we're going the right way?"

"The numbers," he answered matter-of-factly. "They get very hard and bumpy."

"Hard and bumpy, huh? The cot I used to sleep on in the summer was hard and bumpy. Maybe Pi is lying all stretched out on a lumpy mattress somewhere, listening to *Flash Gordon* or *Superman* on the radio."

Early didn't find that likely or funny.

"Pi doesn't have a radio. And if he did, he'd be listening to Billie Holiday, because—"

"It's raining, I know, I know."

It *was* raining, and it was getting dark. The sky rumbled, threatening still more rain.

"We'd better find a rock to crawl under for the night. You pick one and make sure it doesn't look like it's going to roll over on us."

There were lots of nooks and crannies to choose from. Rock formations that had niches and indentations formed by glaciers long ago. But so far there hadn't been any spaces big enough to hold both of us.

"You go left and I'll go right. That way we'll have a better chance of finding something before it starts to pour."

"Okay. I'll go left. I'll yell if I find something," said Early.

"Right. You do that."

"Then you come and find me."

"Okay, Early. I got it."

"Ready, set, go."

We parted ways.

Glaciers are funny things. Great masses of ice that, when they receded, left all kinds of interesting things behind. Waterfalls, gorges, rivers, caves, and deep glacial pools. Early and I must have wandered right into a museum of glacial art. In my search for a place to camp, I had stumbled upon a scene that could have come straight out of a

National Geographic. The wooded path I was on led down to a swiftly flowing stream. The sound of rushing water filled the air around me. It felt good not to be listening for thunder or bears or pirates, or even Early. Stepping from rocks to logs, I maneuvered out into the water and hopped, skipped, and jumped upstream, finding my way to some great slabs of stone surrounded by pools of water that looked deep and dark. A fine mist sprayed my face, but it wasn't raining, and the sound of rushing water grew louder.

The stone slabs were big enough that I could walk around the pools and around a bend. I found myself in some kind of prehistoric gorge, formed by millions of years of water crashing through its cracks and over its sides. And now, after all that time, the water kept coming. A great waterfall lunged over the top of the gorge, pouring an endless supply of icy-cold water into a seemingly bottomless pit.

I closed my eyes, letting the sound and the spray take hold of me. Wanting to be swallowed by it. Wanting to let it wash over me—wash me clean. In church they would call it *being absolved*. But absolved of what? Did I feel guilty about my mom? I hadn't done anything. That was exactly it: I hadn't *done* anything. I wasn't even there—to fluff her pillow, put a cool washcloth on her face, pull the blanket up close. Hold her hand. I wasn't there. I was in the barn. The water crashed around me. How do you get absolved for being absent? In Early's mathematical mind, that would be like taking nothing from nothing. You're still left with—

Suddenly, in the cascade of water, I saw a flash of color, and my stomach clenched in a knot. Had something gone over the edge of the gorge? The color stayed suspended in the waterfall for a brief instant, then disappeared. I waited for it to make its way out of the rush of water and into the current of the stream. But it never did. Had the colored object been pounded to the bottom of the pool? It took me a second to realize why my stomach was in a knot that wouldn't come undone, why I was looking so desperately for the flash of color to emerge from the torrent of water: it was tartan red.

I set my sights on the waterfall. Going over that cliff would probably kill a person, with its water rushing over the top of the gorge and falling in a great sheet. Early couldn't have gotten up there that fast, could he?

Where should I look? In which direction should I go? And now the rain came down, a million new drops of water joining the torrent that churned past me. Anything that had gone over the falls would be carried in one direction. I knew it made sense to follow the water. But that flash of red and the way it had lingered in the falls held me. The color hadn't come from above the waterfall. It had come from *behind* it. My course was set. I had chosen to follow that red tartan jacket on this quest when I had no other beacon or landmark to follow. I would follow it again now. I turned upstream and headed in the direction of the waterfall.

The roar and surge of the water were powerful. Every step was a struggle as I tried both to keep my footing on the rocky bank and to see into the spray pummeling my face. I was heading for the incline leading to the top of the gorge. Just as I was mapping out the climb, looking for footholds and tree roots to grab on to, I noticed a narrow path veering away from the bank and seemingly into the stream. There were footprints.

He wouldn't have walked right into the waterfall. What could he have been looking for? Again, I followed him, three, four, five steps. Then the path ended. All that was left were slippery rocks that jutted out into the water. There were no footprints coming out. Early had not turned back. He had to have walked out onto those rocks. I followed. One rock, two rocks, three rocks.

Just when it seemed the next step would have me swept away by the waterfall, I saw it. A narrow path of rocks, barely visible beneath the dark water, that led behind the crashing waterfall. Frightened yet exhilarated, I placed my feet carefully, one in front of the other, on the slippery path. Then I ran out of rocks. I couldn't see one more step. How do you take another step when you can't see the path in front of you? But wasn't that what I'd been doing all along on my journey with Early? I put my foot out where I could picture Early putting his, took a deep breath, and leaped. I landed on solid ground. The water still crashed around me, filling my ears as it echoed throughout the stone cavern in which I'd found myself.

"Early?" I called, but could barely hear myself. I stepped forward into the cavern. Where was I? What was this place? And where was Early?

"Early? Where are you?" My voice echoed back to me. It must have been bigger in there than I'd thought. And it was dark.

I pulled the flashlight out of my pack, grateful to Gunnar for having packed it in my bag. The light switched on, revealing jagged walls of ancient rock. I found myself looking for cave drawings made by people who had lived here long ago. What would they have drawn? I didn't know much about the native people of the American Northeast. In Kansas, the earliest inhabitants would have drawn bison, and maize, and spears. I supposed that wasn't too far off from what any early artist might have drawn. Animals, food, and weapons. The basics.

I had to think like Early. To him, this was not just a cave that he'd happened upon. He'd looked for it. He'd found it. I moved the light left, then right, and saw that the space or room that I was in led to another, just beyond it. I shut my eyes, then opened them again, trying to view my surroundings as Early would.

I saw the same stone walls, the same dark caverns. And suddenly, I saw what Early saw. *Catacombs.*

Pi had gotten lost in the catacombs.

I ran my hand along the rounded stone of the entrance to the next cavern, still trying to put myself in Early's head. It seemed familiar. Or maybe it just reminded me of something. Maybe it was just like being in Early's head. Lots of interesting nooks and crannies and tunnels from here to there, and there to here. A place where someone could get lost for a long time. But Early never seemed lost. He always knew right where he was and where he was going.

I could still hear the water outside, the river rushing all around this place. But this time I also heard the Allier River in central France. And as I touched the stone archway, I felt the arches of the Gaston Bridge.

The second room led to another. Then another. There

233

was a light up ahead. I shut off my flashlight and walked toward the opening, lit up by a single lantern, which must have been there already, because Early didn't have a lantern. But he did have matches. I entered the room and picked up the lantern—and there was the red tartan jacket. Early lay motionless on the dirt floor.

"Early." My voice sounded raw. He didn't move. I reached down, but just before my hand touched him, I could tell something wasn't right. The jacket was his, but he wasn't wearing it. It just lay on top of him. I raised the lantern and held it a little closer. The shape of the body was wrong. Kind of flat. I lifted the jacket sleeve just a bit.

"Early?" I said again, in a whisper. This time hoping with everything in me that it wasn't him.

The jacket was caught on something, so I gave it a tug, then jumped back as if I'd seen a ghost. Only it wasn't a ghost. It was a skeleton—bony white fingers and all.

"What the—" I jerked back, knocking out the lantern and hitting my head against the low rock ceiling. My heart pounded and my head ached. In total darkness, I touched the back of my head and felt something warm and thick. Blood.

Then I heard a breath in the cave that wasn't mine.

I fumbled around for my flashlight. I must have set it down when I'd come in. Reaching this way and that in the dark, I hoped I wouldn't grab hold of a skeleton foot. *Found it!* I switched it on. The light was getting dimmer, but it was still bright enough to allow me to see the room. And there was Early. He sat scrunched up against the wall, his head resting on his knees. He was crying.

28

Blood and bones. What a combination. I was getting ready to pass out. I bent over at the waist to get my blood flowing back to my brain and found myself counting to ten, out loud. I used to do that when I was a little kid to distract myself from my many cuts and scrapes.

"One . . . two . . . three . . ."

But Early corrected me. "The ones have disappeared."

"Four . . . five . . . six . . ."

"There's only been one five in the last one hundred digits."

"Seven . . . eight . . . nine . . ."

He looked at the body in its shroud. "That's not Fisher, if that's what you're thinking."

"Ten." I stood upright, still feeling a little wobbly but not falling over.

"Of course it's not Fisher. But who is it?"

"Take a closer look," said Early.

"You take a closer look."

"You do it."

"You do it."

This time I wasn't going to give in. Besides, Early already seemed to know the answer.

"Early, who is it?"

"It's Martin Johannsen."

"What? It can't be. He disappeared over fifty years ago."

"Look what's pinned on his jacket."

I didn't want to look. But I had to. Early had looked already, and he'd survived it.

I reached out my hand and pulled down Early's red jacket, just far enough to reveal a blue one. There, pinned to its breast pocket, was a Civil War medal. And there was a bullet hole ripped through his jacket, just below the medal. A piece of paper stuck out of the pocket. It was a receipt. *1894 Winchester Rifle—$18.00.*

Early drew the jacket back up over Martin Johannsen and smoothed the wrinkles out as carefully as if he were tucking the dead boy in for a good night's sleep.

"Who would have done this to him?" I asked. "Shot him, I mean, and then left him here all laid out?"

"It was an accident."

That's the way it was with Early. So sure about everything. No *maybes*. No guessing. No speculation.

"Okay, I'll bite. How do you know it was an accident? Maybe young Martin here walked in on somebody's wrongdoing. Maybe there was a band of hooligans dealing in whiskey or gambling, and they couldn't risk Martin running off and giving away their hideout. So they did him in.

Or maybe Martin got in the middle of some kind of brawl, and two ne'er-do-wells decided they'd rather shoot him than each other."

Early didn't answer.

I crossed my arms over my chest, feeling a sense of satisfaction at having poked a few holes in Early's assessment of what had happened to poor Martin Johannsen. Taking his silence as a rare acknowledgment of defeat, I decided to be a good sport and let it go.

"Well, there's nothing we can do for him now," I said.

"His mother is waiting for him. We have to take him home."

"That's a nice thought, Early, but I don't know if we're exactly the right people to be moving his bones."

"Who else is going to do it?"

Now it was my turn to be a few words short of an answer. Poor Martin Johannsen had lain here for more than fifty years, and we were the ones to find him. Maybe that did leave us with some sort of responsibility to him.

"Okay, but we can't just sling him over our shoulders and carry him out of here. Let's take the Civil War medal. It must belong to Martin's father, and we can give it to Mrs. Johannsen to prove that we found her son. Then somebody else can come back for his . . . remains."

Early carefully removed the medal from Martin's jacket pocket. He looked at me as if sizing me up, then reached a decision.

"You wear it, Jackie." He reached over to pin it on me.

I took a step back and held up my hand. "Just put it in your pocket."

"But this is a medal for bravery. It doesn't belong in a pocket."

"Then you wear it." The medal belonged to someone else. Wearing it would feel like an honor that was unearned. And unwanted.

"I've already got Fisher's dog tags. They're important. You need something important too." Before I knew it, Early had the medal pinned on my jacket, and that was that.

"All right. Now let's get moving before . . ."

"Before what?"

"I don't know." I felt uneasy. "Before Martin here jumps up and wants his medal back." Early and I began making our way back through the tunnels and caves, toward the waterfall. But something was working its way through the series of cogs and wheels that turned in my own brain. Something was missing.

"What's the matter?" asked Early. "You don't really think Martin is going to want his medal back, do you?"

It was in that moment that I realized the reason for my uneasiness. It wasn't that I'd stood next to a dead body—bones jutting out from pant legs and jacket sleeves. It wasn't that we were in a series of tomblike caves beneath a massive waterfall. Strangely, neither of these was the cause of my unrest.

"No, I don't think he wants his medal back. But I think he probably would like to have his gun back. His brand-new 1894 Winchester short-barrel carbine. And I know who has it. The catalog said it was seventeen dollars and fifty cents, and an extra fifty cents for engraving. Martin's receipt shows he paid eighteen dollars, so he must have had his initials engraved on it. Those initials would have been engraved into the wooden stock of the gun—where someone could trace them with their fingers. I recall someone running his fingers over the stock of his gun. Someone we had an unpleasant encounter with at the Bear Knuckle Inn. I wasn't paying much attention to it at the time, but I remembered seeing letters engraved on the stock of that someone's gun."

Just then there was the familiar sound of a rifle lever being cranked, and it echoed throughout the very cavern we were standing in. I stood facing the waterfall, its spray glistening on Martin's medal, until Early tugged on my sleeve.

"Jackie, Pirate MacScott is here."

"I know," I said, turning around to find myself looking down the barrel of a gun. "That's not your gun," I said. "His initials are engraved right on it. M.J.—Martin Johannsen."

MacScott spoke, just above a whisper. "So you think you've got it all figured out, do you?"

"I know enough to know that you're holding Martin Johannsen's rifle. You must be the boy Mrs. Johannsen said had come by to show off his new gun. She saw him with it the day Martin went missing. She said the boy's name was Archibald." MacScott flinched a little at hearing his given name spoken so freely. "What I don't know is why you shot him."

Archibald MacScott's face flushed, and he looked as if he'd been struck with the paddle of a schoolmaster.

"He trifled with me," MacScott said quietly.

"He what?" I asked.

"*Trifled.*" It was Early who answered. "That means 'to treat someone like he's not important.'"

"He was out coon hunting with his shiny new rifle," said MacScott. "Acting so fine and fancy. I come along and wanted to see that gun. Just feel it in my hands. Yes, I'd gotten a gun, too. I bought it secondhand from a traveling salesman." MacScott ran his hand over the smooth, polished wood of Martin's gun handle, still keeping it pointed at the two of us. "But Martin's was fine. I challenged him to a bet. My gun for his. A little target practice. He said he had a piece of paper with a bull's-eye printed right on it. The Winchester Company sent it along with his new gun. So we tacked it up to a big sycamore tree and took aim.

"He took his shot, and I took mine. His hit the bull's-eye. Mine went right of the mark, hitting only the tree."

MacScott breathed deeply, caught up in his own story. "'No harm done,' he says to me. 'You keep your gun, and I'll settle for bragging rights.' Then he tears off that bull's-eye and says he's got to get back home, that his mother will be waiting supper on him. Just like that, and he's off. Like my gun's not even worth taking. And I could hear him already, spreading it around to everyone that Archibald Mac-Scott could barely hit a hundred-year-old sycamore tree. He'd probably be waving that bull's-eye to everyone who'd take a look."

MacScott held the Winchester to his eye. "So I took up my gun again. I was just going to whiz one past him, you see. I shot once. 'You get back here and take my gun,' I called after him. 'I never agreed to bragging rights. You got no call to change our bet.'"

MacScott's breath grew ragged and his voice gravelly. "He didn't answer. 'What's the matter?' I said. 'Just 'cause you got a fancy new Winchester, my gun's not good enough for you?' I walked in his direction and came across the bull's-eye first. He'd wadded it up in a ball and tossed it aside like it was nothing but a game. I walked some more.

"He was lying still when I come up on him. I'd shot him right through."

29

"It was an accident," Early said a second time, only this time I realized he was right. It *had* been an accident. But how had he known? "Why did you put him in a cave?" asked Early. "His mother has been waiting for him to come home. She has supper ready."

MacScott lowered the gun slightly, the weight of it taking its toll. "I put him in the cave to keep animals away while I went to tell Mrs. Johannsen. She'd been my teacher in the eighth grade and had always been good to me. But then I got near the house and saw her calling out for him, searching those woods. She said she expected him home any minute, and I lost all courage. I left and never went back."

"You could still tell her," Early said in his way that made everything sound so simple. "You could still make things right."

The Winchester sagged a little more. I looked at Early,

amazed. Could he actually persuade MacScott to tell the old woman?

"That's an admirable suggestion," he said, the gun and his decision seeming to teeter in the balance. MacScott thought a moment, maybe actually considering the possibility, but then made up his mind—again. He took a partially smoked cigarette from his jacket pocket. Still cradling the rifle in one hand, he ran a match against his pant leg with the other and lit the cigarette stub in one quick motion.

"No, I'm already too far down this road. There's no turning back. Mrs. Johannsen's an old woman who's better off waiting for her son to come home than knowing he's dead. And I'll spend the rest of my days hunting down every bear, coon, and eight-point buck from here to Canada, starting with that Great Appalachian Bear you two have been tracking. He'll bring in a fine bounty."

So that was what he'd been doing all this time. Making up for one missed shot on a bull's-eye by racking up every hunting trophy and bounty in Maine. He was trying to prove to everyone that he could hit his mark. But looking at MacScott's gaunt face and one sunken eye, I could tell that wasn't all. It wasn't just the missed shot at the bull's-eye that he'd been carrying around for fifty-some years. It was the shot he'd made and *hadn't* meant to that had eaten him from the inside out.

He puffed the last of his cigarette, letting it drop to the ground and smashing it under the toe of his boot.

"Hey," Early said, his eyes wide. "You told a lie earlier. You said you never went back to Mrs. Johannsen's house. But you have too been there."

I expected MacScott to deny it and wondered what a back-and-forth argument between Early and MacScott would be like.

But MacScott said nothing. He just shifted his weight from one leg to the other.

"You're the one who's been cutting Mrs. Johannsen's firewood. When I went to get the shovel, the wood was stacked up under the overhang of the shed, and there were cigarette stubs lying all around. They were Lucky Strikes, just like the ones Mr. Wallace, the custodian at school, smokes. Only yours are all burned down to the quick and smashed flat, like that one there."

I shifted my gaze from Early, back to MacScott, still waiting for his rebuttal. He remained silent.

"So you know, then," said Early.

MacScott refused to answer.

"Know what?" I asked, unable to continue being a spectator in this bizarre showdown. One of them had a gun, but the other had words that were apparently hitting their mark. I'd seen everything Early had just mentioned at Mrs. Johannsen's house. The same cut wood and cigarette stubs. It hadn't meant anything to me. Could Early be right? Had MacScott been a sort of caretaker for Mrs. Johannsen, cutting her firewood? Maybe even bringing her food—a box of tea, an occasional chicken, a jar of blueberry jam?

"What does he know?" I asked again.

"He's seen Mrs. Johannsen," Early said. "He knows that she's ready to let go. But she can't. Not until Martin comes home."

"Well, now"—MacScott broke his silence, his voice a

little more gravelly than before—"that's been the problem all along, hasn't it? Her son ain't coming home." He gave the telltale cigarette butt a nudge with his boot. "That was a long time ago, and there's nothing left that can be put right."

Maybe it was the way MacScott stared so intently and with such regret at Martin Johannsen just then, but I had a thought. I reached down and lifted Early's jacket. Then, searching through Martin's other jacket pocket, I pulled out a crumpled piece of paper.

Early recognized it for what it was before I did. "Hey, it's that old bull's-eye." He unfurled it and held it out to Mac-Scott. I thought that was like waving a red flag in front of a raging bull. "There's only the one hole, so you're right. You missed it altogether."

MacScott started to squeeze his finger on the Winchester trigger.

"What he means is . . . ," I said, trying to come up with something else that Early might have meant, something other than *You're a lousy shot, and here's the bull's-eye to prove it.* We had to get out of that cave if we didn't each want to end up another pile of bones, and Early's pointing out MacScott's miserable failure to hit that bull's-eye was surely not going to help us. "I mean, what Early is trying to say is . . ." I grasped for words.

MacScott was obviously reliving this whole story as if it were happening all over again. How many times had he replayed that day in his mind? How many times had he wished he could have one more chance at that bull's-eye? Actually, that was an idea.

245

I stood up a little straighter. "What Early is suggesting is that it's a very small bull's-eye. Maybe you could hit it if you just had another chance. I mean, you probably still wouldn't hit the actual bull's-eye, but you might at least hit the paper."

The dread pirate's eye narrowed. "What are you talking about? I could hit that bull's-eye dead center five times in a row if I wanted to."

"From in here, sure. It's a tiny little cave."

MacScott sneered. "You think I'm stupid, don't you. You don't want me to kill you right here in this cave. You want me to take you outside to prove I can hit this bull's-eye, so that you'll have a better chance of getting away. Is that right?"

I didn't answer.

"Is that right, Jackie?" Early asked.

"Pretty much," I grumbled.

"That's a good idea. I like that idea," said Early. "Do you like that idea, Mr. MacScott?"

"A challenge," he mused. "Marksmanship and a hunt all in one." He seemed to warm to the idea. "All right. Why don't we go outside, get ourselves some fresh air. I'll take four shots at the bull's-eye and still have two bullets left."

MacScott walked behind us, gun at our backs, as we headed out under the waterfall. I nearly lost my balance on the slippery rocks, but Early and I made it to the bank only slightly damp from our efforts.

"There's a good sycamore tree about forty paces off. Tack it up there and you can make your move."

Early and I headed for the tree. Once we were out of

earshot, Early asked the worst question he could possibly ask.

"Which direction should we go in?"

Our lives depended on the answer to that question. And the obvious answer was, in the opposite direction of MacScott and his gun.

Early smoothed the paper bull's-eye and reached to attach it to the tree, stabbing it through with my pocketknife. He paused, looking at me expectantly.

I glanced around in a panic. The first shot was fired, the bullet hitting the center of the bull's-eye, right between Early and me.

"Let's go that way!" I yelled as Early and I ran in the direction opposite MacScott. We started off as the day turned to dusk, and as MacScott raised his gun and took his second shot.

There was no right or wrong way to go. We simply tried to run away fast. Still, you can't just run around like a chicken with its head cut off. I'd seen a chicken with its head cut off, and it didn't get very far. Within seconds we heard two more shots, one after another. The sound echoed in the woods, but Early and I had plotted our course and we stuck with it, tacking this way and that, heading in what we thought was a northerly direction.

It would have been a good course, too. A kind of grand steeplechase that consisted of jumping through bogs filled with wet, rotting leaves, dodging low-hanging branches, crawling under a fallen tree, and scaling a treacherous and rocky slope. But that last part landed us in trouble.

We'd been running hard, our heavy breathing seeming

to echo all around us, when I realized we'd run into a steep and rocky incline. Turning back, we heard a loud thrashing sound not far behind us. We'd had the advantage of youth, and with it speed, but MacScott had the greater advantage: experience in these woods. It dawned on me then that he'd pointed us toward the sycamore tree for a reason. He knew these woods better than anybody and knew how to steer us into a trap. Now it was too late.

"We'll have to climb it." I knew it wouldn't be a problem for Early. He'd proven himself to be a nimble climber back at Gunnar's place. And sure enough, he clambered up and reached the top before I'd gotten halfway there. I stuck my feet carefully here and there, struggling for footing while dirt and rocks skittered down the slope. I grabbed for any root, branch, or handhold I could find.

Panting and perspiring, I reached for a sturdy-looking tree root jutting out from the rock wall. *If I can just get a good hold there and then hoist myself the rest of the way . . .* I reached into the open space beneath the exposed root when I saw a wet clump of leaves move. Before I could react, a snake clamped down on my hand, and I fell down, down, down, landing with a thud on my back at the bottom of the rocky incline.

30

In a flash, Early was at my side. "Jackie, are you okay? I thought we were going to climb up." He must have slid down the hill as fast as I had fallen down it.

"That was the plan." I groaned, looking at the bite marks on my hand. "Do you think it was a poisonous snake?"

"No, it wasn't poisonous."

I breathed a sigh of relief—until he continued.

"Poison is something that is swallowed or inhaled. So, no, it's not a poisonous snake. It might be a *venomous* snake, though. The timber rattlesnake is a venomous snake. It's venom that gets into your body when a snake bites, and that can kill you. Or it might only destroy the muscle and tissue in your arm, and then you'd have to amputate it."

My heart was pounding, probably sending snake venom

racing throughout my body. I tried to calm down. He was already applying some of his lavender-scented snakebite ointment.

"Shh, listen," I said.

"I don't hear anything," said Early.

"Exactly, so let's get out of here. Maybe MacScott cut around to grab us at the top of the hill. Now we can go back the way we came and hopefully—"

My *hopefully* was interrupted just short of the hopeful part when MacScott arrived, blocking our escape. I tried to inch away in the dirt, but I could only scoot a few feet off to the side. There was nowhere to go. MacScott had us trapped, and he knew it. He walked slowly toward us.

"I hit the bull's-eye four times. So I have two bullets left." He cocked the gun. But suddenly MacScott's expression changed. His jaw went slack, and the gun barrel lowered a couple of inches.

Early and I turned our heads to follow the pirate's gaze. It was the bear.

Black as night and bleary with sleep, it lumbered out from a recess in the stone wall behind us. Its massive body swaggered and swayed as if it were shaking the sleep from its back. We'd never actually seen the bear before, just its tracks and droppings. But here we were, face to face. There was no question that this was the Great Appalachian Bear—its left eye was mangled where MacScott said his bullet had ripped into it. *Tit for tat*, as MacScott had said. There was nowhere to run, even if we'd had any running left in us. My hand was screaming with pain, and Captain MacScott did not seem inclined to let us quietly take our leave.

But he was in just as much danger as we were. And this was the bear he'd been tracking for so long. So why was he just standing there?

His face twisted in a pained expression. He stared at the bear with his one eye. And the bear, with its mangled face, seemed to hold an equally pained expression as it stared back, its hackles raised. I wondered if each beast saw something familiar in the other.

We would never know, as MacScott raised his gun, aiming at Early or me—I'm not sure which—and fired. A second later, pain still coursed up my arm, but not from being shot. Had he hit Early?

I was frozen with fear.

The great black bear, awesome as Ursa Major, wagged her head from side to side, and her bellow shook the nearby passage of the Appalachian Trail. I say *her*, but the truth is, we had no way to tell. There were no female markings. No cubs in sight. But I knew. I knew her like I knew my own mother. It was in her bearing—her absolute authority over us two boys locked in her gaze. And it was in her unwavering will to keep us alive.

She raised her body upright, to her full height. MacScott shot again, hitting the dirt just in front of the bear's massive paws. He must've been shaken—he'd missed. He cocked the gun one more time, took careful aim, and pulled the trigger. It only clicked. Empty. Then she was on him. I would have looked away, but I couldn't. It was a sight, like a violent lightning storm, that demands to be witnessed. Mesmerizing and terrifying all at once. Then it was over and the bear was gone. All was still.

Too still.

My head was spinning, and sweat ran into my eyes. I turned my attention away from MacScott's mauled body. Martin Johannsen's gun rested in his upturned palms as if he were presenting a gift.

There was Early, lying on the ground.

The next few minutes played out like a kind of dream, blurry and warped. I made my way over to him. Had he been shot? I checked for blood. There was none. And he was breathing. But his eyes were rolled back in his head, and his body was twitching. He was having a seizure, but this one was worse than any I'd seen before. I tried to lift his head. Maybe he needed water. I ran over to MacScott's pack to see if he had a canteen.

"No, Early . . . ," I said, maybe more to myself than to him.

I was still trying to wrest the pack open when I heard a rustling in the bushes and a grizzled figure emerged from the trees. At first I thought it was the bear returning, but it was a man. A hairy, grizzled woodsman.

He walked over and knelt down, lifting Early's head and cradling him to his chest. I knew I was not seeing things clearly. I could feel the heat of a fever emanating from the bite on my skin, and my body was racked with chills, so I wasn't sure if I was having some kind of dream or venom-filled hallucination. The man tilted Early to the side. After a few more seconds, the jerking stopped. Early's body re-laxed, and he opened his eyes. Then he reached out his small white hand, placing it on the woodsman's bearded face, and said one word.

"Fisher."

31

My vision was a little blurry, and I squinted to see if I could find a resemblance to the youthful face from the trophy cabinet, Number 67. To see why Early would think this was his brother. But all I could make out were the gaunt features and hollow-looking eyes of the bearded man. A lumberjack who'd felled his last tree and hadn't another swing of the ax left in him.

Early smiled a distant smile at me. "See, Jackie? I told you we'd find him. We found Fisher." His words sounded as if they were coming down a long tunnel, and it seemed that by the time they reached my ears, his mouth was already saying something else.

"Jackie, you don't look so good. I knew there were some timber rattlers left in these woods. I just knew it."

After that, I only had snapshots in my mind of the events that followed, and they didn't make a lot of sense. First, the lumberjack picked me up, but then he changed into a great bear carrying me through the woods. I knew my feverish mind was playing tricks on me, but which was crazier—being carried by a great black bear, or by the dead Morton Hill legend and soldier Fisher Auden? Great breaths of air heaved and puffed against my face from whoever or whatever was carrying me. I could hear Early talking in hushed tones as he walked along beside.

"I knew you were alive, Fisher. They said you were dead and that the numbers were all disappearing, but I didn't believe them. You were just lost. But you're not lost anymore, Fisher, because I found you." Early continued, and I heard snatches of his tales of skeletons and caves and waterfalls and bears.

More snapshots of trees and rocks and creeks—then I was in a house tucked back in the woods. Eustasia Johannsen's house. I was in a quilted bed but dreamed of the bear and Early. They were sitting on a bench outside my window. The bear was thin, as if he were on the starving end of a long hibernation. He lowered his shaggy head and shed heavy tears. His shoulders heaved as he cried, and the only sounds I heard were from deep, ragged breaths.

Early put his arm around the bear's sagging shoulders. "You can come back," he said. "Just like Superman did after the kryptonite almost got him. And like Pi did when he kept his eyes on the bright star named for him."

That was when the bear spoke. His words were slow and dreamy, all running together, as in a song on a record playing at slow speed. They made Early cry.

Then Mrs. Johannsen was there in the room with me. She put a hot poultice on my hand. It burned, and my hand felt like it was on fire. Then she brought me tea. It was too hot. She clucked and shushed until I drank it. It was bitter, but I kept it down. She said that I was a good boy and that she had missed me. She had gone back to thinking I was her son, Martin.

"I was by the waterfall. Looking for Early." My mind floated and bobbed like a bottle drifting at sea, but the message inside was unable to get out.

"Don't worry, now. You just need to concentrate on getting better. You know how you get when you don't get enough rest. Cranky as a bulldog."

Her voice sounded so much like Mom's. I blinked, trying to make my heavy eyelids stay open, to focus on her blurred face.

She put a cool cloth on my forehead, and I saw her eyes gazing into mine. She held her hand to my face. It was so familiar. Her look. Her touch.

"Mom?"

I blinked. It couldn't be her. It was the fever playing tricks on me again. It was just Mrs. Johannsen talking to her long-lost son. But it wasn't. Maybe it was the way she held my hand. Maybe it was the way she smelled of talcum powder. Maybe it was her voice—a mother's voice.

Which was crazier—Mrs. Johannsen talking to her dead son, or me hearing my mother's voice?

"*Mom?*" Just saying the word, I no longer felt like I was adrift. The listing motion I'd felt inside subsided. I could see myself stepping onto Dinosaur Rock on Fisher's steeplechase, the current of water surging beneath me.

"I got lost."

"I know, but you found your way back. Finding your way doesn't mean you always know where you're going. It's knowing how to find your way back home that's important."

I ventured out further.

"And then I was mad. I shouldn't have gone off like that." Another step.

"It's all right. Sometimes boys have to stretch their wings a bit. That's hard for mothers."

"But I wasn't there. I was gone."

"We all lose our way once in a while. I knew you'd come back. It wasn't your fault."

I hadn't realized how much I wanted to believe that. To hear those words of absolution. They washed over me with as much force as a great waterfall, cleansing me from head to toe and carrying me away in a peaceful current.

"I miss you, Mom."

"I've missed you too. But, you know, I've been here the whole time. Just a hop, skip, and a jump away." She smiled and kissed my forehead, her hair brushing my face. "Now, you get some rest. You're tired as the day is long. And it's been a *long* day. Sleep well. You're not lost anymore."

"Good night, Mom," I whispered as the door shut, and I knew she was gone. And I slept a deep, motionless sleep.

The next morning my hand still hurt like a son of a gun, but the sweating and chills were gone, and my head was clear. I knew in the light of day that it was Mrs. Johannsen who'd put a cool cloth on my forehead, whispering words of love and forgiveness to her son, Martin. I knew I had

257

chosen to see her differently. But how had her words meant so much to me, when she was speaking them to the son she thought had returned? Because she let me hear them as if they were being spoken to me. And, I guess, in a way I let her speak to me as if I were her son. Neither of us was fooling the other. But if a soothing balm is administered by someone other than a doctor, does that make it any less soothing?

I put on my shoes and went into the main room of the cabin to find Early. There he sat, at the kitchen table. I knew what he was going to say as sure as if I were saying it myself. Early was going to say he'd found Fisher. He probably had the woodsman tucked away somewhere, ready to be displayed as proudly as the picture in the trophy case back at Morton Hill Academy. I could see it all.

So when Early did open his mouth to speak, I was struck dumb by what he actually said.

"Mrs. Johannsen is dead."

"What?" I said, even though I'd heard him loud and clear.

Early didn't elaborate. That's when I noticed he was sorting his jelly beans. I walked over to the table. I'd been around Early long enough to know that his sorting meant different things. If he sorted in groups of ten, that meant he was trying to organize his thoughts or solve a problem. If he sorted by color, that meant he was upset and trying to calm himself.

I watched as he took each jelly bean and scooted it with one finger into its place. Today he was sorting by color—red, yellow, green, blue, orange—and grouping them in columns of ten. He was upset *and* trying to figure something out. It had to be about Fisher.

"Early," I said, avoiding any mention of Fisher or the woodsman from the previous night, "what happened with Mrs. Johannsen?"

"Last night, after she got you settled, she was beaming like a lighthouse." He studied his columns of jelly beans as if they were magic beans that held the secrets of life. "Not really. That's just an expression. No one really beams like a lighthouse. Most lighthouses use five-hundred-watt lights, so that would be very bright. She was beaming more like a candle. A candle set in a window, but a closed window, so there's no breeze to make the candle flicker. It was a steady glow like that."

"What did she say?" I asked, keeping my voice low and calm to match Early's, but his had a hint of pain in it as well.

"She just hugged me to her bosom—that's what ladies call their chest—and she thanked me for bringing you to her. Then she blew out that lantern she keeps up in the window and went to bed. This morning I went in to ask if she'd like me to put some coffee on. And there she was. All laid out, so peaceful and still. It was just like she said. Her body had done the work of living, and then it did the work of dying."

"And that man?" I asked tentatively. "The one who carried me here last night?"

"He's gone," Early said quietly, staring at his tidy rows of colored jelly beans, all sorted neatly by color. Everything was in order. Everything should have made sense. But I could tell by the look on Early's face that it didn't make sense. For what might have been the first time in his life, he couldn't figure it out. Just then, a tear rolled down Early's face, and in one motion he swept all the jelly beans onto the floor in an explosion of color and chaos.

32

I knelt down, gathering the jelly beans, wishing I could put them back in some order that would make sense. But I couldn't, so I just dropped them in the jar, one after another after another, and screwed the lid back on.

I found Early on the porch steps, tears streaking his dirty face. He had papers and news articles from his journal strewn about. Early must have realized that the woodsman wasn't Fisher. I opened my mouth to say what he'd already figured out. That his brother wasn't coming back. That he was gone, lost forever near a bridge in France. But instead, I kept quiet, because I didn't want it to be true. Besides, who was I to tell Early anything? He said we could build a boat, and we did. He said that Martin Johannsen's death was an accident, and it was. He said there were timber rattlesnakes in Maine, and even with the swelling and redness gone from my arm, I knew that there were. Of course, he could be wrong about some things. He had thought I was

Mrs. Johannsen's son. He had thought there was no color in Kansas. He had thought he could trust me before the regatta. There *were* times when Early was wrong.

But I of all people understood the need to believe that a loved one is alive, standing in front of you, loving you.

Early was surrounded by his array of articles and notes. His arsenal of reasons why Fisher was still alive. He stared at a particular newspaper clipping as if he were looking right through it. It was the picture of the bear hunter from Early's bulletin board at school—the bear hunter I now recognized as Archibald MacScott when he still had two eyes. He was standing proudly by his prize, smiling a big smile, thinking he had killed the Great Appalachian Bear and won the bounty.

Seeing the picture made me wonder.

"He must have been a good hunter—a good shot, I mean. How is it that he missed the real Great Appalachian Bear yesterday, at point-blank range?"

"He wasn't trying to hit her," said Early.

"That's crazy. I don't know that much about hunting bear, but I do know that if you go shooting at a bear like that, *not* trying to hit it, you're asking for whatever you get."

Early just nodded.

"What?" I said. "You think MacScott wanted that bear to kill him?" Even as I said it, it made sense. MacScott had lived a long time carrying the guilt and shame of what he'd done.

"Didn't you see it in his face?" Early asked. "He was asking that bear to put an end to his pain."

I looked back at the picture from just a few months ago.

"I wonder how long it took for him to find out that he had killed the wrong bear back then," I said. "Do you think he had to read it in the paper?"

"I don't know, but Fisher knew it right away."

"What do you mean? What does Fisher have to do with it?"

"Look at his eyes. He knows there's a big fuss being made over the wrong bear."

I looked at the picture more closely.

"What are you talking about, Early? There's nobody in the picture except MacScott, the bear, and that"—my voice caught in my throat—"bearded lumberjack." I stared at the face and, strangely, I recognized it. Not as the face in the trophy case, but as the bearded face of the man who had helped Early during his seizure yesterday.

"You think this is Fisher? So you saw this picture and thought Fisher was in these woods, and that's why you set off on this wild-goose chase?"

"It *is* Fisher!" said Early, clearly frustrated that he'd been telling me the same thing over and over and I still didn't seem to understand. "I've shown you!" he yelled. "It says it right here"—he grabbed a loose piece of notepaper—"and here and here and here." He held a stack of crumpled articles and pages with notes in his clenched fist. "But you won't listen." Then he hunched his head down into a green jacket that he must have borrowed from Martin's closet, looking for all the world like a turtle in an oversized shell.

I had no words left to argue with him. And they wouldn't have helped, anyway.

"Fine," I said. "You keep looking for your dead brother.

But for now, we've got to bury Mrs. Johannsen." I grabbed the shovel that was propped up against the porch and set off to finish digging Mrs. Johannsen's grave. "And then I'm done. I'm going back to Morton Hill. And I'm going to sleep in a bed. And I'm going to stay dry. And I'm going to mess up my sock drawer. And I'm going to listen to Billie Holiday when it's not raining. Better yet, I won't listen to Billie Holiday at all. I'll listen to—"

I stopped short as I reached the clearing where I'd expected to find Mrs. Johannsen's mostly dug and empty grave. Instead, where there was supposed to be a hole in the ground, all the empty space had been filled in with the dirt we'd set off to the side, and there was a cross made out of wooden planks positioned as a grave marker.

I took a tentative step forward, half wondering if Mrs. Johannsen had buried herself.

Early came up behind me. "You can't listen to Billie Holiday when it's not raining, and your socks— Hey." He looked at the grave. "How'd she get buried so fast?"

"Good question." I walked toward the cross to see the name that had been carved into the wood.

MARTIN JOHANNSEN

It was as if all the jelly beans in Early's jar had exploded all over the place. This made no sense at all. And on the tree stump just beside the newly filled grave was a red tartan jacket, folded up and placed just so. I looked back at Early. He was wearing a different jacket, because he had left his back in the cave behind the waterfall, covering Martin

Johannsen's bones. That was why he had been shivering during the night.

"Where'd you get that jacket?" I asked.

"I'm not going to tell you. You don't believe anything I say, anyway."

"Mrs. Johannsen probably gave it to you. It's Martin Johannsen's jacket."

"Is not."

"Is too."

"Is not."

"Then where'd you get it?"

"I'm not telling you."

There was something familiar about the jacket. That drab olive-green canvas—very functional, very durable. Very military. I tugged at Early's arms to see the front of the jacket where a name would have been sewn. At first he resisted, but then he let his arms go slack. There were capital letters, lined up neat and clear. Five letters.

AUDEN

My dream from the night before came to mind. Suddenly it seemed important. Early and the bear had been talking. What did they say?

Early had put his arm around the bear's sagging shoulders. He'd said something to the bear, and his voice was small and sad. What was it? I struggled to recall. It was like trying to find the words of a song, guessing where to place the needle on the record.

Slowly the dream replayed itself in my mind.

You can come back, Early had said. *Just like Superman did after the kryptonite almost got him. And like Pi did when he kept his eyes on the bright star named for him.*

I remembered the bear speaking back. I moved the needle forward in my mind.

The bear had lifted his sad face and said, "I'm not a superhero. And I don't look at stars anymore."

The needle skipped ahead, and Early was crying. Then the bear got up, took off his heavy coat, and placed it on Early's shivering shoulders. "Go home," he said, and walked away, leaving Early alone. And the dream in my mind moved into the empty space, whirring and crackling, with no more words and no more images.

I realized it wasn't a dream. It was a scene I had witnessed playing out through the bedroom window, only there hadn't been a bear. It had been a man. And that man was Fisher Auden.

In that moment, it was as if all the fallen jelly beans had lined up in neat, colorful rows, just like those letters on the olive-green jacket. The bearded onlooker from the newspaper clipping. The woodsman covering Early's skinny shoulders with his jacket. The dream that wasn't a dream. Even the walnut shells that I saw scattered at my feet near the newly dug grave. Fisher Auden was alive. He had been following us, keeping watch over us in those woods. And he had buried the bones of Martin Johannsen.

And now the silence. The painful, absolute quiet.

Again, in that moment of strained silence, I was reminded that Early was not just a strange oddity of nature who counted jelly beans and read numbers as if they were a story. I knew he could feel hurt and disappointment, but before he had been fairly quick to bounce back. This time, something was different. During this whole long journey, Early had known his brother was alive, because in his mind, Fisher was a superhero. And superheroes never die. But now, tears streamed down Early's face because his brother *had* come back. Only it wasn't the brother he remembered.

I had grown accustomed to Early being in the coxswain seat. He had been the one calling the commands, adjusting our course, directing, guiding. Now, strangely, our roles were reversed. *I* was the one who had traveled down this road before. I knew its twists and turns, its rocks and pitfalls. I knew what it felt like to be lost. But I didn't know if I could guide us out.

Early took off his brother's jacket and put on his own. There was only one thing I could think of to say.

"Tell me how you knew."

"You won't listen."

"Yes, I will."

"No, you won't."

I took Early by the shoulders. "I'm listening. Tell me."

Early set his backpack on the leafy ground and took out his crumpled stack of notes. "The explosives had a detonator. The German tank hit the shed where Fisher's men were hiding. Then the tank was destroyed on the bridge. That means someone had to still be alive to push the detonator. Fisher would have been the one in the water, placing the charges, when the German tank blew up the shed. Fisher was still alive. *He* pushed the detonator. He was a hero."

"But his dog tags. They were found among the dead."

"He would have given them to another soldier to hold. He swam with his shirt off, and he didn't want the dog tags to reflect in the moonlight."

That's the way it was with Early. He could have the same information as everyone else, but it all meant something different to him. He saw what everyone else missed.

"I see" was all I could say. And I did see. More than I wished I did.

Yes, Fisher was alive. But he'd been wounded. Probably on the outside at first, back in France, but now, even more, on the inside. I didn't know what had happened to Fisher between France and the woods of Maine, but the brother, the hero, that Early knew and idolized was gone. I knew what that was like. Poor Early. He was only now realizing that there are no such things as superheroes. But then, we both should have known. Superman doesn't have a son. And Captain America doesn't have a brother.

"He was sitting right next to me," said Early, "but it was like he wasn't *really* here. I told him to come back with me. That he would be all right. He was raining inside and there was no Billie Holiday. No music at all. He told me to go home. And he left."

I searched for the right words to say, but they didn't come. So I just took up Fisher's jacket, folded it with the care and precision I would use to fold a flag, and put it in my backpack.

Early wiped his eyes and said, "Let's bury Mrs. Johannsen and go home."

For the second time that week, I put shovel to earth and began digging a grave.

33

Mrs. Johannsen was laid to rest next to her son. We covered her in the quilt off Martin's bed and pinned the Civil War medal on a bright-yellow square. It was the sunniest part of the quilt, and we thought she'd lived with so much sadness in her life that she could use a little cheer.

But cheer was something sorely lacking as Early and I walked, mile after mile, back through the woods of Maine. Our steps were heavy and labored. It took me a minute to calculate what day it was. Friday. We'd been gone for six days, living on little food and even less sleep.

We reached the covered bridge that we'd crossed earlier in the week, but this time our footsteps were slower, and we didn't shout to hear our voices echo. Halfway across, Early rested his arms over the railing and stared into the water. He reached into his jacket pocket and pulled out Fisher's dog tags.

I recognized the look on his face. Not only had Early

lost his hero, he'd also been sent home. Dismissed. And I knew what was coming next, even before Early cocked his arm back.

"Early, no!" But it was too late. He'd already cast the dog tags into the air.

The shiny metal disks on the chain landed in the river with barely a splash.

Something in me broke loose, and before I knew it, I'd shed my backpack and jacket and jumped into the swiftly moving water. My mom used to say *Still waters run deep*, and fortunately I landed in the water with enough force to send me down to the still waters.

The sun penetrated far enough for me to make out fish and rocks and branches. I pulled and kicked my way down. Searching. Hoping. Then I saw it. A little shiny something. It swayed in the water, catching the sunlight and twinkling like an underwater star. I don't know if I swam to it or if the current moved me in the same way it had moved the tags, but I found myself reaching, straining, to catch the small metal plates, snagged as they were on a branch. Why had Early cast Fisher's dog tags away? He had said that Fisher was empty. That he was raining inside. Couldn't Early see that his brother was wounded? I knew Early felt dismissed and abandoned. But couldn't he see that Fisher's scars hadn't healed? Why didn't Early hang on?

The metal tags shifted, reflecting the light in a different way. As my lungs began to strain for air, I realized I'd been here before. Underwater, searching for something small and shiny and just out of reach. My navigator ring. I reached for the tags as I had for the ring I'd thought I'd seen in the swimming pool that first week at Morton Hill. As I had when I'd seen it in the stars that night with Gunnar. I wanted to take it back. Wished I could take it *all* back.

I remembered the day of my mother's funeral. It was raining outside, and I could see my dad lingering at her grave in the downpour. Could it have been raining even harder inside him?

A couple of weeks after the funeral, my dad and I had sat in silence at the breakfast table. The house was kind of messy. Mom had always taken great care around the house. She wasn't fussy but seemed to keep up with all the cleaning, stitching, mending, tidying, fluffing, and sprucing.

On occasion she'd ask me to help with drying the dishes or cleaning out the attic. She'd say, *If we all pitch in, it might take twice as long, but it'll be more fun.*

Now none of that was getting done. Dad looked around him as if trying to figure out his role in this strange place. He hoisted himself from the table and declared it was time for us to get off our duffs and get the place shipshape.

He started in the kitchen, with a bucket of soapy water and an assortment of rags and sponges, scrubbing down every inch of tile, cabinet, and stove from top to bottom. In his clearing of counters, shelves, and drawers, he tossed out old calendars Mom had saved because she liked their pictures of mountain streams and wooded forests. He boxed up crocheted pot holders, flowered aprons, and the special dish towels, embroidered with the days of the week, that Mom used only for show. Then he moved on to the rest of the house with a broom and a dust rag, packing up pillows, doilies, tablecloths. Anything that was not functional or practical, anything that impeded his dusting, mopping, or swabbing of the decks, was boxed up, tossed out, or basically thrown overboard.

I mostly stayed out of the way and participated only when given specific orders. *Dump this trash outside. Take that box to the attic. Pour out this dirty water and fill it up with fresh.* And I watched as he stripped away all the softness in our house. The color, the warmth, the memories. Until all that was left was cold and hard. And clean. Very clean. I tried to look busy, afraid that if I sat still too long, I might get packed up or thrown out as well. But it wasn't until he pointed to a box of miscellaneous items for the Salvation Army that I snapped.

The box was filled with assorted screws, door hinges, and mason jar lids, and a yo-yo. Another difference between my mom and dad. My mother was a saver. My father apparently kept only the bare essentials. But on top of the screws, the hinges, the jar lids, and the yo-yo was a teacup. Not part of a set. Nothing fancy. Just a chipped teacup with little red flowers. It was my mother's, and it had its place on a hook right next to the kitchen sink. She drank out of it every day. Coffee in the morning, tea in the afternoon, and a special concoction of hot cider, honey, and a little of what she called *the stuff for what ails you* when she felt the chills coming on.

"We don't need to get rid of all this," I said, my voice shaking.

"A place for everything and everything in its place," he answered, without looking up from his task at hand.

"Then you can take it out yourself. I'm not doing it."

This time my dad stood up to his full height. "You'll do as you're told. Now, hop to it."

I was treading on thin ice, but I took another step.

"You can't just get rid of everything." The ice groaned beneath me.

"Son," he said in a cautioning tone, hands on hips.

I'd seen a drill sergeant one time in a movie, dealing with a new recruit who wasn't following orders. That drill sergeant in the movie got in the soldier's face and yelled, *YOU UNDERSTAND ME, SON? 'CAUSE IF YOU CAN'T, I'LL SPEAK IN A LANGUAGE YOU CAN UNDERSTAND*. I didn't know exactly what that language was, but I had a feeling I was about to find out.

I didn't care.

Disobeying my father, I picked up the teacup.

"You may want to forget about her, but I don't!" That was when it happened. My hurt and anger made their way to my trembling fingers, and the cup slipped from my hands, shattering on the kitchen floor.

The captain squared his shoulders and barked out one more command. "You are dismissed!"

Dismissed. I was a civilian and did not speak the language of soldiers. But I understood that loud and clear. There was a great rending as the ice cracked, and my dad and I were set adrift and apart.

And that was when I went outside and threw my navigator ring in the river behind our house.

My lungs were bursting, and the river current tried to sweep me away. I plucked the dog tags from the underwater branch and kicked my way to the surface, gasping and sputtering for air. Early met me at the bank.

"Why did you jump in, Jackie?"

"Because," I grumbled, handing him the dog tags. "I wanted to go for a swim."

"Fisher's dog tags!"

"Yeah, I just happened to come across them in the river . . . where you threw them. You should keep these. They're Fisher's. And he's still your brother. Come on. I need to find a place to dry off before I freeze out here." I had seen a shack just downriver from the bridge, and we headed that way.

It might have been an old hunting cabin from fifty years ago, but now it was just a run-down shack with a few broken fishing rods, a paddleboat in the corner, and another boat, turned upside down, with a tarp draped over it. But it had plenty of light coming through the windows, and a potbellied stove in the middle of the room.

We scrounged around for wood scraps and quickly got a fire going. I was glad my jacket and backpack had been spared another dunk in the river and stripped off my denims and shirt to dry by the fire. Wet again. It seemed like I'd spent most of the past six days wet.

Early and I sat on the overturned boat and ate the last of the beef jerky and biscuits we'd packed up from Mrs. Johannsen's house.

Early studied Fisher's dog tags, letting them dangle and turn in the firelight. "He doesn't want me. I tried to tell him to come home. But it was like he didn't even understand me. Like that part in Pi's journey where he landed on the island and they were speaking another language."

My heart ached for Early. He had come all this way, believed the impossible could be true. And it was true. But he was still going home without his brother.

I took the dog tags and studied them myself. I couldn't read numbers in the way that Early could, but those raised letters that spelled out FISHER AUDEN and BETHEL, MAINE told a story that even I could understand.

"He does want you. He's just so hurt and sad. Think about it, Early. You're always comparing his journey to Pi's. You know how Pi went on his great adventure but then lost his whole family? Well, Fisher's men at that bridge in France were like family to him. And he lost all of them. And you know how Pi carried his burden into the catacombs? Fisher is carrying his own burden over not being able to save his men. He's mourning the loss of the people he loved and the life that he knew." My eyes stung a little bit. Those dog tags might as well have read JACK BAKER—USED TO BE FROM KANSAS. "Fisher has lost his bearings. He doesn't feel like he belongs anywhere."

I ached, feeling my own loss. And Fisher's. And Early's. I searched for some way to help Early understand why Fisher wasn't coming back. "Maybe he just needs more time in the empty space—to think things through. Get his bearings." I shook my head at my own pathetic tale. "Remind you of anyone?"

"Your dad."

"What?" I said, my head jerking up so fast, I could have gotten whiplash. "No, Fisher is not like my dad."

"Yes, he is."

"No, he isn't."

"Yes, he is."

"No, he isn't!" I yelled. "Early, you don't even know my dad."

"Yes, I do. You told me about him. Remember when you told me about your soap box car and how it got warped in the rain and it got fixed? When we started building the boat, you didn't know how to cut an angle or glue a joint. You said it got so late when you were fixing your soap box car that you didn't remember finishing it. Your dad finished it. He took care of you, just like Fisher took care of me.

"And when we were looking at the stars with Gunnar? You knew Orion and the Pleiades and Cassiopeia. You learned them when you were a kid. But you said your mom didn't know those names. Your dad is a navigator. He taught you the names of the stars. And I know your dad is a soldier. He did his job and worked hard and wanted to come home. Just like Fisher. But something happened that made everything different. And he got lost. Just like Fisher." Early crossed his arms, standing his ground. "He made your bed and sorted your sock drawer. He loves you."

I supposed that to Early, sorting a sock drawer would be an expression of love. Maybe my dad looked at it that way too.

I didn't answer. Early's retelling of all that I had told him over the past couple of months hit me like a slap in the face. My face flushed. Was it from shame or anger?

"But he also took down all of Mom's stuff in the house,"

I said. "He was trying to get rid of anything that reminded him of her. He packed it all up. What about that?"

Early didn't say anything. I'd stumped him on that one. Not even *he* could come up with an explanation.

He thought, then answered quietly. "Maybe he packed it up and is carrying it. Like it's his burden."

Now I was the one left without a response. I stood and checked the clothes by the fire. Just then there was a clatter and the sound of loud voices outside. We peeked out the window. Up the hill, maybe thirty feet from the shack, were MacScott's men, Olson and Long John Silver.

"What are they doing here?" I asked.

"They've probably been at the Bear Knuckle Inn, having some spirits and vittles. That's what pirates call drinks and food. I like the way that sounds, *spirits and vittles*. It sounds so much nicer than *ale and ham hocks* or *bourbon and liver*. Now, *milk and cookies*, that sounds okay—"

"The Bear Knuckle Inn?" I interrupted Early's wordplay. "You think that's around here?"

"Yes. It's just over that hill. It was right at the bend of the river where the maple and oak trees were in full color. Remember?"

"No, Early, I don't remember. But it would have been nice to know before we camped out in this shack. We've got to get out of here."

"Maybe we could ask them to give the *Maine* back. Now that Captain MacScott is 'no longer with us,'" he said, using finger quotation marks. "That means someone's dead. Or you can also say *kicked the bucket* or *bought the farm* or *cashed in his chips* or *gave up the ghost*—"

"Early! I know what it means! But it doesn't mean they're going to just hand over the boat. And now that their captain is 'dead,'" I said, using my own finger quotes, "they'll probably kill us for good measure." I put on my clothes, which were still a little damp.

"Where do you think they put it?" asked Early.

"The *Maine*?" I pulled on my jacket and peeked out the door of the shack to make sure no one was nearby. "How should I know? They're pirates. They wouldn't keep pulling it behind their boat, in case someone was looking for it. They've probably stashed it away somewhere near their hideout."

"Yeah, somewhere near their pirate lair," Early whispered.

We must have thought at the same time that the Bear Knuckle Inn was very much like a pirate lair. And that the very shack we were in would make a good hiding place for any hidden treasure. Early and I both turned away from the door. We took a corner of the tarp we'd been sitting on and gave it a tug.

The deep blue of the *Maine* seemed to flood the dingy room with color. We turned the boat over and found the oars tucked underneath.

By then, the voices outside seemed much closer, and one of them said, "Hey, there's smoke coming out of the shed." Early and I didn't wait for the *On your mark, get set,* or *go!* We threw our backpacks over our shoulders, hoisted the *Maine,* and busted out of the shed. The river was just down the hill, but running with a boat on your shoulder while carrying the oars is harder than a three-legged race.

Dogs were barking. Olson and Long John were yelling. But they were either too drunk or too lazy to catch us. Early and the *Maine* and I made it safely to the river and were already pulling away from shore when the dogs and pirates arrived, panting and cussing.

I smiled. "Do you think those dogs are still smelling menthol?"

Early didn't respond. Not to me, anyway. "The empty space," he mumbled to himself. "There has to be a mistake in the numbers. Pi needs more time in the empty space."

Then Early buried his head in his notebook, jotting down figures or numbers or notations as if he'd had a revelation.

With my hands firmly on the oars and my legs and arms pumping in Fisher Auden's boat, I had a revelation of my own.

Early had said he felt as though Fisher didn't understand him back at Mrs. Johannsen's house. As though he were speaking a language that Fisher couldn't understand.

Fisher might have once been a school hero and a legend. But now he was a soldier. And I needed to find another person who could speak the language that a soldier would understand.

34

We arrived back at Morton Hill on Saturday to a strange mix of reprimands and cheers—the reprimands coming from teachers and the cheers coming mostly from boys who appeared equally awed and envious. Earlier in the week, the weather at sea had cleared enough to allow my dad to arrive on campus on the Wednesday of fall break, which left plenty of time for Early and me to be declared missing. Apparently, our absence had caused quite a stir, and there were lots of folks out looking for us. But when my dad laid eyes on me, he didn't seem mad. He just hugged me for a long time. I think he didn't want to let go because he was crying.

The next day, Dad drove Early and me north, into the woods of Maine. Of course, there was no way to know if we would find Fisher, but we figured the best place to start was at the logging camp. And there he was, chopping wood in the chill, misty air as the sky clouded over and threatened rain. Early and I got out of the jeep but hung back. Fisher stood up straight at the sight of a naval captain approaching, and saluted. It was admirable but sad, too. He was so thin, and his saluting hand trembled.

Dad saluted back. "At ease, son."

Fisher's shoulders relaxed.

The two of them sat on a couple of stumps and leaned toward one another in quiet conversation. I heard only bits and pieces, but, judging from the way they each listened and responded, I knew that these two men, these soldiers, were speaking a language they both understood. One of duty, honor, and loss.

Eventually, I learned that Fisher had been wounded by debris from the bridge explosion, and after nearly drowning in the Allier River, he was found by a French farmer and taken to his home to recuperate. While there, he learned that the army had commissioned eight markers to be placed in the town square to commemorate the eight fallen soldiers. They thought he had died along with his men. By then the war was drawing to a close. He had suffered a great trauma and couldn't bear the thought of suddenly reappearing and being hailed as a hero for having destroyed the bridge and enemy tank when his fellow soldiers had died in the mission. But mostly, he couldn't bear the fact that he'd been absent from the shed when his friends were killed. *I should have been there with them*, he'd said.

I remembered Early saying that no one knew where Mozart was buried. That maybe he'd wanted it that way—to be unencumbered by praise and accolades. Fisher wanted it that way too, but while he was still alive.

So he wandered alone through France and England, then hopped aboard a cargo ship and made his way back to Maine. The army had declared him dead, and in that he found his only comfort. And the woods of Maine were his resting place.

After some time, Fisher and Dad stood, and my father placed his hand firmly on Fisher's shoulder.

"You've had a tough go of it, Lieutenant," my dad said—a statement rather than a question.

"Yes, sir."

"You had a mission, and you carried it out to the best of your ability."

"Yes, sir."

"And a lot of good men were lost."

"Yes, sir."

"I've known good men like that. And I can tell you, as bad as that loss is, the only thing that makes it worse is losing another one. Your mission is over, son. It's time to come home."

There was a long pause. Fisher looked up, letting the wind breathe a cool sigh through his shaggy hair, and the authority in my dad's words seemed to settle into him like a warm bath on a cold day. His tears mingled with the first drops of rain.

"Yes, sir."

We headed toward the jeep, and I found myself marveling at my dad—at the ease he had in communicating with Fisher. But I think I also felt a tinge of envy and wondered if my father and I would ever have that same ease and understanding.

My dad looked up, letting the raindrops touch his face. Maybe he had a few tears he was trying to hide. After a moment, he looked at me and said, "We'd better get a move on before the rain washes all the dry off."

I smiled at the phrase. It was my mother's. Hers was a language my dad and I could both understand.

Fisher looked better with his beard shaved and his hair cut, but he was still weak and shaky and very malnourished. We took him to the hospital in town, where he would get a lot of rest and eat three squares a day. Early and I visited every day after school, sneaking in maple fudge and assorted jelly beans to round out his three squares.

A few days later, Dad drove us—Early and me—to Boston for the culmination of the Fall Math Institute. Fisher couldn't go, but he told Early to give that numbskull mathematician the what-for.

The sun streamed into the great oak-paneled lecture hall while we sat quietly, watching as Professor Douglas Stanton wrote out more than two hundred digits, which, he explained, were the most recently calculated numbers of pi. He talked long and loud and wrote lots of symbols and equations on the chalkboard, highlighting the fact that there were no ones in the most recently calculated digits of pi. He explained that, based on this disappearance of the number one, he'd concluded that other numbers would also disappear and that pi would eventually end. When he finished, there was a great deal of fuss and applause, and Professor Stanton raised his bushy eyebrows and said he would entertain questions or rebuttals if anyone was so inclined.

Early *was* inclined. He stood up, all four feet seven inches of him, and walked to the chalkboard. Without saying a word, he began making markings of his own, crossing out some of Dr. Stanton's figures. Then, with his little piece of chalk, he drew a vertical line after one number in the series and then drew a horizontal line through the remaining numbers, replacing them with a new series of numbers that actually began with and included the number one. The entire audience sat in stunned silence. I can't even pretend to explain the notations he made, but there were a few gasps, and a steady murmur spread throughout the room. Judging from the reaction, I assumed Early had just delivered a devastating blow to Professor Stanton's theory. But Early wasn't done.

He turned to face the auditorium and spoke without the use of the microphone. He didn't need it, as his voice was already loud and the room was pin-drop quiet.

"Proof by contradiction," he began. "Professor Stanton says there are no more ones in the number. Unfortunately, his numbers are wrong. The one did disappear for a while, but Professor Stanton didn't know that Pi was just lost. He was sad and had a big hole in his heart. He'd lost so much and didn't have his mother or father or any friends. He just needed more time in the empty space. Until"—Early pointed to the sequence of numbers that had made the crowd gasp—"someone would find him."

Finding Pi

FOR A LONG TIME, Pi lay hurt and alone, drifting between life and death. His thoughts meandered from memory to dream. His hands, his arms, and his whole body were so translucent that he was certain he could no longer be counted among the living.

Until he heard a sound. It was a voice, hoarse and raspy. "Is someone there?"

Pi sat up, or thought he did, although he could barely feel the rock beneath him. His head ached where he'd cracked it. He touched the trickle of blood that made its way down his scalp. If he could feel his head ache and his blood still trickled, then he must be alive, he reasoned.

"Hello," he croaked. "I am here."

A shadowy figure peered over the ledge above him. Another tortured soul whose burdens had led him to this place.

"Take my hand," the voice said.

Pi got to his feet and thrust the pack up and out of the

hole. It landed with a thud. He reached for a rock jutting out above his head, then found a foothold and hoisted himself up a few inches. He searched for another rock and another foothold. Finally, he was able to grab hold of the hand that reached for him. The hand was firm and strong and pulled him out of the hole.

Pi had many questions to ask. *What are you doing in this desolate place? Can you really see me? Am I still alive?*

But before he could speak, he gazed into the face of the one whose hand he still held. Pi stared, dumbfounded.

"Father?"

The man looked equally surprised and held his son in a long embrace. "Pi," he answered in a whisper.

Standing in his father's arms, something shifted in Pi. He took in what seemed like his first real breath in a very long time. The air around him felt different on his skin. Pi wasn't sure if he had earned the name Polaris or not—but it no longer mattered. He had longed to hear the name his mother called him. *Pi.*

Words flowed out, and Pi learned that his father had been hunting when their village was attacked. He returned to find such devastation that he'd wanted to leave along with the other survivors. But he stayed for many months, waiting for his only son to return. His son did not come back. Heartbroken, he felt that his burden was too great to bear, and he, like Pi, was drawn to the place of lost souls.

Now that father and son had been reunited, they needed to find their way out of the winding catacombs. But how? It was dark, and they had been wandering in the maze of tunnels and caves for so long. Then Pi saw the drawings on the rock wall. The drawings were simple and moved from one cave to the next, telling the story of an ancient people on a journey. The people in the story followed the sun until it grew dark. Then, in another room, the drawing showed them following the stars, until finally, there was a bear. A great black bear, shown leading her cubs. The people followed her. And so did Pi and his father.

As they walked, the air gradually got cooler and sweeter. The whispers and sighs faded away, and eventually the light of day replaced the darkness. Pi and his father passed through a misty waterfall and found themselves on dry ground.

Both of them took a moment to breathe in the fresh air and warm their faces in the sunlight. Pi's hands were no longer translucent. They were flesh and blood.

35

When Early finished, the auditorium was silent.

The moderator stared at the chalkboard and then back at Early. "Well, you've given us a great deal to think about, young man. I'm sure there are many of us who would like to take a closer look at your figures and ask a few questions."

Professor Stanton's face grew red. "This is absurd. He's a boy!" He turned his attention to Early. "You can't come in here with your silly story and prove that my theory is wrong."

"Yes, I can," Early replied without emotion.

I could see it coming like a freight train.

"Cannot."

"Can too."

Professor Stanton didn't know what I knew all too well. There is no arguing with Early Auden. But the good professor was a learned man, and he'd figure it out sooner or later.

"Can*not*."

"Can too."

Probably later.

The story of Pi seemed to be one that could conjure up a lot of different memories and connections. Pi's story was a journey, like that of Fisher. But as Early talked this time of Pi being hurt and losing his way, it reminded me of someone else. During the ride home, I glanced sideways at my dad and noticed for the first time the worry lines on his face. He wasn't in uniform, and his body seemed to relax without the weight of his medals and brass. I thought about the way he had clung to me when Early and I returned to Morton Hill—like a sailor who'd been washed overboard and found a life preserver to hold on to. Could it be that my father, the navigator, had been washed overboard and lost his bearings, just like me?

I could imagine my navigator ring at the bottom of the river, and I was sorry I'd thrown it in. But I also knew I didn't need a navigator ring to find my bearings.

When we were back on campus at Morton Hill, my dad gave Early a warm handshake.

"You did a fine job back there, son," my father said. "I haven't the faintest idea what you were talking about, but you seemed to have all your *i*'s dotted and *t*'s crossed."

Early smiled. "Yes, sir."

Early passed me on his way back to his workshop. "I don't think your dad was paying attention," he said in a whisper that was loud and clear. "There weren't any *i*'s or *t*'s in the equation."

My dad shook his head as Early walked away. Then he leaned against the jeep and crossed his arms. It felt like when he'd talked to Fisher. Easy and open. Like he'd just taken a deep breath and was letting the words exhale out instead of holding them back.

"I should never have brought you so far from home," he said. "I guess I just didn't know what to do. Imagine that. I give umpteen commands all day long and navigate a ship all over the ocean, and I couldn't figure out what step to take next." He shook his head. "I'm sorry, Jack, about packing up all of your mom's stuff. I just thought if I could put things in order, if I could make things right—but I couldn't."

He raised his face to the sun for a long minute. "Well, what do you say? Maybe it's time to pull up anchor and head home."

I leaned up against the jeep, next to him, and crossed my arms. "I don't know. I don't mind it here. And, see, the thing is, I sort of wrecked a boat a while back." I raised my face to the sun. "You want to help me build a new one?"

EPILOGUE

Connecting the dots. That's what Mom said stargazing is all about. *It's the same up there as it is down here, Jackie. You have to look for the things that connect us all. Find the ways our paths cross, our lives intersect, and our hearts collide.*

Once I started paying attention, I noticed all kinds of crossings, intersections, and collisions. For one, Fisher showed great improvement under the watchful care of a certain young candy striper at the local hospital. She had curly red hair and green eyes and answered to the name of Pauline. But that was only because that's what Early had called her the first time we met her at the Bear Knuckle Inn, and she thought it was prettier than her real name, which was Ethel. She took Fisher for long walks and even held his hand, which hardly shook anymore.

Then there was Gunnar's letter to his sweetheart, Emmaline. Gunnar had given me that letter, asking me to do what he couldn't bring himself to do—mail the letter. So I did mail it, with my address on the envelope, just in case. It came back with a handwritten note that said *Return to Sender*. Apparently Emmaline had moved on. So the letter went back into the little rose-colored book of poetry in my desk for some time, where it would have stayed indefinitely, had I not chosen Hopkins as the topic of my famous poet essay and had I not acquired some of Early's deductive reasoning skills of putting two and two together. Although, with Early's method, it was more like putting together two and two plus a pinch of this and a dash of that.

It happened one day in the library. I had to write a paper on a famous poet, and being familiar with Gunnar's *firefolk*, I chose Hopkins. Miss B. said she might have just the thing. She reached into her desk and pulled out a very old-looking book. It was a collection of poems by Gerard Manley Hopkins. She told me I might look at the volume in the library but could not check it out, as it had been a gift to her.

"Yes, ma'am," I said. Taking the book to an open table, I glanced at the inside cover. In a masculine hand, it read: *To E. from G. Christmas 1928.* The date rang a bell. Gunnar had given a book of poetry to Emmaline for Christmas. Had it been in 1928? I took the *Journal of Poetry by Young Americans* from my book bag and studied the name on the envelope. *Emmaline Bellefleur.* Inching my way closer to Miss B.'s desk, I hoped to spy something with her full name on it.

She looked up from her work. "Can I help you, Mr. Baker?"

"Um, this is a very nice book," I said, handing it back to her. "Do you have a favorite poem?"

She looked surprised by the question and seemed to catch her breath. "Well, yes, I do," she said softly. "I have a special fondness for 'The Starlight Night'—all that talk of stars and fire-folk and circle-citadels." She seemed to get lost for a moment in the poem or in her memory.

I carefully lifted the letter and said, "I think this is for you, Miss Bellefleur."

She looked at the handwriting on the envelope, then back at me with tears in her eyes. I didn't stick around to watch her read it, but I knew I wouldn't be surprised if Gunnar Skoglund showed up on the grounds of Morton Hill Academy in the near future.

Then there was Archibald MacScott. The night of the cave, and the snakebite, and Early's seizure, and a million other things, Fisher had gone back to the site of the bear attack to bury a second body—MacScott's—but the one-eyed man and the 1894 Winchester were gone. There was a good deal of blood on the ground that led away from the site, but the trail ended at the river.

We'd thought the bear had killed him right there on the spot. But in light of this new evidence, Early thought maybe MacScott had wanted to have a proper burial at sea, so he had mustered what little life he'd had left to drag himself to the closest body of water and dropped dead as he plunged into the river. Then Early thought better of it and decided that the Winchester, which had been the great burden of MacScott's life, had become too heavy to bear and maybe he'd just bent to drink from the river but the gun's weight had pulled him to a watery death. Early seemed to find both scenarios equally gruesome and interesting and never declared which he liked best.

Back at school, the boys of Morton Hill Academy were always eager to hear the tale of Early's and my journey. As I told it, over and over, I realized what an adventure it had been. Who would have thought a motion-sick kid from Kansas would have embarked on a journey that included pirates, a volcano, a great white whale, a hundred-year-old woman, a lost hero, a hidden cave, a great Appalachian bear, and a timber rattlesnake—in Maine!

My mom was right. Our stories are all intertwined. It's just a matter of connecting the dots. I keep looking for her to pop up somewhere in this story. To somehow, mysteriously, be a part of the connections, intersections, and collisions. I keep feeling that I should have something more than just the broken fragments of her teacup tucked away in a box in my closet. But I know Elaine Gallagher Baker, the civilian; she'll turn up somewhere. And when she does, I'll hear her say, *There are no coincidences. Just miracles by the boatload.* In the meantime, I have a piece of paper on my wall. It's a drawing of my own constellation, with stars named Dad, Gunnar, Miss B., Fisher, Martin, Eustasia Johannsen, Early, and me—Jackie Baker. With a red pencil, I connected each star. And not so coincidentally, it formed the shape of a teacup with little red flowers.

As for Early—in the weeks following our journey he was invited for pie in Sam and Robbie Dean's room once in a while. And he even showed up for class once in a great while, especially after Mr. Blane quit talking about pi ending. But he preferred to stay a little off the beaten path. He and I still went for our early-morning and late-afternoon rows, and he still called out the commands, even though I could row a pretty straight line on my own. He always ended our rows by giving the command to let it run, and we'd stare out over the bay, admiring the endless ocean.

Early Auden could not keep the ocean out. I figured he realized this too, because on a walk down to the shore one day, not long after our Appalachian trek, Early started opening his stacked sandbags, emptying them onto the beach. I asked him if he'd given up trying to keep the ocean out. He said he was never trying to. He'd been using the sandbags to build a lighthouse, where he planned to raise a great bonfire so that Fisher could find his way home. *Semper Fi*, Early. *Semper Fi*.

I stood on the shore that day, with the salt water pushing closer to me with every wave, and recalled how, just a few months before, I had stood on this same spot, so disoriented I'd thrown up. I marveled at the vastness of the ocean. I stood in awe of its depth and mystery. And I realized I was equally in awe of Early Auden. Yes, he was strange. Yes, he could be maddening. And yes, he was my friend.

As the ocean tugged at my feet, I realized that Early Auden, that strangest of boys, had saved me from being swept away. By teaching me how to build a boat, that numbers tell stories, and that when it's raining, it's always Billie Holiday.

The Journal of Poetry
by Young Americans—1928
2ND-PRIZE WINNER

The Beauty of a Single Star

by Elaine Gallagher
Abilene, Kansas

The stars in their courses
illuminate and guide,
for voyagers and wayfarers
to seek far and wide.
But before Pleiades and Orion,
Before minors and majors,
They were just stars in their courses,
Singing their praises.
In one star alone is beauty enough
For awe and splendor and wonder
To lift up one's eyes, with arms outstretched,
And gracefully, humbly stand under.

AUTHOR'S NOTE

The idea for the story that became *Navigating Early* came to me several years ago when my mom told me about a vivid dream she'd had of a young man with an extreme talent for playing the piano. In her dream, the young man had no training but could play even the most difficult piece after hearing it just once. Her dream was more about a friendship between this young man and a young woman. But the idea of writing a story about someone with an unexplainable gift stayed in my head. What would that person's gift be? How would it affect the rest of his life?

My first order of business was research, so I read a book by Daniel Tammet called *Born on a Blue Day: Inside the Extraordinary Mind of an Autistic Savant*. In it, Daniel tells his story of growing up with autism and the amazing ways his mind works. He can perform extraordinary calculations in his head. He memorized more than 22,000 digits of pi. And he sees numbers as shapes, colors, and textures. His story was a springboard to that of Early Auden.

By our standards today, Early might be diagnosed with a high-functioning form of autism. He would also be considered a savant, a person who exhibits extraordinary ability in a highly specialized area, such as mathematics or music. I chose not to use the terms *autism* or *savant* in the book because most people in 1945 would have been unfamiliar with them, and most people with autism would have been undiagnosed. A person like Early would have just been considered strange.

Early is not meant to be a representation of the autistic child. He is a unique and special boy with an amazing mind, a beautiful spirit, and an unexplainable gift. Like Daniel Tammet, he sees the number pi in shapes, colors, and textures. But as Early developed in my mind and in the story, I realized that his amazing gift went even further. To him, the numbers in pi also tell a story.

That brings up the next area of research. Pi.

Irrational. Transcendental. Eternal. Those are all words that describe the number pi. But people—who have been fascinated by the number for thousands of years—also use words like *beautiful, mystical, holy.* How can a number have conjured up such imagery and even controversy over the centuries?

Early Auden has savant abilities in mathematics. He can perform extraordinary calculations in his head. He calms himself and organizes his thoughts with patterns and sequence, sorting by color and quantity. And for him, the number pi is the most special and beautiful of numbers, and that number tells a special and beautiful story.

In my story there is, of course, a certain amount of fact

alongside a fair amount of fiction. So, because I am a game-show lover, let's play a game called:

PI: FACT OR FICTION?

Fact or Fiction: Pi is a never-ending, never-repeating number.
A: Fact. Pi is an irrational number, which means it cannot be written as a fraction. Its decimal numbers will never repeat in any sort of pattern and they will never reach an end.

Fact or Fiction: The sequences of numbers mentioned in *Navigating Early* are real sequences found in the number pi.
A: Fiction. The number pi does start with 3.14, but the sequences I mention in the book are fictional. If they do exist in the number pi, it is purely coincidental.

Fact or Fiction: The numbers in pi really tell a story.
A: Fiction. I made that part up, but who knows? If a person can see numbers as shapes, colors, or textures, maybe someone else sees them in other amazing ways.

Fact or Fiction: Someone once found a mistake in the numbers in pi, as Early does in the story.
A: Fact. In 1945, D. F. Ferguson found a mistake in a previously calculated value of pi from the 527th place onward. In my story Early happens to find the mistake first. But Early is a fictional character, so Mr. Ferguson deserves all the credit.

Fact or Fiction: There are numbers that have stopped showing up in the digits of pi.
A: Fiction. No numbers have gone missing. In fact, the numbers zero through nine are fairly evenly and consistently represented throughout the known numbers of pi.

AND FINALLY,
A FEW NON-PI-RELATED QUESTIONS.

Q: Is hippopotamus milk pink?

Q: Is Maine really the only state name with one syllable?

Q: Did the regatta originate as a gondola race in Venice?

Q: Are there timber rattlesnakes in Maine?

A: Yes. Yes. Yes. And most sources say no, but I tend to side with Early on this one.

RESOURCES

Beckmann, Petr. *A History of Pi*. Boulder, CO: Golem Press, 1970.

Berggren, Lennart, Jonathan Borwein, and Peter Borwein, editors. *Pi: A Source Book*. New York: Springer-Verlag, 1997.

Blatner, David. *The Joy of Pi*. New York: Walker, 1997.

Grandin, Temple. *Thinking in Pictures: And Other Reports from My Life with Autism*. New York: Doubleday, 1995.

Strickler, Darryl J. *Rowable Classics: Wooden Single Sculling Boats and Oars*. Brooklin, ME: Wooden Boat, 2008.

Tammet, Daniel. *Born on a Blue Day: Inside the Extraordinary Mind of an Autistic Savant: A Memoir*. New York: Simon & Schuster, 2007.

ACKNOWLEDGMENTS

This book is about many things, not the least of which is stargazing. The Kansas state motto is *Ad astra per aspera*—"To the stars through difficulties." It's no wonder we have stars in our motto, because we have such a wide-open sky in which to view them. But stargazing is an underappreciated opportunity in today's world. So, a few words of thanks to many people who have encouraged me to not only look at the stars, but to stand under them in a spirit of wonder, awe, and gratitude.

First of all, to my mother. Early Auden is a boy with an amazing mind and an incredible gift. But the initial interest in a story like his was planted years ago and slowly took root before the first words came out. So special thanks to my mom for telling me of a dream she'd had one night about a young man with a remarkable gift for playing the piano. She probably said, "You should write a story about that." And I did. Early doesn't play the piano, but my mom is a piano teacher and I'm sure she could have him up and running in no time.

And to my dad, for enjoying everything I do.

A very special thanks to my sister, Annmarie Algya and our wannabe sister, CY Suellentrop (pronounced "C-Y," not "Sigh"), for accompanying me on a "research" trip to Maine. We always put the "research" part in quotes because the trip was way too much fun to be so narrowly categorized. We haggled with the rental car lady, had an "incident" in the hotel lobby, got addicted to *NCIS*, and sampled lots of chowder. Research at its finest . . . and funnest.

To the following people, who are the dream team of my professional life: My agent, Andrea Cascardi. I am so lucky that you said yes to my initial query. That started this whole wonderful ball rolling and it wouldn't have happened without you. My editor, Michelle Poploff, and her assistant, Rebecca Short. Thank you for fostering, shaping, and loving this manuscript into its final form. You are the best at what you do. And thank you, Michelle, for the special Saturday phone call. My publicist, Elizabeth Zajac. Simply put, my daughters love you, and they are great judges of character. I hope they grow up with your kindness and optimism.

To Vikki Sheatsley and Alex Jansson for a beautiful and intriguing book cover.

To my writing colleagues, Christie Breault, Beverly Buller, Dian Curtis Regan, Lois Ruby, and Debra Seely. Our writing group doesn't really have a name, but I always look forward to seeing the entry I use in my calendar to remind me of an upcoming gathering. The Writer Gals seems an appropriate name, as they are a wonderful group of both.

To Jack Devries and his mom, Sarah. Jack is a great kid who has been in my son Paul's class since kindergarten. Jack is on the autism spectrum, and he has been a model for developing a character with a great heart and a gentle spirit. And thanks to Sarah for being a good friend and adviser in the writing of this book.

To a few other important people who offered their words of support and constructive criticism: Diane Awbrey for a great critique. John Kindel, Leroy Kimminau, and Darryl Strickler for their rowing and boatbuilding expertise. Tinka Davis and Paul Sander for their mathematical minds and insight into the pi element of the story. They all certainly know their stuff, and any remaining mistakes or intentional variations from the factual are my own doing. In fact, why don't we just say any variations from the factual *are* intentional and call it good.

To Tucker Kimball and Justyne Myers at Gould Academy in Bethel, Maine, for giving a great tour of their beautiful campus and providing me with wonderful insight into the boarding school world.

To my many friends at Eighth Day Books and Watermark Books. Two slices of heaven for any reader, and they are both within walking distance of my house.

Being somewhat of a vagabond writer, I have many people to thank for providing me with the space in which to write this book. To Matt McGinness for providing many a place to write over the years, but especially for being a supportive and encouraging voice during my many "yet to be published" years. To Steve and Mary Algya for letting me use their treehouse apartment above my sister's garage. I can work for hours, then sneak into Annmarie's house and pilfer candy from her children without them even knowing it. To Bob and Jan Hall, for offering their lovely home over Christmas break so I could finish a draft. That was a big deal. And to their daughter and her husband, Carrie and Jon Hullings, for designing the most awesome office space—just for me. Yes, it is in the lobby of their orthodontics practice, but that's okay. With the number of kids I have in braces, I get plenty of use out of the area, and free coffee. And a big shout-out to Warren Farha at Eighth Day Books for giving me the key to the store for early-morning writing, and for having a wonderful poetry section in the front window where Early Auden's name was born.

And to my favorite four—Luke, Paul, Grace, and Lucy. I'm a lucky mom. My only complaint is you're all growing up too fast. So all birthdays are canceled for next year!

And Mark. My north star—and a true gentleman.

ABOUT THE AUTHOR

CLARE VANDERPOOL loves to read, research, and travel. Writing *Navigating Early* gave her the opportunity to do all three. On a research trip to Maine, Clare explored lighthouses, walked on sandy beaches, visited a boarding school, and even took her own trek on the Appalachian Trail. Unfortunately, she did not run into any bears. That would have been some *research*!

Clare started reading at age five and writing at age six, when her first poem was published in the school newspaper. Her first novel, *Moon Over Manifest,* was awarded the John Newbery Medal for the most distinguished contribution to American literature for children.

Clare lives in Wichita, Kansas, with her husband and their four children.